...elling author **Anna J. Stewart** can't remember...
...asn't making up stories. Raised in San Francisco, she
...ly found her calling as a romance writer when she dis-
...red the used bookstore in her neighbourhood had an
...e wall dedicated to the genre. Her favourites? Mills
...oon books, of course. A generous owner had her re-
...g her bag of books every Saturday morning, and
...her pen met paper and she never looked back—
...ch to the detriment of her high school education.
...na currently lives in Northern California, where she
...ntinues to write up a storm, binge-watches her favourite
.../ shows and movies and spends as much time as she
...n with her family and friends… and her cat, Snickers,
...ho, let's face it, rules the house.

Also by Anna J. Stewart

Reunited with the P.I.
More Than a Lawman
Gone in the Night
Always the Hero
A Dad for Charlie
Recipe for Redemption
The Bad Boy of Butterfly Harbor
Christmas, Actually
"The Christmas Wish"

Discover more at millsandboon.co.uk

THE RANCHER'S HOMECOMING

ANNA J. STEWART

MILLS & BOON

First Published in Great Britain 2019
by Mills & Boon, an imprint of HarperCollins*Publishers*
1 London Bridge Street, London, SE1 9GF

The Rancher's Homecoming © 2018 Anna J. Stewart

ISBN: 978-0-263-27217-8

0219

For my Blackwell sisters: Melinda Curtis,
Cari Lynn Webb, Carol Ross and Amy Vastine.
I will follow you women anywhere.

And our fearless wrangler and editor, Kathryn Lye.
I hope we've done you proud.

CHAPTER ONE

CHANCE BLACKWELL MISSED a lot about performing.

He missed the way the room went silent as he sang words he'd painstakingly chosen. He missed the oddly intoxicating smell of beer, perfume and rejection. He missed the way the lights were dim enough for him to pretend he was alone, that it was just him and his guitar.

What he didn't miss was walking off stage to find his long-time, long-suffering agent ready to pounce. Given the sour expression on Felix Fuller's face, there wasn't an "atta boy" in Chance's future.

"I thought you had new material." Felix's disappointment was clear and cut almost as deep as Chance expected. Only five years older than Chance, who'd just turned thirty, Felix was as short as Chance was tall, pudgy where Chance was toned and was determined while Chance was…

Well, Chance didn't know exactly what he was anymore.

Chance sighed and gripped the guitar he'd received as a gift his first Christmas after leaving the Blackwell Family Ranch ten years before. His wife, Maura, had worked a second waitressing job on the sly to buy it from a local pawnshop that Christmas they spent in Nashville. He could still remember her sitting on the floor next to the scraggly tree he'd dragged out of the back of a tree lot, her freckled face alight with excitement as he unwrapped it. The instrument had been the greatest gift he'd ever received. Until Rosie was born, at least.

"The new songs aren't ready," Chance lied. "And the crowd seems happy enough." Applause was applause, right?

"The crowd was being polite." Felix followed Chance down the narrow hallway. "You can't launch a comeback on old songs, Chance. Sentimentality will only get you so far. We need something new, something fresh. Something from the heart."

From the heart? Chance swallowed against the wave of grief-tinged nausea. If that's what was needed, no wonder his creative spark had been doused. "I need more time."

"You don't have more time." Felix nipped at his heels like an overanxious puppy. "Unless you don't have any interest in keeping a roof over Rosie's head. Or yours, for that matter."

Chance's gut knotted. He could live in his car and be fine with it, but no way did he want anything less than complete stability for his daughter. "I can't write from a dry well, Felix." And that's exactly what he had. A dry, dusty well of inspiration. *Ashes to ashes...*

"Okay, okay, so let's look at the bright side." Felix's voice dropped as he gestured toward the frayed, dark green curtains. "They've missed you, Chance. Your fans, your audience, they want you back. Which means we've got to strike—"

"I told you before this gig, I'm only dipping my toe." Chance accepted the congratulatory slaps on the back and positive comments from patrons as he made his way to the makeshift dressing room, which, over the years, had been occupied by far more talented and popular musicians than himself. Apparently *they* didn't care that he was singing songs from five years ago. "I'm not diving in all the way again. I'm not ready."

He knew what he should be drawing on, but the idea of writing about Maura, about her illness, her death, scraped his heart raw whenever he plucked the first notes. The paralyzing grief over losing his wife had faded—for the most part. He'd come to terms with her being gone, but only because he didn't have a choice.

Rosie needed him. And when it came to his daughter, nothing else mattered.

Sadly, that meant going back to the only thing he'd ever been any good at: songwriting and performing.

"What do you mean you're not ready?" Felix moved around the band as they dodged around him, instruments in hand, semipanicked expressions on their far too young faces. "All evidence to the contrary, man. You belong on that stage. Look, Chance, I get it. This is tough, and it's a big change for you, but you and I agreed you weren't done. You promised after enough time passed—"

"You don't get to decide when I've had enough time." Chance stopped with his hand on the tarnished doorknob and looked over his shoulder. "What's this really about, Felix? You threatening to jump ship if I don't get on board? Have another hot new act waiting in the wings for your full attention?"

Felix shook his head, a bit too enthusiastically for Chance's taste, as a strand of slicked-black hair fell over one suddenly anxious eye. "Not full attention, exactly."

"Felix?" Chance urged. "We've been together long enough for you to be honest with me." Lord knew Chance had certainly been honest with him. "I know it's been tight for you with me taking this much time off right when things were getting good for us. But you knew when you signed me Maura was my top priority." And she had been, right up until the end. Only now that the haze around his heart had cleared did Chance have the slightest inclination to perform again. Writing was a different story. "You have somewhere else you need to be, just say the word."

"I've come across a couple of acts I'd like to sign, sure." Felix shrugged as if they didn't matter much. "One's singing in a club in New York, another group out of Orlando. There're...possibilities."

And Felix was all about possibilities. "I'm not going to begrudge you needing to move on," Chance said. "I'd never want to stand in your way."

Losing his agent certainly didn't hold much appeal, especially without another one showing any interest. And no one would as long as he didn't have anything new to offer. Felix had been his only agent, and traversing this crazy music business had never been on the top of Chance's to-do list. Then again, anything was better than being stuck back on the family ranch, saddling horses, baling hay and mucking out stalls while his dreams died a silent death. Maura had always been the one to believe in him, encourage him. Understand him.

Other than his grandmother Dorothy, Big E's first wife, who had bought him his first guitar—a guitar his grandfather had ripped out of Chance's hands after Dorothy left and Chance declared his intention of leaving ranch life behind. How Big E thought taking away the one thing that brought Chance any happiness would punish anyone other than Chance was beyond him. Then again, Big E had considered Chance's dreams a phase he'd outgrow. Without his brothers' support, the wedge between Chance and his family had grown too big to overcome. Which is why ten years away didn't feel nearly long enough.

"Maybe we should talk about this inside," Felix said

with a bit of a cringe on his face as he gestured to the dressing-room door.

"Oh, hey, Chance! Great show!" Greg Kennedy, owner of Tuned Up, one of the lesser known but better respected dive bars in downtown Los Angeles, darted down the stage stairs and headed for him. His compliment sounded forced, even to Chance's tone-deaf ears. "Did your brother find you? I told him he could wait backstage for you."

Chance froze. "My brother?" Every teenage insecurity slammed back at him like a slingshot. "Which brother?" *Please don't let it be Ty. Please don't let it be...*

"Which one?" Greg chuckled. "That's right, I forgot you have four. I think his name was—"

Chance jumped back as the door swung open. "Ty."

"What's going on, baby brother?" That twinkle-eyed grin was always the first thing anyone noticed about Chance's twin. That and the way he could charm the stickers off a cactus with a wink and a smile. That his brother appeared to have traded in his tailored executive suit for more cowboy-friendly attire set every warning bell in Chance's head to clanging. Nothing good ever came of a Blackwell brother showing up. "Been a while." Ty aimed that smile of his at the almost five-year-old in his arms.

"Daddy! It's Uncle Ty! See?" Rosie, all bouncy red curls, freckled nose and skinny arms, patted her hands against Tyler's cheeks as she blew a raspberry. "He's funny, Daddy! Just like you!"

"Just like me, huh?" As disappointed as Chance was in Felix's reaction, and as irritated as he was by his brother's unexpected arrival, everything about his beautiful Rosie made him smile. "Where's Claudia?" Chance handed his guitar to Felix before he reached for his little girl. The instant she settled in his arms, his pulse calmed. His world righted itself. He could breathe again.

"I'm here!" The graduate student from UCLA who had been Rosie's nanny for the last year leaned over to peek and wave from behind Tyler. "Tyler was just telling us all about your ranch in Montana. It sounds amazing."

"A ranch with horsies and cows, Daddy," Rosie told him with a firm nod. "And Uncle Ty says there are kitties and a dog and a goat named Billy. And when I come visit I get to learn to ride and maybe even rope! But I will need boots. I would like pink boots, please. When can we go visit the kitties and dog, Daddy?"

Chance patted his daughter on the back of her purple shirt and stifled the familiar urge to strangle his brother. "Why don't you let me talk to Uncle Ty about that? Claudia? Would you mind taking Rosie out for a bit? Maybe you can listen to the next band. Felix will go with you." The last thing he needed, or wanted, was for his two worlds—however detached he was from one of them—to collide. "Just hang on for a sec."

Chance pushed past his brother and ducked into the room. He rummaged through one of Rosie's bags and pulled out her pink headphones. Like a seasoned pro, Rosie snatched them and plunked them over her ears.

"Okay, Daddy?" she yelled.

Chance laughed and nodded. "Go with Claudia, okay?" He set her on her feet, tugged up her jeans, which were too short in the legs and too big in the butt, and exchanged his daughter for the guitar. "I'll just be a few minutes."

"Okay." Felix didn't look convinced as Rosie grabbed his hand. Claudia followed with an expression of uncertainty on her round face. "But we still have to talk about this."

"Looking forward to it." Chance set down his guitar, watched as Rosie skipped her way between his agent and nanny and quietly, slowly, closed the door. "What are you doing here, Ty?"

"If you answered your phone once in a while this might not be such a surprise." Ty dropped down into the ripped, green faux-leather sofa that was wedged tightly between the walls. "Man, this place is a hole. I thought showbiz was supposed to be glamorous."

"It can be." But starting over meant starting at the bottom and it didn't get more bottom than where Chance was standing at the moment. "Out with it already. What's Big E done now?" He busied himself gathering up the books and games strewn about that Claudia and Rosie had occupied themselves with during his show. Right now all he wanted was the safe, quiet surroundings of the small two-bedroom bungalow he called home.

"I'd fill you in on the details." Ty sighed. "But you told your boy Felix you would only be a few minutes. You need to come back, Chance. You need to come home."

His stomach pitched. "I don't think I do." And the ranch had never felt like home. Not since their parents died.

"Do you really think I'd have flown all the way out here, left my beautiful bride-to-be with those brothers of ours, if I didn't think this was important?"

"I don't really know what to think about any of you." Ty engaged? The idea still had the power to render him speechless. "I'm the black sheep, remember?" He jammed Clyde, Rosie's worn, crazy-eyed stuffed monster into her rainbow backpack. "The last place I belong is on the Blackwell Family Ranch."

"Whether you think you belong there or not, it's your home, Chance. And like it or not, we're your family. We need you."

The Blackwell brothers needed him? Chance got to his feet and faced his brother. "What's wrong? Is Big E dying? Do you need me to sing at the funeral? Oh." Chance snapped his fingers. "No, wait. I forgot. Last thing our grandfather would want is to ever hear me sing. You were never one for barrel racing, Ty. Out with it."

"Jon and Ben want to sell the ranch."

"Good. Great." One less thing to have to ever think about. "Fabulous. Enjoy whatever cash you get out of it." He'd relinquished any hope of seeing Blackwell money long ago. As far as he knew, Big E had disinherited him the second Chance eloped with Maura Montgomery.

"Ethan and I don't want to sell," Ty added.

Had stubbornness not kept Chance on his feet, he might have passed out. "I'm sorry, what? *You* don't want to sell. You. The Blackwell brother who had one foot over the property line the second he could walk?" Had Chance stepped off stage and into an alternate reality? He sat in the only other chair in the claustrophobic space. "This ought to be good. Why don't you want to sell?"

Ty shrugged, stretched out his legs. "It's our legacy. It's Big E's legacy. And we've made some really good progress with the guest-ranch aspect of the business. It's picking up with all of us working together. Plus Hadley's nuts about the place. FYI, we couldn't have done much without Katie. She's been amazing to work with. Girl knows just about everything there is about ranching, especially our ranch."

"Katie's still there?" Chance shouldn't have been surprised to hear his sister-in-law hadn't moved away. She and Maura had been raised on that ranch. It was as much the Montgomerys' home as the Blackwells'. "Guess Maura was right. She always said Katie would never leave that place." Thinking of his late wife's kid sister brought up memories Chance honestly wasn't ready to deal with.

"Yeah, well, Lochlan's getting up in years. He's still our foreman, but it's pretty much in name only. Katie's picked up his slack to cover for her dad." Ty ducked his head, but not before Chance caught the flash of concern on his brother's face. "Lochlan's sick, Chance. Katie's tried to keep it quiet, telling us he'd gone to visit friends, but we all just found out. He's fading. And, well, I know it's none of my business, but he wants to see his granddaughter before he dies."

"You're right," Chance snapped. "It's not your business." Dormant anger he'd long buried threatened to boil over. "That old man refused to see his own daughter when she was dying. Wouldn't make the trip. Not even to say goodbye. He didn't even take her calls." It was the one thing that still kept Chance up at night. That he'd been unable to grant his dying wife's final wish. Not that he'd been able to accomplish much over the phone, but between Maura and Rosie, he couldn't leave. *Stubborn son of a...* "Would you like me to tell you what her father's rejection did to her? Would you like me to tell you in excruciating detail how she cried for her father at the end?"

"I'm not even going to try to understand that one, Chance." Ty shook his head and Chance was relieved to see a flash of sympathy come across his brother's face. "And I'm certainly not going to excuse it. Not even Katie can."

"Ah." Chance nodded. "So that's what this is about. Katie sent you to plead Lochlan's case. You know I wouldn't put it past the old man to have put her up to it."

"Clearly you haven't seen Katie in a while. She doesn't do anything she doesn't want to. And for the record, no, she didn't put me up to this. I can tell you I've caught her on more than one occasion looking at those pictures you send her of Rosie. Might be smart of you to remember that while you lost your wife, she lost her sister. Pictures and videos aren't any substitute for holding that little girl in her arms."

"She lost her sister when Lochlan disowned Maura for marrying me. Because she walked away from everything Lochlan planned for her." Chance held up his hands. "If that's the reason you came all the way here—"

"It's not that. It's not only that," Ty corrected. "We need your vote."

Tyler wasn't making any sense. "My vote for what, exactly?"

"For what happens to the ranch. We're tied, which means it's up to you. So let's set aside the opportunity you have to be the bigger person and let an old man go to his death in peace. How about you come back long enough to help me keep this ranch where it belongs? In the Blackwell family."

CHAPTER TWO

"Ooh, Daddy! Look! Horsies! Tshey're everywhere!" Rosie's excited squeal from the back seat of the minivan announced his daughter was wide-awake. After four days on the road—because making the twenty-hour trek from LA in one stretch would have been a recipe for disaster—he was ready for a break. Given Rosie's ear-splitting tantrum at the motel last night, he wasn't the only one.

Not that Falcon Creek, Montana, was going to give him anything close to a respite. Driving through town had already been like sliding through a time portal. Near as he could tell, nothing had changed. Other than a new coat of paint on the diner and new planks on the walkways. A shiny new sign over Brewster's. Sure there were some new businesses and shops and, undoubtedly, new people. Everything else… Exactly. The. Same.

"Do you see the horsies, Daddy? Oh, they're so pretty. Can I ride one, please, Daddy?"

"I think they're a bit too big for you, Bug." He glanced in the rearview mirror. His heart swelled at the excitement shining in his little girl's eyes. "But I bet Aunt Katie will be able to find you the perfect pony." Katie had always been magic with horses.

"Oo-o-oh, a pony." Rosie rolled her head against the back of her car seat and kicked her pink-booted feet against the back of the passenger seat. "I'll get my very own pony?"

"We'll have to see." Chance winced as the headache throbbing in the back of his head shifted to his temples. He'd run out of coffee—and thus, caffeine—about two hundred miles ago, and judging by the ache in his jaw, he'd grind his teeth to dust before they reached the ranch. "For as long as we're here at least, I think we can work something out." Chance shifted his attention back to the endless dirt road.

He slammed his foot on the brake.

Rosie squealed as if they'd just taken a dip on a roller coaster. Chance's hands gripped the steering wheel as his heart hammered in his chest. The iconic gateway to the Blackwell Family Ranch loomed overhead. Its rusted, weathered sign—nearly as old as the ranch itself—welcomed visitors and guests.

And nearly had Chance turning around and heading home.

Nausea churned in his stomach. What was he doing here?

"Do that again, Daddy!" Rosie ordered.

"Once was enough." He powered down his window and allowed himself his first breath of Montana air in more than a decade. The combination of pristine oxygen, green grass and leftover moisture from last night's storm hung slightly tinged with manure and hay. Or maybe that was just his mind playing tricks on him. It had taken him years to forget the smell of the ranch, as if it had seeped into his blood the day he'd been born. He shifted the minivan into Park and unhooked his belt.

"Are we here?" Rosie shifted in her seat, turning her head so fast her red curls slapped her cheeks. "Are we at Grampy's?"

"Almost." He never should have told her they were going to visit her grandfather. It seemed every word out of Rosie's mouth in the two weeks since Ty had delivered his invitation of doom had been to ask about Maura's father. Every word was like a knife to Chance's heart.

He couldn't care less what Lochlan Montgomery thought of him. But if Ty was right, if the old man was dying, Lochlan deserved to see his only grandchild once before he met his maker. If for no other reason than it was what Maura would want.

But if the old man did or said one thing that gave Rosie a moment's sadness or despair...

Chance slipped out of the van, his sneakered feet hitting the dirt road with enough force that dust immediately covered him. The silence hurt his ears as it shouted its welcome. He stretched, groaned and waited for his muscles to stop screaming at him as he tried to shake feeling back into his extremities.

The midafternoon sun was still moving toward its peak, but was beating down hard enough to remind him that he—and Rosie—would be needing hats. He'd left his Stetson—the one Big E had given him on high school graduation—on his bed when he left the ranch for good. No doubt one of his brothers had found use for it. It would fit one of them better, anyway. "You want to get out for a while?" He rounded the minivan and slid the door open, only to find Rosie standing on the floorboards. She grinned up at him. Chance bit back a sigh as he reached down and picked her up and got bopped in the face by Clyde. "When did you start unbuckling your belt?"

Rosie grinned and hugged Clyde against her chest. "Surprise!"

"You are full of them." He pressed a kiss against the side of her head and lowered her to the ground. "Let's not do that again, okay?" The second her feet hit the dirt, he swore the earth quaked. She darted to the fence line and stared out at the endless pasture dotted with horses and cattle.

Chance lost his breath. His little girl barely reached the middle section of barbed wire, but the sight of her standing before the Montana sky, the Rockies framing her in purple-hazed perfection, her new jeans and bright yellow shirt shining and the sunlight catching against her hair, he wondered where the time had gone. Had it really been almost five years since the doctors had first set her in his trembling hands? Chance took a long, deep breath. Whatever the next few days, weeks or years brought, this was what he needed to remember. This moment. This sight.

Not that he was already counting the minutes until he could leave. Frustration edged its way around the calm. What was he thinking, letting Ty goad him into coming back? There was nothing for him here. Nothing except bitter memories of a place where he never belonged and a family he'd never fit into. Forget being a square peg in a round hole. For Chance, he'd always felt like a banjo in an orchestra. How many times had his brothers and grandfather teased him that he was, in fact, the worst cowboy to ever saddle a horse?

Now, as irony often snagged the last word, it would be up to him what happened with the place? As far as he was concerned, they should sell to the highest bidder and be done with it. It would ease the financial pressures building up on him and possibly help him decide which school Rosie would attend next year. Although Felix had high hopes this place would reignite that creativity he'd been thirsting for.

Yep. He stared out at the emptiness of the land. They needed to sell.

Which meant this was going to be a very short visit.

Besides, he had three weeks before Felix was back from

making the rounds on his search for new talent. If Chance had new material by then, his star just might rise again. If he didn't…

His career would be over.

The land stared back at him, accusing. He didn't want the memories. Not of his brothers, or the parents he barely remembered, not to mention his grandfather, who had only berated or ignored Chance's interest in music. He certainly didn't want to think of Maura and how she was as ingrained here as much as she was in his heart.

But it was the thought of his late wife that loosened the tension in his jaw. For an instant, he could all but see her, red hair flowing behind her, as she rode Fairweather, her favorite horse, across the rolling hills, her laughter ringing in the air like wind chimes in a summer storm. Huh.

Chance blinked and pulled out the notebook he kept close at hand. He scribbled down the thoughts, on the off chance they might lead to something productive. Something that would ease Felix's doom-and-gloom protestations that Chance's career might never resurge.

"Daddy, look!" Rosie's cry shot him out of his reverie. He looked up to find Rosie pointing to a horse and rider in the distance headed toward them. A smaller animal trotted alongside in a scene straight out of a Zane Grey novel.

Chance joined Rosie at the fence, his pulse hammering as he debated which brother would be the first to welcome him home. Not that he expected much of a welcome. Jon had his own organic spread, the JB Bar Ranch, nearby. Ethan was just getting his veterinary practice off the ground. Ben was currently lawyering with his new wife, Rachel, and living at the Double T, and Ty…well, Ty knew better than to be the welcoming committee.

As the horse drew closer, the pounding of hoofbeats vibrated across the land. If he squinted, he could make out the rider's features. Along the edges of the worn tan hat, a flash of red caught the sun. His mouth went dry as the rider came to a halt on the other side of the fence. For a long moment, they stared at one another, Chance nearly falling into the bottomless green eyes so reminiscent of Rosie's and Maura's. But while the color was the same, the independent, determined spark could only belong to one person.

"Hello, Katie." Chance rested his hand on Rosie's curl-topped head as his heart skipped a beat.

"Chance." Her smile seemed a bit strained, her freckled face a bit pale, and her hands gripped the reins hard enough that her knuckles had gone white. Apparently he wasn't the only one apprehensive about his homecoming. The black-and-white Australian cattle dog woofed and quirked its head as if suggesting introductions were in order.

"Aunt Katie?" Rosie looked up at him.

Chance nodded and drew Rosie against him as Katie Montgomery bounded off her horse and removed her leather gloves. She stuffed them in the back pocket of her snug, worn jeans and walked toward them. "Well, who do we have here?" She narrowed her eyes and leaned over to peer closer at Rosie, the trepidation on her face fading as she looked at her niece in person for the first time.

"It's us, Aunt Katie!" Rosie broke free of Chance's hold and darted forward. "It's me, Rosie and Daddy!"

"Careful, Little Miss!" Katie chided as Rosie wedged herself under the bottom line of wire.

Katie gave Chance a quick glance before she dropped to her knees and wrapped her arms tight around his daughter. "Oh, Rosie." Katie dropped kisses on both of Rosie's cheeks before hugging her again. "I'm so happy to see you. I'm so glad you're here. Careful, Hip." She brushed a quick hand over the dog's back in reassurance.

Chance saw the tears in Katie's eyes before she squeezed them shut. She may have had her older sister's eyes and the same fire-red hair, but the resemblance ended there. Where Maura had been soft around the edges, girly, flirty, tall and willowy, Katie was compact, edgy, curvy and all cowgirl. Maura's dreams had been focused on being any-where but Montana, while Katie had been firmly situated on Blackwell land, working alongside her father for as far back as Chance could remember. She loved this place just as much—and probably more—than any Blackwell brother ever had. She'd bled, sweated and worked for it. When they sold the place, he hoped the new owners would realize the prize they had in her and keep her on.

But for now, all he could do was watch as Katie and Rosie giggled and hugged and giggled some more. To see his daughter this giddy made the excruciating drive worth it.

"You're as beautiful as you are in your pictures." Katie rocked Rosie back and forth until the little girl squirmed. Rosie knocked Katie's hat off her head as Katie got to her feet and swung Rosie around in a circle. Katie's dog barked and hopped along with them.

"Daddy said you'd be happy to see me." Rosie looked back at Chance when she was back on her feet. "You said so, right, Daddy?"

"I did." Chance barely recognized his own voice. See-ing them together, he couldn't help but imagine the same scene with Maura. Maura, who had died just before Rosie turned three. Maura, who, once the chemo had taken its talon-sharp hold, hadn't been able to swing her daughter in her arms or smother a giggling little girl with kisses. But Katie wasn't Maura. As his lips pulled into a wide, genuine smile, the regret melted away. She wasn't Maura. No one ever would be. And that, he realized, was okay.

"Welcome home." Katie grinned, but he suspected it was more for Rosie than him.

He glanced at his minivan, which had yet to cross the border onto the family property. "Not quite."

"Close enough." Katie shrugged. "Ty wasn't sure when you'd be arriving. Or if you'd show up at all."

"I said I'd come." Chance cleared his throat. "Unlike some people, I keep my word when I give it."

"Should have known you'd arrive with your foot in your mouth." Irritation flashed across Katie's sun-kissed round face before she turned her attention back to Rosie. "Things aren't always so cut-and-dried, are they? Let's see those boots, Little Miss." Katie stretched out her arms, still holding Rosie's hands, as if afraid to let go. "You are all cowgirled up, aren't you?"

"Daddy bought them for me." Rosie kicked one foot in the air, then the other. "I told him they had to be pink. I like pink. Do you like pink?"

"I like pink just fine," Katie said with a bit of a snort. "And if you're planning on staying at the main house, I think you're going to find it suits you perfectly. Unless you made other arrangements?" She glanced back at Chance.

"No arrangements." Chance shook his head. "We packed the car and headed out. Given what Ty told us about all the changes to the place, I figured there would be a free bed or two."

"More than that. Little Miss here can have her pick of rooms if she'd like. Not sure you'll recognize yours."

Meaning Big E had probably turned his room into a smoking room or bowling alley. He'd have bet good money his grandfather would have done his best to erase any trace of Chance's existence once Chance left. Guess he was right.

"And if you don't like the main house," Katie contin-

ued, "you can always stay with me and Dad. I made up
Maura's room for her." Katie didn't blink as she spoke, as
if gauging Chance's reaction.

"Grampy!" Rosie squealed. "I have a room at Grampy's
house?"

"Of course you do. You always have had," Katie added
with a pointed look at Chance.

"The main house will do just fine." No way would he
ever sleep under the same roof as Lochlan Montgomery.
Nor was he going to be made to feel guilty about not coming back before now. Lochlan had gone out of his way to
make certain Chance was not welcome in his home. In that,
Chance was more than content to oblige him. "Rosie, how
about you get back in the car? We can meet Aunt Katie
down at the house."

"Or she can ride back with me." Katie stooped down in
front of Rosie and tweaked her nose. "What do you say,
Little Miss? You want your first ride on a horse?"

"Oh, Daddy, please!" Rosie asked in that almost whining tone of hers.

Chance looked to the horse standing nearby, its shining
gold coat glistening in the sun. He hadn't been kidding earlier when he'd suggested a pony. Personally he'd been hoping for more of a miniature version when the time came.

"Guess we'd best find out if she takes after me or her
mother when it comes to horses." For Rosie's sake, he
hoped it wasn't him.

"She'll be fine," Katie said. Chance met her challenging
gaze, as if she was expecting him to say no just to spite her.
Daring him to do so in front of his daughter only stirred up
old resentments he'd never attributed to Maura's kid sister.

Katie Montgomery, however, was no longer a kid. She
was a fully grown woman who had spent more time on and
around horses than Chance had spent walking. She looked

every bit the professional ranch foreman her father had been. In fact, Chance would bet she was far more capable than Lochlan had ever been, especially in recent years.

"Daddy, can I go with Aunt Katie, please?"

He was reluctant to let Rosie out of his sight, but this was one of the reasons they'd come back to Falcon Creek. For Rosie to meet and get to know her mother's family. For Rosie to get acquainted with her aunts and uncles and cousins. "Sure, Bug. You want Clyde to go with me?"

"Yes, please. Daddy says it's always polite to say 'please.'" She raced over and smacked Clyde into Chance's hand.

"Your daddy's a smart man," Katie agreed. "Now hold on! Good girl, Hip." Katie raced after Rosie when the four-year-old made a beeline for the horse as fast as her little legs would carry her. The horse dropped its head and let out a chuff, as Hip placed herself in front of Rosie. "Good girl, Hip." Katie gave the dog a good pat. "Let's get the introductions out of the way. Rosie, this is Hip. Short for Hippolyta. Hold out your hand, Rosie. Let her smell you so she can remember you're a friend."

"'Kay." Fearless Rosie stuck her hand out right under the dog's nose. Hip gave a good sniff, then angled to shove her nose up under Rosie's hand as if demanding a pet. "Rosie, Hip. Hip, Rosie."

"Her nose is cold." Rosie's eyes went wide.

"There you go. You're friends, now," Katie laughed.

"Hippo!" Rosie threw her arms up and lunged in for a hug.

"No!"

Chance nearly dove through the fence as Katie lunged for Rosie, but Hip let out what Chance could only describe as a sigh and let Rosie wrap her arms around her neck and squeezed.

Hand against her heart, Katie held her other palm out to Chance. "It's okay. Whew." That she appeared so relieved was more concerning to Chance than he liked. "You surprise me, girl." She crouched and looked her dog directly in the eye. She sank her hand into Hip's fur and rubbed. "I thought you didn't like being called Hippo."

Chance heard the dog growl in the back of her throat.

"Rosie, come here, please." Katie pulled her away from the dog and motioned for Hip to stay. The dog blinked big black eyes at them as if to ask where they were going. "Say 'Hippo' again, please, Rosie."

"Hippo!" Rosie giggled as Hip dropped to the ground and stuck her butt in the air, wagging her tail back and forth.

"Chance, would you try, please?"

"Uh, sure." Chance cleared his throat. "Hippo."

Hip shot back up, stood on all fours at attention and barked, then growled.

"Unbelievable." Katie chuckled and shook her head. "First she gets herself a goat boyfriend, now this. Okay, Rosie, I guess for you only, it's…um, you know."

"Hippo!" Rosie doubled over with laughter as the dog came over and jumped into her arms to lick her face. "Doggie kisses!"

"They are the best kisses," Katie assured her. "You still up for that ride?"

"Yes." Rosie gripped the dog's fur in her hand and looked up at her aunt with such admiration Chance's chest constricted.

"We need a few bits of information before you go climbing up there. Riding a horse isn't just for fun. It's also a responsibility." She looked over her shoulder at Chance. "We'll meet you back at the house in a little bit. I need to go check on the ranch hands fixing fence line out along the south pasture. Shouldn't take more than an hour."

Chance nodded. "Yeah, I'll see you then." Feeling as if he was leaving his heart in the pasture, he forced himself to return to the minivan. Seconds later, he started the vehicle and stared down the road. Before he changed his mind, he floored it and shot forward under the Blackwell Family Ranch sign. And headed down the road to home.

CHANCE BLACKWELL HAD come home to Falcon Creek.

Katie checked her saddle, cinching the stirrups, and stalled as her mind raced in time to her pulse. Life hadn't always been kind since he'd been gone, but the years looked good on him. The boyish good looks that had girls spinning in their saddles had transformed into solid, handsome features. Along with his charm, he had a complete arsenal of weapons to use in all that show-business stuff of his.

Of all the brothers, Chance had always stood out with his too-long dark hair and equally dark eyes that she suspected saw more than most. He hadn't been as rough-and-tumble as the other boys, who'd teased Chance that he'd been switched at birth, given his less than enthusiastic proclivities toward anything ranch-related.

Technically Chance was still her brother-in-law, meaning she shouldn't be noticing the way his jeans fit or the way his blue button-down shirt molded over a toned torso and arms. All she should care about was the love and pride that shone in his eyes whenever he looked at his little girl. She attributed the fluttering in her chest and knots in her belly to the continued stress over being caught between the brothers and their grandfather, Big E, who was pulling so many strings he may as well start a new career as a puppet master.

She should know. Big E had been pulling her strings

for the past six months. Dread tightened her throat. If she wasn't careful, one of those strings was going to snap. And Katie was going to find herself pitched out of the Blackwell Ranch—and family—forever.

Which was why it was far less stressful to think about Chance Blackwell. She was banking on the fact that his good memories of the ranch would outweigh the bad and he'd side with the brothers who wanted to keep the place. Not only because she couldn't imagine this place not being owned by a Blackwell, but also because she needed this job. She was this close to officially being named foreman. Her father had lived his entire life on this ranch. Moving him now, when he had so little time left, would break both their hearts. And send Lochlan Montgomery into his grave.

Of course, she and the ranch would be in a better position if Big E had given her any control over the ranch's finances. But no, the old coot couldn't imagine a woman running his family ranch, which was ironic since that's exactly what had been going on for the past two and a half years, as controlling every aspect of the business fell in line with his plans to get his grandsons back where he wanted them.

When it came to manipulation, there were few who excelled more than Elias Blackwell.

And no one else excelled at unnerving Montgomery women more than Big E's grandson Chance.

Given how unsettling the idea of Chance returning had been, she thought she was managing pretty well so far. Of course, she'd been working overtime to make certain her father didn't hear the rumors. The last thing she needed was to have Lochlan diving even further into a whiskey bottle in the hopes of drowning the never-forgotten resentment over the fact that his older daughter had chosen Chance over her family.

Seeing Chance in person again after all these years sent a tidal wave of memories and emotions sweeping through Katie. She squeezed her eyes shut and struggled against the pulls of happiness, grief and hope. She'd talked to him over the years, of course. Sometimes every day when Maura had been sick, then less frequently as Chance had settled into life as a widower and single father. Communication soon dwindled to text messages and photo exchanges, an occasional phone call with her niece, who had quite a lot to say for a four-year-old. And Katie hung on to every word as if they were priceless pearls.

"Aunt Katie, are we going to ride?"

Katie looked down at little Rosie, who was running her tiny hands down Starlight's flank just as Katie had taught her. The second she'd seen Rosie her heart had nearly exploded in her chest. As much as she'd dreamed of holding Maura's little girl, those dreams hadn't come close to the reality. It hadn't taken more than ten seconds to realize that Rosamund Maura Blackwell had Katie wrapped around every finger Rosie possessed. And she always would.

The determined expression on Rosie's freckled face told Katie two things: one, Rosie was indeed her mother's daughter, and two, Chance Blackwell had both his hands full. "We are indeed." Katie bent down and gripped Rosie around the waist. She'd been teaching kids to ride since she was ten, but she couldn't recall any lesson feeling quite this personal before. "You remember everything I told you?"

"Uh-huh." Rosie nodded so hard her curls bounced. She gasped as Katie lifted her up to the saddle, but she didn't squeal. While Starlight was a very docile horse, Katie had seen the horse twitch at Rosie's high-pitched excitement over Hip.

As instructed, Rosie grabbed hold of the saddle horn and inched herself forward so Katie could climb on behind her. Boots solidly in the stirrups, she settled Rosie and reached around her for the reins, which she trailed through Rosie's hands to give her a sense of control. Katie made a clicking sound and kicked her heels against Starlight's flank and off they went, walking, rather than trotting at Katie's normal speed.

"We're riding!" Rosie cried in between bouts of laughter. "I'm riding a horse!"

"You are!" Katie kept the reins loose in her hands against Rosie's hips, but she could tell, as the little girl shifted in the saddle and leaned into the movement of the horse, that Rosie was a natural.

Not her father's daughter in this respect, for sure. Katie had to pinch her lips together to stop from laughing as she recalled Chance's multiple attempts at riding. She knew what his problem was: he didn't trust horses. The trouble was, the horses sensed it, so whenever he approached, they'd do their best to get away. He'd been bucked off so many saddles the ranch hands had started calling him Ricochet. Something told Katie that wouldn't be a problem with Rosie. She might be Chance Blackwell's daughter, but Rosie was also a Montgomery. And Montgomerys lived their lives in the saddle.

"Are there lots of horses to ride?" Rosie asked.

"Lots and lots," Katie assured her. "And your uncles and aunts have animals, too. Cows and dogs and cats. Your uncle Ethan has a rabbit named Coconut and a hedgehog named Pixie."

"Pixie," Rosie laughed. "I want to meet them."

"I'm sure you will. And, of course, there's the zoo."

"You have a zoo?" Rosie turned her head and Katie saw her eyes go wide.

"A petting zoo, yes." Katie resisted the urge to roll her eyes. The whole petting-zoo idea had been Zoe's—she was

Big E's most recent ex-wife. And while Katie had been re-
sistant to the idea initially, she'd quickly jumped on board
when she understood what a draw it would be for guests.
Besides, she'd developed an affinity for the creatures in
residence. She glanced down at Hip, who trotted along beside them, tongue hanging out, occasionally glancing up at
the two of them as if to confirm they were still on board.
"We have rabbits and llamas, and there's Billy of course."
Hip barked. "Hip and Billy are quite close," Katie chuckled. "You'll see when we get back to the house."

"I love animals." Rosie sighed. "I've been wanting a
kitten for the longest time."

"Did your dad say no?"

"I didn't ask yet. I heard him and Uncle Felix talking
and Daddy doesn't have a lot of money. Daddy says he
only has enough to feed two mouths."

Panic gripped Katie's insides and slid to her toes.
Chance had money issues? If that was the case, he'd probably be leaning toward selling the ranch rather than keeping it. Given his history with the place, it was going to
take a lot of convincing—or a minor miracle—to get him
to change his mind.

"Uncle Ty said there are lots of kittens." Rosie stated.
"Maybe I can have one?"

"Well, they were kittens. Mostly we have cats now."
The last thing she needed to do was alienate Chance by
giving his daughter a pet she'd have to leave behind. Especially considering she needed to find a way to convince
him that selling was the absolute worst thing he could do.

"Does that mean 'we'll see'?" Rosie slumped in the saddle. "That's what Daddy always says when he means no."

"Well, for me, it means maybe. And you know what?
Your grandpa and I have a cat at our place. Snicklefrits.
You can come play with him whenever you'd like." Not that

Snicklefrits had been played with much over the years. He mostly shadowed her father, and that meant moving from one chair to another depending on the sunrise, sunset or what was on television.

"Snicklefrits." Rosie giggled. "That's a crazy name for a cat."

"Well, the cat's kind of crazy. I think he'll like you." Katie glanced down at Hip. "Something tells me you have a way with animals. You ready to try a gallop? Go a little faster?"

"Yes, please." Rosie nodded and bounced higher in the saddle. "I want to go as fast as we can!"

"Well, hang on, then." Katie kicked Starlight once more. Seconds later, Katie pushed her worries aside and lost herself in the sound of the wind rushing in her ears.

And the joyous laughter from her niece in her arms.

CHAPTER THREE

THE WINDING ROAD to the main house gave Chance the kick in the pants he needed to get his head on straight. Wallowing over having to come home because his grandfather was messing with the family—again—wasn't going to do anyone, least of all Rosie, any good. Whatever the circumstances, she deserved a great trip and visit with family. It wasn't as if all the memories about this place were bad. When it came down to it, he loved his brothers. He might not know them all as well as he would like, but they were blood. Even a decade away couldn't negate that.

They'd seen each other through a lot, including the death of their parents and a string of stepgrandmothers that made Big E look like a serial groom. Chance's conversations with his grandfather had dwindled over the years, something the old man must have kept to himself given each of his brothers had called him in the last weeks to ask if he'd heard from Big E. As if. It was difficult to talk to someone about your life when they made no secret of their disapproval. At least Rosie gave them something to talk about without getting into a knock-down-drag-out about when Chance was going to put this music silliness aside and come home.

"Well, I guess you finally got your wish, old man." Chance parked the minivan around the side of the house he'd grown up in. The paint had been refreshed—white with pale green shutters. The front porch had served as both haven and escape on more than one occasion. He popped open the back and pulled out his guitar case, then tucked a carved wooden box under his arm before grabbing Rosie's Hello Kitty suitcase. The sooner he got his daughter settled in the house, the easier it would be to get her into a routine. The sound of crunching tires behind him had him closing up and heading around the corner to the front porch.

A slow smile spread across his face as he watched his oldest brother, Jon, climb out. The dog that hopped out behind him looked as if he was used to being part of the welcoming committee. A ranch man from the tips of his booted toes to the hair on his hat-covered head, Jonathan Blackwell looked every bit the cowboy on a mission. And was a reminder of what Chance had done his best to leave behind.

"Look what the storm blew in." Jon pushed back his hat and angled a smile at Chance that made the last ten years melt away like butter in a cast-iron skillet. "Figured a lot might have changed with you, but Hello Kitty is a new look."

"A man's only got so many choices when it comes to his little girl's luggage. As you well know." Chance set the case and his guitar on the steps and embraced his brother. The hearty back slaps they gave one another could be considered the first in what would no doubt be many competitions during his visit. "Good to see you, bro."

"You, too." Jon gave him another smack before dropping his hands on Chance's shoulders. "It's been too long." He gave him a hard shake. They'd never seen eye to eye—at least not literally—before Chance had left, but they did now. And Chance recognized the uncertain expression on his brother's face. He'd been expecting it. And dreading it. "I'm so sorry about Maura, Chance."

"Yeah." Chance had finally reached the stage where the mention of his wife's name didn't make his heart seize. His hold tightened on the box under his arm. "I know. I appreciated the letters. And the flowers. And the pictures." Jon had sent care packages for weeks after Maura's death, including photos of all of them growing up on the ranch. Chance had started an album and framed a number of them for Rosie. They had helped. "Thanks for understanding about not coming out."

"As long as you know any one of us would have been there in a heartbeat." Jon squeezed his shoulders. "All you had to do was ask."

There hadn't been any point in his brothers—and extended family—descending on him. There hadn't been a memorial service. Maura had donated her body for cancer research and once he'd received her remains, a service felt like moving backward. Not to mention he hadn't decided what to do with her ashes. Besides, by that time he had an almost three-year-old to focus on and even though he had no doubt Rosie was aware something was wrong, it didn't change her demands or her needs one iota.

"I had Rosie," Chance said. "She was all I needed." His little girl had saved his life. "So who's this?"

He bent down and offered his hand to the dog, who trotted right over and gave instant approval.

"Trout. My shadow." Jon chuckled.

"He's great." Chance scrubbed his hands into the dog's fur and earned a friend for life. "Has, um…?" Chance cleared his throat and stood up to retrieve his guitar. "Has there been any word from Big E? Have we located him yet?"

"Nothing new since my last email." Jon, a father of five-year-old twin girls himself, picked up Rosie's suitcase without a second glance. "Gotta admit, there's some-

thing that's been bugging me about this from the start."
Jon scrubbed a hand across his whisker-stubbled chin. "At
first I just thought it was Big E being Big E. Disappearing with Zoe like that. Going wherever the wind blows.
But abandoning the ranch without making sure it could
financially sustain itself, making things ten times more
difficult on Katie than they should have been, kicking her
to the curb without any warning…?" Jon shook his head.
"I think Ben's right. I think the old man's finally lost it."

"I would have thought tossing Zoe out on her, ah, ear,
would prove just the opposite," Chance said. Hearing their
grandfather had dumped wife number five on the side of
the road outside Las Vegas had seemed like karmic retri-
bution given Zoe's machinations.

"Ben isn't exactly objective where Big E is concerned."
As if their lawyer brother and Big E didn't have enough
issues, Zoe had, only weeks before her marriage to their
grandfather, been engaged to Ben. Their grandfather had
been the culprit behind a lot of shenanigans over the years,
but stealing Ben's fiancée had been the last straw for the
Blackwell brothers. You mess with one, you mess with
all of them. Or so the family motto was supposed to go.

The sentiment had applied to Ben.

But not, it seemed, to Chance and his dreams.

"Where do you stand on selling the ranch?" Might as
well start confirming the information Ty had previously
provided.

"Honestly? I'm all for it." Jon stepped in front of him
and opened the front door. "I've got my hands full with
the JB Bar, Lydia and the girls. I'm not inclined to push to
save something Big E can't be concerned with."

"Ah, yes. I've got soon-to-be sisters-in-law to meet,
don't I? What was it Ty called Lydia? 'Nanny Fantastic'?
Seriously, dude, you're marrying your girls' nanny?"

Jon reached out and dragged Chance over the threshold. "You're darned right I am. And when you meet her at dinner tomorrow night, you'll understand why." He moved back to close the door and watched as Chance took in the interior of their childhood home.

"What. The. Ever. Loving—" Chance couldn't move. He could barely breathe. What he could do was blink. He had to in order to avoid going blind from the neon pinks, blaring whites and glittering silvers sparkling from nearly every inch of the two-story house. Glitter and sparkles and feathers and sequins. There weren't any memories to be found. Anywhere. "I think I may throw up."

"We have a special trough outside for that. It's been bedazzled." Jon smirked. "Zoe."

"Yeah, well, who else?" Chance finally found the strength to move, but as he walked from the hall into the dining room, he nearly tripped over his feet. What the heck was that hanging from a ceiling? It was like a Muppet had been mounted as a chandelier. He shivered. This was what nightmares were made of. And he said that as the father of a pink-obsessed four-year-old. Make that four-and-three-quarters. "This might be too much even for Rosie." At least he hoped so. Otherwise she'd be calling interior decorators once they got back to Los Angeles.

"Do I hear voices?" A young woman poked her head around the corner from the kitchen, her pretty, friendly face alight with curiosity and amusement. "If it isn't two of the Blackwell brothers. You must be Chance. As you're the only one I haven't met yet." She finished drying her hands on a dish towel and reached out to greet him. "I'm Hadley."

"Ty wrangled you on to stay in this place, huh?" Chance said, keeping a leery eye out for his twin. "He around?"

"He'll be back in a couple of days. Went into Bozeman with Ben to talk to a company about adding zip lines to our activities here." Hadley's smile was contagious. "And you know what they say. Fall in love with the man, fall in love with the land. As Jon can attest with Lydia. Welcome home."

"Such as it is," Chance said, then, seeing Jon's disapproving look, shifted his attitude. "Nice to meet you, Hadley. Welcome to the family."

"And such an interesting family it is." Hadley's eyes sparkled. "Did I hear you two talking about Big E? Are there plans in motion to finally get all this settled?"

"By 'all this' do you mean do we know if we're going to keep this place, sell it or hope Big E comes back and resumes running it?" Jon asked. "Ah, I don't know. Have we decided, Chance?"

"I'd like to know all the particulars before I cast my vote." It was the right thing to say. But it wasn't what he planned to do. The sooner they unloaded this place, the sooner he could stop worrying about money and being hounded about coming home. Make the break clean, final and profitable. That was his goal. "Ty's made an initial argument about keeping it. I hear you're a fan of the place, Hadley?"

"I am. I love it here." If she was concerned about Chance holding her future in his hands, she didn't say. "Come on back. I unearthed your mom's old cookbook a few weeks ago. Just made some of her iced-tea lemonade. You want some?"

Chance's stomach growled as if it had a memory. "Yeah." The air whooshed out of him. How many pitchers had he watched her stir and pour in those early years. "Yeah, that would be great." He followed her as if in some sort of trance. "This isn't some kind of enhanced manipulation technique, is it?"

Jon jabbed an elbow into his back. Chance grunted.

"Not at all." If Hadley was offended, she didn't show it. "I'm trying to work as many Blackwell family elements into the business as possible. Also working on testing some of her recipes for the upcoming weddings. Grace's mother and I have been going back and forth on choices. And don't worry." She set a frosty glass in front of him. "When I'm manipulating you, you'll know about it." She grinned before turning away.

"Touché, and noted." Chance drank eagerly, not realizing how thirsty—or hungry—he was. Which no doubt meant Rosie was as well. The Golden Arches, apple slices and chicken nuggets were a lot of miles ago. "Don't mean to be obnoxious. Been a long few days."

"A four-day road trip with a four-year old." Jon shuddered. "My sympathies. You could have made it easier by flying. One of us could have picked you up."

"Rosie and I made stops along the way." Chance took another drink to avoid admitting the truth. Even with the hotel stays and gasoline, it put him ahead in the budgeting department. A budget that would keep them in their house for the next six months. After that…?

"Speaking of Rosie, where is she? Don't tell me she's off roaming the place like her Uncle Ty used to." Jon smiled and nudged his elbow.

"She's with Katie." Chance was already getting a little worried about letting his daughter go off on that monster of a horse with her aunt. Not that he didn't trust Katie, but somehow it felt wrong sharing the responsibility of his daughter with anyone. It had been the two of them for so long, he wasn't sure he knew how to share her. He didn't know if he wanted to. "We made a quick stop at the turn-off to the ranch before heading down the main road. Katie was on her way to the south pasture."

"She's been so excited about seeing her," Jon told him.

"Glad you bit the bullet and came back. If for no other reason than to let her meet her aunt and grandfather in person."

Chance avoided his brother's disapproving gaze. He didn't need a lecture, nor did he want one.

"Gen and Abby can't wait to meet her. And their famous uncle. They have a surprise planned for tomorrow night." Jon knocked his glass against Chance's. "I have a feeling the terrible two are about to become the terrifying trio."

"Bite your tongue," Hadley said. "Your girls are angels."

"They are now," Jon chuckled. "You two get the after-Lydia product. If you'd like to hear tales of the before, just ask around town. You'll get an earful."

"When did we turn into the kind of men who sit around talking about their kids?" Granted, Chance preferred that topic over anything horse-related.

"And all girls no less," Jon added. "If only Big E could hear us now. So you saw Katie. Everything okay there?"

"Sure." Chance shrugged. Here it comes. "Why wouldn't it be?"

Hadley seemed inordinately concerned over a spot on the counter.

"First time you've been back since you ran off with her sister. That's gotta be awkward."

"For her or me?" Chance asked. "It is what it is. Nothing to be done about it."

"Maybe something could have been done." Jon pinned him with a stare. "Before it was too late."

Chance's knuckles went white around his glass.

"I think I'm going to take this upstairs." Hadley scooted around the counter for Rosie's bag. "Or at least take it to the stairs. Be nice, boys. One of you just got home. You need each other." She patted Chance's arm as she passed. "And blood would clash horribly with this tile."

Chance watched her leave, doing his best to swallow his temper along with any words that might come back to bite him. "If you're meaning to take Lochlan's side in what happened, I'd advise you to keep your nose out of it."

"I've always been on your side, Chance." Jon sat back on the bar stool and studied him.

"Not from where I sit." Chance finished his drink and carried his glass over to the sink. Had any of his brothers ever gone to bat for him with their grandfather? Had any of them ever defended his dreams or his desire to leave? But that wasn't what this was about. This argument was about Maura and the pain her father had put her through when she was already in enough to kill her. "That bitter old man refused to talk to his daughter for ten years. Ten. Years." The anger he'd fought so hard to bury surged back with the force of a tornado. "And why? Because she fell in love with me? Because she wanted something more than the legacy of the ranch her father lived for? Because she chose to leave this dead-end place rather than wither away and turn to dust like her sick mother did? Like everyone who stays here does?"

"Like Katie's doing? Or me? Or my girls?" Jon arched an eyebrow and folded his arms over his chest.

"That's not what I meant and you know it." Even for them, brothers with a penchant for knock-down-drag-outs, this conversation was devolving fast enough to break any record they had of a truce. "Your life, your decision. I don't begrudge you or anyone else that. I gave Maura the option of staying. I told her I'd come back after taking my shot. I said we could make a long-distance thing work. But she wouldn't hear of it. She wanted to leave. She wanted to go with me and live our dreams together. And I wasn't about to tell her no." As if she would have listened. Montgomery women cornered the market on stubbornness.

"I'm just saying the phone works both ways, little brother. She could have—"

"She did." Chance slammed his fist on the counter. "Who do you think she called the day after we found out—" His breath caught in his chest and threatened to suffocate him. "The day after she was diagnosed. Maura wanted her father. She wanted the man who had held her as a child, the man who rocked her and told her everything was going to be okay. Even though we knew it wouldn't be. Do you know what Lochlan did?" Chance rounded on his brother and felt relief at the shock on Jon's face. "He hung up on her. So don't you dare sit in judgment of me and my decisions. He broke his little girl's heart. And for that I will never forgive him."

"I'M HOT," ROSIE whined and slumped against Katie as they crested the hill.

"I bet you are, Little Miss." Katie pressed a kiss to Rosie's head, an excuse to check and make sure she wasn't getting overheated. "Ranching and riding is hard work. We need to get you a hat." And about a gallon of sunblock. Fortunately the sun had been trapped behind clouds for most of their ride and Katie could provide enough protection against the rays.

"Are we going home now?"

"The main house is just down there." Katie pointed to the two-story, weathered white house with green shutters sitting among the outcropping of buildings and the barns. Nearby, the guest cabins loomed, with more than thirty rooms, a dining hall and an activity facility. Checking in on the workers had taken a little longer than expected, which meant Rosie had gone from entertained to bored in about sixty seconds. Even Hip and Starlight hadn't been enough to distract her. Katie should have known better:

the last place an almost five-year-old would want to be was out in the middle of nowhere with a bunch of strangers and a seriously distracted aunt.

Katie wrapped an arm around Rosie and squeezed. She hadn't been able to help it. Once she'd gotten a hold of Rosie, she couldn't bear to let her go. Seeing as Chance was in a more amenable mood than she'd expected, she'd taken every advantage.

"I bet Hadley's made some of her yummy lemonade. Do you like lemonade, Rosie?"

"Uh-huh. Daddy and I make the powder kind out of envelopes at home. But only for special occasions. I like milk. Cows give milk. Daddy says there are cows here."

"There are. And I can teach you how to milk one if you'd like."

"Maybe." Rosie sighed. "Not today. I'm sleepy." She rubbed her eyes.

"I bet you are." Katie choked back tears as Rosie closed her eyes and relaxed against her. Katie kicked Starlight and increased to a gentle trot, but she caught herself looking down into the little girl's face. Grief washed over the hole that had been hollowed out of her, a hole left empty by the loss of her sister.

She missed Maura so much sometimes she ached. Even though they hadn't seen each other in years, they'd talked all the time, texted, teased and informed. Maura had been Katie's best friend since the moment Katie had been born, only eighteen months behind her big sister. They had been inseparable. Opposites in nearly every way, but inseparable nonetheless.

Until Maura had discovered boys. Even then, only one boy would do.

From the time she was fourteen, Maura Montgomery knew she would marry Chance Blackwell. Anyone who ever saw the two of them together knew it as well. Katie had lost count of the number of times she'd come across them after they'd sneaked out together, or when she'd followed them down to Falcon Creek Lake, where Chance would play his guitar and sing to her. Their feelings for one another had always fascinated and confused her.

Katie didn't remember a time her parents were happy. Ranch life was hard on a marriage, especially when one spouse—their mother—wasn't a particularly strong person. Watching Maura and Chance fall in love had created a longing inside Katie she'd since decided simply wouldn't be fulfilled. No one would ever love her the way Chance loved Maura. No one could ever love the land, the work, the business as much as Katie did.

And she could never tolerate anything less.

Which was why this job, this ranch, meant everything to her. She didn't have anywhere else to go, and if she looked, she'd probably have to start at the bottom. It might be the twenty-first century, but the idea of hiring a female foreman still didn't sit well in the male-dominated world of ranching. Besides, she didn't want to go anywhere else. This was her home, her…everything. And the Blackwells were her family. Which was one reason why she'd been willing to help Big E.

"This plan of yours better work…and fast, Big E," Katie whispered into the breeze. "I don't know how much longer I can keep going."

She'd keep going as long as she had to, Katie told herself. She didn't have a choice. Everything was falling into place just as Big E predicted and planned. All the Blackwell brothers were home now. She only hoped things worked out before someone learned the truth.

Rosie let out a sleepy sigh that had Katie smiling. The little girl had Maura's spirit, her enthusiasm and vivacity.

And her propensity for being easily bored. That "bring on life 'cause I can take you" attitude oozed out of every pore. The tiny dimple in Rosie's chin? That was all Chance, as was her nose. The poor kid had been saddled with a double dose of stubbornness from both sides of her gene pool. Katie could only hope Chance would be as amenable to Rosie seeing her grandfather as he'd been letting Katie take her for a ride.

By the time she reached the stables, Rosie's weight was taking its toll. Katie's arms ached as she called Conner, her main stable hand and trail leader, over for help in handing her niece off so she could dismount. She removed her gloves, stuffed them into her pockets and picked up her hat before taking back Rosie, a sliver of love winding through her as Rosie linked her arms around Katie's neck and settled into sleep. She whistled for Hip, who bounded dutifully over to escort them back to the house. Beyond the braying of the miniature donkeys, she heard the bleeting of Billy the goat in the distance. That little guy always knew when Hip came home.

"Right tired one there, Katie." Connor tipped a finger to his hat and grinned. "You're hiring them awful young now, aren't you?"

"Start them early, you know that, Conner." Katie laughed. "Everything good here?"

"Yes, ma'am. Chuck and Dally are heading out to check on a bull we think might have broken through the fence line. Nothing serious. We'll get it taken care of."

"Great. I'll be heading home soon. Need to check on Dad. I should be back around after dinner." There were some minor repairs that needed doing on the guesthouse and the activity calendar needed filling and updating. Ranching was a 24/7 occupation. What downtime came, chances were it wouldn't last long. There was always something that needed tending to. Not that Katie had any idea what to do to relax. She was one of those people incapable of sitting still when there was work to be done.

Katie hummed as she made her way across to the main house. Funny how a seemingly little girl weighed more than a newborn calf. As she rounded the corner she saw Chance standing on the front porch, lounging against the post by the stairs.

Katie's boot caught in the dirt and she tripped, catching herself before they both toppled to the ground. It wasn't seeing him there so much that startled her, but the unusual tingling that electrified her heart and had her catching her breath. The way he stood, looking out over the land, sipping a glass of Hadley's lemonade tea, made Katie think of what it would be like to come home to someone like him after a hard day's work on the ranch. Would he turn his head, smile at her and be happy to see her, even covered in mud and grime and smelling of cows, horses and worse? Would he hold out his arms to welcome her home, take the child from her and hitch her into his own grasp and kiss them both hello?

Katie gasped, guilt sweeping the thoughts from her mind. This was Chance she was thinking about. The man who had—to hear Lochlan tell it—destroyed their family. What was she thinking putting Chance in any role other than that of Rosie's father? And her late sister's widow.

She was thinking she needed a tall drink and long hot bath. She needed to get her head screwed back on straight. Now was not the time for muddled thinking or distractions. She had to be on top of her game now that Big E had gone from man with a plan to overconfident. She had to be prepared for anything. And anything could not include Chance Blackwell.

She shifted her path and made a show of coming into

view. Katie knew the instant he saw them. He went from relaxed contemplation to a soldier at attention. He set his glass on the porch rail and walked down to meet her.

"She okay?" Chance reached for Rosie with firmness and care.

"She's just pooped." Katie shook out her arms and laughed. She stopped herself when she realized the sound echoed falsely in her own ears. "I'm not sure she's as enamored with ranch life as she once was."

"Good." Chance winced. "Sorry. Didn't mean that to sound quite so—"

"Rude?" Katie tried not to be offended. Of course Chance didn't want Rosie liking this place. The only reason he'd come back in the first place was because Ty convinced him he didn't have a choice. "Don't worry. I'll get used to it."

"I'm sorry." Chance rubbed a hand up and down Rosie's back. "You're right. That was rude. It's hard. Being back here." He shifted to look out onto the Rocky-tipped horizon. "I keep expecting her to come riding along, hair flying, those ridiculous boots of hers barely clinging to the stirrups."

"The purple-and-blue boots Dad special-ordered from Bozeman?" Katie's heart flipped. "She almost wore out those things. Bugged him for months until he gave in." She reached up and caught one of Rosie's curls around her finger. "I know you don't want to be here, Chance. I know you hate us. But that doesn't stop me from being grateful you brought her here."

"I don't hate you, Katie."

"Just my father." Didn't he know that hurt her just as much. "I know he's a difficult man, Chance."

"Understatement of the century." Chance cradled Rosie's head in his hand. "He did everything he could to control your sister's life and yours. He could never accept Maura choosing me over him. Or that she left."

"No, he couldn't." Katie shook her head. "I know that. Just as I've always known I came in second where she was concerned."

"Katie." Chance's gentle admonishment wasn't something she wanted to hear.

"You think I don't know?" Katie asked around a too-tight throat. "You think I don't know she was the one he wanted to follow in his footsteps? That she was the one he doted on, spoiled and loved?" She looked into Chance's face, part of her wanting him to correct her, to tell her she was wrong. As much as it hurt when he didn't, she was grateful he didn't lie to her. "I know he cares about me in his own way. I can only hope he's proud, but I won't count on that. I'm all he has now. Even if I'm not what he wants."

"That's the saddest thing I've heard in a long time."

"That better not be sympathy I hear in your voice, Chance Blackwell." Katie stepped back and pointed an accusing finger at him. "I wouldn't trade my life for the world. This place is everything to me. It's where I belong. It's where you all have made me always feel like family."

"You are family, Katie."

She forced a smile. If he only knew. Family didn't lie to one another. Family didn't deceive and manipulate. "I appreciate that. I need to get back and make sure Dad eats something. And I think you should probably get her into bed."

"Which pink cloud shall I choose?" Chance asked. "That place is…"

"Hideous." Katie would give anything to have seen his face when he first walked inside. "Yep. I am well aware. Just imagine Rosie's face when she wakes up and finds she's living in a cotton-candy dispensary."

"Hadley left us dinner. Why don't you come back and join us?"

"I can't. Have to fix Dad his dinner and then I'll be doing another walk-through of the stables. I'll be in the north paddock in the morning, though. If you want a riding-lesson refresher course," she said, then began backing away.

"I'm not getting on a horse, Katie Montgomery," he called after her as she headed toward her truck, which she'd left parked at the back of the house.

She turned and laughed. "We'll see, Chance. We'll see."

CHAPTER FOUR

CHANCE CARRIED A still-sleeping Rosie up to his old room. A room that had undergone a massive personality transplant. He blocked his mind to the frilly canopy bed—he didn't know they still made those—and the swirly pink wallpaper. His old scarred dresser had been transformed, as had the desk that had gotten him through grammar school and high school that sat wedged beneath a window and looked out onto endless pastures and countless cattle. His closet, now stuffed with boxes and junk that had no connection to him, was ajar because of the slightly uneven floor.

And there, on his bed, sat his old hat.

"Subtle, Jon." Or Hadley. Or maybe his veterinarian brother, Ethan, or his new bride, Grace, had gotten sneaky and creative? Ben wouldn't have been so subtle; despite his brother's formal lawyerlike tendencies, Ben would have been more likely to smack Chance in the face with the Stetson. Ty would have put him in a headlock and shoved the hat on his head.

Maybe it had been Katie. That grin on her face as she'd backed away from him had been full of more than humor. He might not have dwelled on a lot of memories from the ranch, but he'd known Katie well enough to know when something was amiss. And despite her easygoing smile and steely-eyed determination, something hovered beneath the surface. She was worried.

No. Chance held Rosie a moment longer than necessary as he watched out the window as Katie hiked over the hill and up toward the foreman's house. She was scared.

"Daddy?" Rosie mumbled and sighed as he laid her down on the creaky mattress. "I rode a horsie."

"I know you did, Bug." Chance kneeled on the floor beside the bed and stroked her hair and sweaty face. "Did you like it?"

She blinked sleepy eyes at him and smiled. "Yes. But my butt hurts."

"It won't hurt so much next time."

"Tomorrow?" Rosie yawned. "I can ride again tomorrow?"

"We'll see." He pressed his lips to her forehead and squeezed his eyes shut to ride the wave of emotion that swept over him. "You take your nap and we'll have dinner later, okay? Then tomorrow you'll start to meet your family. Your aunts and uncles and cousins."

"I have family." Rosie beamed at the thought as her eyes drifted closed. "I love having family. Where's Clyde?"

"In the car. Here." He reached for his hat and pushed it into her hands. "You keep this safe in dreamland for me and I'll go get him. Be careful, though. This hat is special."

"It is?" Rosie hugged the gray hat to her chest and patted it like a pet.

"Your mommy helped Big E pick it out just for me." Or so the story went. Probably Big E's way of making sure Chance held some appreciation for it.

"Mommy liked it here. I like it here." Rosie's arms went lax and she dropped back into sleep, her mouth open just wide enough to emit little-girl snores.

He pulled the folded blanket from the bottom of the bed and draped it over her before leaving the room. Chance stood in the hall, brushing off ghosts and an early-evening chill. The house felt…different. Not at all what he expected after all these months, all the years of dreading returning. His mother and father had doted on this place, but that had been when appliances went on the fritz and the wallpaper peeled from the corners of the room. It hadn't been perfect, or designer chic. But it had felt like home.

He peeked into the bedroom next to his old one, the one Ethan had once occupied, and decided he could settle for that. The floorboards still squeaked in familiar spots, the sound an echo from the past that made his lips curve. The bones of the house were still here. He could hear them creaking as he headed downstairs, as if calling to him, and begging for help. It was the house's soul that was barely hanging on as its heartbeat slowed beneath the avalanche of emotionless detachment and overwhelming color.

The house was no longer a home. But it wasn't only Big E and Zoe who had done the damage. It was as if it had lost its will to live after the boys' parents had been killed, truly gasping its last breath when the final Blackwell brother left.

"Good riddance," Chance whispered. Because Chance, more than anyone, knew there was no turning back time. No matter how hard one tried.

"DAD!" HIP NIPPING at her heels, Katie pushed open the back door, wiped her boots on the porch mat and stepped inside. "I'm home!"

Silence greeted her, as usual, and drew her into the darkened, dated kitchen. She snapped on the light and sighed. There went any hope of a long soak in the tub before she headed back to the ranch to lock things down. Not one item had shifted since she'd left before sunrise and the mess had only been added to. Yesterday's dishes were stacked in the chipped farmer's sink. Toast crumbs sat like dead ants on the counter, mail and bills were piled on the breakfast bar. A pot on the stove proved her father's talents with oatmeal had not progressed in his sixty-eight years and had, in fact, deteriorated to the point that she'd need to buy new cookware. She smelled burned food and sour milk, due in part to the half-empty milk container left out on the counter.

"At least *you* lick your plate clean," Katie told Hip, who was sitting patiently at her eating spot, waiting for the rice-and-chicken dinner Katie stored in the fridge. After a quick zap in the microwave, she set it down, refilled Hip's water bowl and smiled at the dog's grateful whine when Katie gave her the all clear to eat.

Disgust mingled with despair when she returned to the refrigerator and found only two bottles of beer left in the door. She couldn't remember when beer hadn't been considered a food group in her home, which meant it must have started before Katie's mother had died twenty years ago. Only a few months before the Blackwell brothers' parents were killed when their car got caught in a flash flood on Blackwell property.

She was down to the last containers of guest-ranch leftovers, which meant it was time for another pilfering run. She wasn't entirely sure what she'd do in the off-season for belly-warming, delicious food. But she'd worry about that later. For now…

"He can go through a case of beer but won't touch the lasagna." Katie's mutter echoed in the kitchen. Part of her knew she should ask the manager at White Buffalo Grocers to stop making the deliveries, but was that a battle with her father she wanted to wage? She'd given up cursing long ago. What was the point of turning the air blue when it didn't change anything?

Hip, done with her dinner, wandered over to her plush

bed by the sliding door and settled in to watch the sunset. *Ah, the life of a dog*, Katie mused. *Must be nice.*

"Dad?" she called louder this time and headed into the living room.

The large-screen TV Big E had given Lochlan last year for Christmas was on but muted. The shopping channel displayed some gaudy jewelry set that made the Blackwell house look tame by comparison. Newspapers going back a week were strewn on the floor and crinkled under her feet as she approached where her father slept in his easy chair. A half-dozen empty beer bottles were lined up like soul-sucking soldiers on the coffee table that years ago had displayed family photo albums and certificates of merit.

Years ago. A lifetime ago. Losing their mom had started Lochlan on his rapid descent into depression and alcoholism. Maura leaving had shifted him into warp speed.

She dropped down and gripped the arm of the leather chair. "Oh, Dad."

Tears burned the back of her throat. Lochlan Montgomery, fourth-generation ranch foreman, the biggest and—once upon a time—the best man she knew, sat slumped and snoring in his chair like a shell of a human. Snicklefrits, all tufted orange fur and big black eyes, blinked lazily at her before rolling over and going back to sleep.

Lochlan's onetime hefty frame appeared more skeletal now thanks to the diagnosed heart condition that had landed him in the hospital more than a dozen times in the past three years. He cursed his doctors, insulted his nurses, threw any sympathy Katie or anyone offered him back in their faces and raised holy hell if Katie even mentioned bringing in a home-care worker to help keep the house and watch over him.

Katie rubbed her fingers against her temple and tried to center herself. Why was it that the harder she tried to hold on, the more things slipped through her fingers? She was so tired. Tired of worrying about her father. Worrying about the ranch. Worrying about whether Big E was going to put an end to these plans of his and finally get back to where he belonged. Yet all that paled in comparison over being trapped in a mounting pile of secrets and lies.

Secrets she had to keep, lies she had to tell if she had any hope of keeping her job and home.

Lies like Lachlan had gone to visit friends rather than admit he'd become a reclusive alcoholic unable or unwilling to leave his own home.

She was one person and with only twenty-four hours in a day, something had to give. Cracks had begun to form in the foundation of her life: in the knowledge she'd always have a roof over her head, friends to laugh with. A ranch to run.

The ranch. That odd bubble of pride and responsibility bounced inside her chest, like a level searching for balance. The Blackwell Ranch had been her first love for as long as she could remember. Since she'd first placed a booted foot in the dirt; since she'd first sat astride a horse. It might not be hers by blood or ownership, but all the sweat and blood she'd shed in her twenty-seven years had soaked into the ground, connecting them forever.

Once upon a time, her father had felt the same way. Before he'd let anger and grief overtake every emotion living inside what had at one time been a full heart.

Nights like this, Katie couldn't help but wonder if it was her will alone keeping her father alive. Nights like this, she was glad her mother and sister weren't around to see him.

"Dad." Katie dropped a gentle hand on Lochlan's flannel-covered arm and squeezed. "Dad, hey, I'm home. How about we get you something to eat?"

Lochlan mumbled and moaned and turned his head toward her. Katie's stomach roiled against the stench of beer and his growing disdain for hygiene.

"Dad, come on. Wake up, please." She shoved a bit harder to jolt him awake. "Hey, there you go. Hi there." She blinked through the tears and smiled. For an instant, familiar, fatherly gray eyes looked back at her from sunken sockets. His weathered, wrinkled skin shone a bit more brightly as he opened his mouth to speak. "Yeah, it's me. It's Katie. You awake now?" She tugged his hand and he pushed his legs down to close the chair. "Come on, Dad. Let's—"

"Leave me be!" Lochlan roared as his other hand shot out. The smack caught Katie hard against the side of her face. Snicklefrits hissed and leaped off the sofa to disappear into the back bedroom.

Hip's bark split the air as pain exploded across Katie's cheek and shock jolted her system. She tasted blood in her mouth and swiped a hand at her lips before she caught Hip by the collar and pulled her back. Even as her heart broke into a million pieces, Katie whipped her head around as anger overcame sympathy. "Dad, stop it! Stop!"

As Hip growled, Katie scrambled toward Lochlan as he struggled out of his chair. "You're going to hurt yourself, Dad. Please." She crouched in front of him and locked her hands around his wrists, keeping him in place. She couldn't stop the sob from escaping her lips. "Daddy, please."

The haze clouding his eyes seemed to clear. He sat up straighter, blinked rapidly and stared into her eyes. "Katie-girl? That you?"

"Yes, Dad, it's me." She ran her tongue across her teeth as relief sank into her. "You were asleep." There was no telling what he might have been dreaming. "Are you awake now?"

"Course I am. I know when I'm sleeping. What happened to you, girl?" He pushed out his chin. "One of those bulls get the better of you? Ferdinand on the loose again?"

"Something like that." She couldn't bear to tell him the truth. Not when he wouldn't remember it in the morning. Not when he might not care. Hip came up behind her and pushed her nose into Katie's arm. The small, concerned whimper from her loyal friend was like a balm to her bruised heart. "Are you hungry, Dad? You want me to heat you up some pasta?"

"I want a steak," Lochlan grumbled. "Not that that doctor of mine will let me have one."

"I can fix you one, Dad. The doctor won't know." Katie kept a stash of rib eyes in the cold storage for nights like this: when she knew it was the only thing he'd eat. What harm could it do him now when there was so little that made him happy? "It'll be our secret."

"You're a good girl, Katie."

Katie eased her hold and pushed to her feet. There wasn't any point in being angry. Not when her father was living in his own personal hell. "How about you go in and get cleaned up. Meet me in the kitchen in a few minutes and we'll have dinner together." Not that she was hungry now.

She watched closely as he pushed himself to his feet. He'd always been larger than life, towering over her for as long as she could remember. Even now that she was grown, he still did. But only as a shadow of his former self. Sometimes she missed her father so much she ached.

"Go in and change your shirt, okay? You've spilled beer on it."

"I have?" Lochlan plucked the material with his finger. "Sorry about that, girl. Makes for a right mess of laundry, I know."

"I'll take care of it." Laundry. Right. "Just put it in the

hamper in your bathroom, okay?" She kept an eye on him as he regained his balance and wandered into his bedroom, just off the living room. The room had been his office at one time, back when he ran the Blackwell Family Ranch with the precision of an army general. But Katie realized soon after taking over the majority of his tasks at the ranch that it made more sense to move his bedroom here. Now, rather than move everything upstairs, her office was crammed into a corner of her smaller bedroom down the hall. And if she needed to do more extensive work, she used Big E's office.

And that was an office she had to tread carefully in now that the Blackwell brothers and some of their significant others used it for paperwork. Katie's mind buzzed. She'd come to hate that office. With the phone calls she'd endured, the orders she'd taken. Big E's plotting and planning against his own grandsons had moved through that place like a virus, infecting Katie as an accessory. When had everything gotten so complicated?

Katie stood stone-still until she heard the running water in her father's bathroom sink. Only when she was in the kitchen did she press a hand against the side of her face. She rotated her jaw. "Ow." She grabbed a bag of frozen peas from the freezer along with her father's steak.

She threw the meat into the microwave to defrost—an act of sacrilege as far as she was concerned—and went about cleaning up the kitchen. Only when the microwave buzzed and the butter sizzled beneath the raw steak she set in the cast-iron skillet did she duck into her own bathroom to examine the damage.

"Well, you have had worse." She pressed tentative fingers onto the red welt stretching from her eye all the way down to her lip, which had split open. "That's gonna bruise big-time." Katie took a deep breath. Maybe no one would notice.

Bruises, cuts and scrapes were part of ranch life. She'd been kicked and smacked and thrown off more horses than she could count. She'd had busted ribs, a broken wrist and sunburns bad enough to send her to the ER. But this bruise? That was a first. She rubbed a hand against her chest. "Oh, Daddy."

Hip whined from the doorway. Like Pavlov's dog, Katie dropped to her knees and wrapped her arms around the dog, much like Rosie had done earlier that day. Burying her tearstained face in Hip's fur, she held on.

What was she going to do about her father? Put him in a home? That was out of the question. He'd lived on the Blackwell Ranch ever since he was a boy. He was one of the reasons she'd agreed to Big E's plan in the first place. Being officially named foreman of the Blackwell Ranch meant more than job security and achievement. It meant she wouldn't have to worry about breaking her father's heart. She'd do whatever she had to in order to ensure he drew his final breath on this land. He'd lost so much else in his life. This was the least she could do for him.

An odd sentiment for sure, but when all was said and done, Lochlan Montgomery was the only family she had left.

Except Rosie.

Katie released Hip and sat back on her heels, starting to smile as some of the pressure lifted until her lip split open again. "Rosie." The whispered name jarred her back to reality and drew Hip close again. "Yeah, you like her, don't you, girl?" Katie scrubbed her hands deep into the dog's coat and earned a comforting lick across her arm.

Rosie.

Chance had brought Rosie to meet her grandfather.

Until a few minutes ago, Katie believed Rosie might be the solution she was looking for. Lochlan needed something—someone—to live for, as it had been clear for years Katie wasn't enough. She'd seen his reaction whenever Katie gave him a new picture of his granddaughter or showed him one of the videos Chance had sent her. Katie had only been able to dream of seeing the two of them together in person.

Katie's stomach rolled. If Lochlan was in this kind of condition, if he was striking out—physically now—there was no way Katie could let that little girl anywhere near him. It wasn't safe. And Katie would do anything to protect her niece—her sister's only child.

"Katie-girl, you gonna cook that steak or cremate it?"

"Coming!" Katie choked through her tears. "Maura, I'm going to need some help here." She lifted her chin and stared up at the ceiling. She wasn't a religious person. She didn't know what she believed about the afterlife, but she did know there were times she could feel her sister's presence as if she was standing right over her shoulder. Besides, Kate was out of options. Ghosts and memories might be her only solution right now. "You hear me, sis? I can't trust him around your baby. You gotta help me out. Give me an answer. Please." Katie wiped away the tears. "Show me what to do."

CHAPTER FIVE

IF THERE WAS one habit Chance had never broken, in spite of leaving the ranch, it was rising with the sun. Coffee in hand, feet bare, he stepped onto the front wraparound porch and, closing his eyes, took a long, deep breath. The deep pink-and-orange haze stretching across the horizon of the Rockies gave an odd, welcoming kind of warmth as it drew him forward. Colors of the sunrise, kissed with gold, easing the world into another day.

Chance smirked, pulled out his notebook and set down his coffee to scribble the line. *That's two thoughts in two days.* At this rate he'd have a new song in about a year and a half. But he didn't push it or force the words and thoughts into coalescing into anything they weren't ready for. Inspiration would strike. He'd have a new song soon.

He had to. And not just because his bank account demanded it. Chance Blackwell had never been able to do anything other than write and sing. And that felt completely empty without Maura as his muse.

Chance took a long drink of coffee, giving reluctant silent thanks to Zoe for at least knowing to provide a state-of-the-art machine. It was an updated version of the one Maura had bought him their last Christmas together. She'd teased him that he'd need help during those long nights when he was dealing with a teething Rosie and Maura's chemo. They'd laughed about it together. Maura through a sheen of regretful tears.

Chance through a broken heart.

With the animals providing nothing but white noise, the silence of the land pressed in on Chance, driving him back into the house to retrieve his guitar. He took a seat on the chair by the door, set his coffee on the rectangular wooden table and braced his feet on the railing.

His fingers fell into place along the neck, the strings pressing against his fingertips with comforting familiarity. As his other hand brushed down the body and he began playing, the thoughts and worries and fears that had accompanied him on the trek home settled into dormancy as music filled the air.

Chance smiled, dropped his head back and closed his eyes. He let his hands take over and go where they wanted, where they needed to. The melody found itself, as it always did, skipping and hopping its way through his mind like stones across a still lake. He stopped, almost irritated at the thought. Chance sighed and opened his eyes, and after writing it down, left the notepad beside his cooling coffee.

Before he returned to the music and let himself get lost.

"Boy, this brings back memories."

Chance's fingers stilled on the instrument as he dropped his feet to the floor.

His brother Ethan leaned his arms on the porch railing and tipped up the brim of his ball cap. "Sounds good, Chance. Sounds like home."

Sounds like home.

"All that's missing is a hangover and the smell of frying bacon on the stove." Ethan's smile didn't quite reach his eyes, as if he wasn't sure his intrusion was entirely welcome. "Good to see you."

"You, too." The same throat-tightening emotion that had struck yesterday when Jon had turned up caught Chance again. "Wasn't sure when I'd be seeing everyone."

"We're taking shifts. Easing you back into things." Ethan's smile shifted into that quirky grin that had gotten him out of more trouble than in. "Some brothers I can tackle to the ground the second they hit town. Others take a defter touch."

"You make it sound as if I'm made of angel glass." Chance set aside his guitar and choked down cold coffee. "I'm not."

"We know. I know. You're the strongest of all of us, Chance. Always have been." Ethan clomped up the stairs and held out his hand. When Chance grabbed hold, Ethan yanked hard and pulled him out of the chair and into a hug. "Missed you, music man."

"Guess that makes you 'animal man,'" Chance joked when Ethan slapped him on the back. At this rate, by the time he saw Ben and Ty, he'd be black and blue. "Congrats on the degree. Just what you always wanted."

Ethan shrugged, as if becoming a vet wasn't that big a deal. "Hit a few bumps along the way. Things should get easier once we settle this whole thing with Big E and the ranch."

His brothers had definitely not learned the fine art of subtlety over the years. "I haven't made up my mind, Ethan."

Ethan looked confused for a moment, as if he'd forgotten Chance held the deciding vote on whether to sell.

"Not what I meant, actually." Ethan picked up Chance's coffee cup and frowned when he found it empty. "I think it's best we save that discussion for when we're all together. And after you've reacclimated a bit."

"Ethan Blackwell, family diplomat. This Grace's influence?"

"Maybe."

The only way to describe the expression on Ethan's

face at the mention of his fiancée was goofy. So much so, Chance's melancholy lifted.

"She's been amazing," Ethan said. "Turned on all the lights in those dark spaces, you know?"

Chance rolled his eyes to the sky and grabbed his notebook. Now even his brothers were getting in on the songwriting act. "The right woman will do that."

"Tell me you know how to operate that monster coffee machine in there," Ethan said as he headed for the door.

"I do. You want to place an order?"

"The biggest cup you can manage would be awesome. I'm doing my weekly check in on the horses and residents of the petting zoo this morning before I head into town." He pulled open the screen door and jumped back. "Well, hello, little one." Ethan looked down at Rosie, who was wearing her superhero pink pajamas and had done a stellar sleep job on her hair. "You must be Rosie."

"Hi." Rosie rubbed her eyes with one hand and gripped Clyde with the other. "Daddy, I'm hungry."

"I bet you are, Bug." Chance had decided to let her sleep through the evening, mainly because he was exhausted. He'd dropped into the sleep of the dead well before nine. The glamorous life of a single parent. "This is your uncle Ethan. He's an animal doctor."

Rosie's eyes went wide as Chance stooped in front of his brother to pick up Rosie.

"I like animals," Rosie told Ethan over Chance's shoulder, as he tried to scoot into the kitchen before she saw too much of the— "Oo-oh, Daddy! Look at the pink!" She shot straight up, practically standing in his arms as they walked through the house. Chance heard his brother chuckle.

"Keep laughing, bro. Word is we Blackwell brothers only make girls and karma is their friend."

Ethan shut up.

"Daddy, did you ever see so much pink?" Rosie's squeals shot through his skull even as her excitement made him smile. Maybe the pink wasn't so bad. Chance looked at the pink-and-white grouted-tile backsplash and countertops. Then again…

"What's for breakfast, Daddy?" Ethan took a seat at the breakfast bar next to Rosie.

"Kitchen's stocked." He'd done a thorough inventory last night after doing the dishes. "What would you like? *Rosie?*"

"What do you like, Uncle Ethan?" Rosie turned those big green eyes of hers on her uncle.

Oatmeal, Chance mouthed when Ethan looked to him.

Ethan grinned. "I think pancakes sound scrumptious. Perfect start to a day on the ranch. Who's your friend there, Rosie?"

"Clyde."

She slapped her stuffed monster on the counter as Chance muttered under his breath. Griddle. Where would he find the…

"Clyde is very fun-looking." Ethan picked him up to examine. Crooked eyes and crazy patterns on the fabric, the creature's arms flipped and flapped, as did his short little overstuffed legs.

"Mommy's friend Judy made him. She makes a lot of them, but Clyde is the best. Right, Daddy?"

"Yep. Right." Chance found the griddle, now he just needed… "Hey, Rosie. How about you take Uncle Ethan up to your room so he can help you get dressed?" Ha. That should show his brother. Besides, Ethan needed some in-house training given he and his wife were expecting their first child in a few months. "And maybe unpack your bag? Fill up those drawers, Bug."

"I would love to help Rosie unpack," Ethan said. "Miss

Rosie, would you show me to your room while your father toils over breakfast for us?"

"What's 'toils'?" Rosie slipped her hand in his and hopped off her stool.

"It means works hard," Ethan explained and looked at Chance over his shoulder. "Which is what we all do around here. Whether we want to or not!"

"AUNT KATIE!"

Rosie's high-pitched squeal from across the round yard had the horse rearing up to the point where Katie almost lost her grip on the reins. "Whoa, girl. It's okay. You're okay. Calm down." Katie forced herself to relax as she loosened her hold and eased up, staying where she was as the horse readjusted to being handled. The three-year old palomino had been deemed untrainable by her previous owner, who wasn't known for equine patience. Thankfully word had reached Katie, who had, since ranch funds were stretched to the limit, put a hole the size of Montana in her savings account and bought the horse herself. She'd renamed her Gypsy. The horse could fit in nicely once she got over her fear of strangers. And noises.

"Sorry, Daddy. I forgot not to yell."

Katie's irritation melted away at the sadness in Rosie's voice. Part of her wanted to head over immediately and snuggle the little girl to bits, but she couldn't abandon her current charge. Being on a fully operational cattle ranch was a difficult adjustment for anyone, but especially a little girl who knew nothing but city life. Gypsy wasn't the only one who was going to need some additional time and training.

Chance must have understood, because she heard him talking in a low tone. Out of the corner of her eye, Katie saw Rosie nod and press a finger to her own lips.

"I think that's enough for today, girl." Katie dropped her arm and took a step forward, her free hand outstretched. It took a moment, and Katie, looking Gypsy directly in the eyes, silently urged the horse toward her. A few clomps and a cold nose nudge later, Katie wrapped her arm around the horse's head, giving her a good pet and a kiss. "You're an amazing creature, Gyspy-bell. I'm so glad you came to live with me. Maybe one day soon we'll get you out on a run."

The horse gave a neigh and kicked up her head as if agreeing.

"Let's get you back to your stall and brush you down. Good morning, Little Miss." Katie led the horse to the fence where Rosie, wearing jeans, a bright blue shirt and her fancy pink boots, was shiny-faced and peeking through the fence. Hip, patiently waiting as always, sat on the other side of Rosie, looking between her and Katie in canine expectation. Chance had one hand on his daughter's back while he talked to Ethan, who did a double take as Katie approached.

Katie ducked her chin and wished she'd headed straight for the stables.

"What happened to you?" Ethan asked, cutting off his brother in midsentence as he came closer.

"Nothing to worry about," Katie said in what she hoped didn't sound as rehearsed as she'd practiced. If makeup and ranching made a good mix, she could have hidden the bruise with a layer of concealer, but given she couldn't remember the last time she'd slathered anything other than sunblock on her face, showing up at work fully made up would have only kicked up other comments. "Just an accident."

"That's a big owie," Rosie said. "Does it hurt?"

Only her heart. "Not really. Ethan, you here to check on the horses?"

"Among other things." Ethan didn't look nearly convinced by her explanation.

Katie looked anywhere but at Chance. She couldn't, because after one glance, she saw the stony anger flash in his eyes. "Rosie, I'm glad you realized you shouldn't be squealing. That's really important, especially around animals like Gypsy here. She's had a rough go of things and loud noises scare her."

"They scare me, too," Rosie said. "I'm sorry. May I pet her?"

Such a formal, polite request from such a little girl. Chance really had done her sister proud with their child. "Climb on up so you can hold out your hand. And hang on with the other, okay?" The sooner they got her acclimated to climbing fences, the better. Katie tried not to notice Chance draw his brother away so they could talk. She had no idea what they were saying, but she saw Ethan nodding in agreement. "Just like you did with Hip, you need to let her get used to you. There you go. You remembered to pet gently and with the way her coat grows. See that, Gypsy?" Katie nuzzled the horse as she took a step closer to Rosie. "You've made a new friend today."

"Hey, Rosie." Now it was Ethan who avoided eye contact with Katie. "Would you mind coming with me to visit the horses and animals? I could use your help with a few things."

"Really? Oh, Daddy, can I?" Rosie gave Gypsy a final pat and hopped off the fence.

"Of course you can," Chance said. "And after we'll head into town to get you a hat at Brewster's."

"I—" Rosie slapped her hands over her mouth and looked guiltily at Katie. "I get a hat today?" she stage-whispered instead. "Thank you, Daddy."

"Mind your uncle Ethan, you hear me?" Chance called

after them as Ethan took Rosie's hand and led her toward the stables.

"I think Ethan needs to mind Rosie," Katie joked.

"What happened, Katie?" Chance had his hands locked around the top fence rail as he started to pull himself over. Hip growled and shifted into protective mode once again. The dog knew better than to leap into the paddock, but given what had happened last night, she wouldn't put it past Hip to ignore the rules if she thought Katie was in trouble. Katie held out her hand in an order to stay.

"I told you, it's nothing. I need to get Gypsy back in her—" But she cut herself off as one of the ranch hands came over to claim Gypsy. "Thanks a lot," Katie muttered before she turned her back on Chance and headed to the other end of the paddock. She whistled for Hip and circled her finger in the air. The dog took off running around the perimeter to meet her on the other side. The last thing she needed was Chance sticking his nose into something he'd only make worse.

"Katie." Chance caught her shoulder.

"You can still hop fence faster than a jackrabbit," Katie snapped as he spun her around. "It's nothing, Chance. Really." He caught her chin in his fingers, pushed the hat off her head and tilted her face into the morning sun. Her jaw and under her eye throbbed. "Ow. Careful."

"Lochlan did this to you, didn't he? Don't lie to me, Katie." Despite the words, his tone remained gentle. But there was nothing gentle about the fire raging in his eyes. "I know what being backhanded looks like."

She should at least try to lie to him, if only to avoid World War III. But the second she opened her lips, the second she saw the silent challenge mingling with sympathy in those suddenly beautiful brown eyes of his, she surrendered. "He didn't mean it, Chance. He'd been drinking and was asleep. I shouldn't have—"

"You mean he was passed out and too drunk to know what he was doing." His hold eased and he stroked his thumb across the cut on her lip. "Katie, why didn't you tell anyone this was going on?"

"Because it hasn't been," Katie insisted. "I swear, Chance, this is the first time anything like this—"

"It will be the last." Chance took a step back, but she already saw what he didn't want her to see. He was shaking in rage.

"Chance, please, leave it alone!" Katie called after him as he jumped back over the fence and yelled at his brother for his keys. Ethan didn't hesitate. Before Katie got out of the paddock, she was too late.

Chance was already driving away.

CHANCE MIGHT BE many things, but impulsive wasn't one of them. Even at age seventeen, when he'd begun to make plans to leave the ranch to break into music, he'd plotted and planned every step. To do otherwise would only beg for trouble and allow the unexpected to derail him.

There were times, however, when impulsivity was necessary.

Chance skidded Ethan's truck to a gravel-grinding stop outside the foreman's single-story house. A few seconds later, he took inordinate pride in pounding his fist against the rickety door before he yanked it open and walked inside. "Lochlan!"

Darkness welcomed him. Along with the musty smells of dust, body odor and a layer of alcohol so thick he nearly choked.

"What's with the bellowing?" a man's voice echoed from farther inside the house. Chance kicked aside the newspapers and magazines to reach the curtains and ripped them open. "And who's there?"

Sunlight streamed in and illuminated every speck of dust flying in the room. However Chance had once planned on greeting his former father-in-law, it flew right out of his mind as Lochlan Montgomery came around the corner, an amber bottle in his gnarled hand.

"Chance Blackwell."

The change in the old man hit Chance like a gut punch. Chance had grown up intimidated by the ranch foreman, especially after Chance had begun dating Maura. Size aside, there had always been something in the father's face that acted as a warning to Chance to keep his distance. Lochlan stood at six foot six, and it wasn't until Chance turned eighteen that he could almost look the old man in the eye. And even then he'd done it with absolute reluctance.

Now he did so with resolution.

As hard as he stared, Lochlan stared back. Slowly, gradually, the old man straightened, puffed out his chest and locked his jaw so tight Chance could see the muscle pulse in his cheek. "So. You're back then."

"I'm back." It took every ounce of control Chance had not to swipe that smug smirk off his weathered face. The resentment and anger and sorrow of the last ten years swelled up inside of him, nearly cutting off his air. He could feel his body shake as it had when he'd held a crying Maura in his arms, listening to her wonder helplessly how her father could hate her so much. The sound of Maura's chest-deep sobs echoed in his mind. Until the image of Katie's swollen and bruised face pushed aside the memories. "As despicable as I always thought you were, you've managed to surprise even me. Clearly it wasn't enough to throw one daughter out of your life. Now you've taken to smacking Katie around?"

"What foolishness are you talking about?" Lochlan lifted the bottle to his lips, hesitated for a moment, then drank. "Never hurt a hair on my girls' heads." He headed for his chair.

Chance moved in, ripped the bottle out of his hand and, for the first time, stood eye-to-eye with the man who had caused Maura more pain than the cancer ever had.

He set the bottle on the table and took one more step forward, just to make sure Katie's father heard every word. "You're a disgrace of a man, Lochlan Montgomery. And I'm not talking about how you treated Maura after she left. I'm talking about the way you've given in to hate and let it eat at you from the inside out. I'm talking about the way Katie works herself to the bone doing your job and still comes home to take care of you. And what do you do in return? You keep this place looking like a sty as you drink yourself into oblivion and then backhand your daughter so hard you split her lip."

"I did no such thing." His breath reeked of alcohol as he tried to stand up to Chance, only to back away and grab for his chair. "I...did..." His eyes glazed over as he frowned. "Not."

"You did." Chance shoved aside the sympathy. He recognized that helpless, hopeless expression. But Chance had never had the luxury of surrendering to it. Not when he had a little girl to care for. "I want you to listen to me, Lochlan. I want you to hear these words in your dreams." He bent down so Lochlan had no choice but to meet his gaze. "You will not lay a hand on Katie again. Ever."

"I couldn't have done that." Lochlan pressed a hand against his chest, shook his head. "I love my Katie. I love both my girls."

"All evidence to the contrary." Chance kept his voice low and even. "Katie's not coming back here until you're stone-cold sober. You hear me? And if that's not incentive enough, you're not coming ten steps within your granddaughter until I'm convinced you aren't a danger to her."

"Rosie," Lochlan gasped, and for the first time since Chance entered the house, he saw a glimmer of life on his father-in-law's face. "Rosie's here? In Falcon Creek? You brought her...home?"

Home was a relative term. "She's here. But I'm not letting her near you in this condition. You have to earn the right to see her. And from where I'm standing, you're nowhere near close."

"Maura's little girl. My Maura." Lochlan's breath hitched in his chest and for an instant, Chance worried he was going to have a heart attack. "I never thought you'd come back."

"Neither did I." Something he had Big E to thank for. Not that he would. He hated this place as much as he had growing up. He didn't fit. He didn't want to fit. It wasn't home. And now what had Chance done? Not only had he succumbed to Ty's demands he come back and cast the deciding vote on what would become of the family ranch, but he'd also set up his daughter as a pawn in the futile hope her grandfather could be saved.

"You stole my girl. You stole my Maura. All my plans. All my dreams." Lochlan was practically whimpering as he buried his face in his hands.

"I didn't steal anything. She couldn't wait to be free of this place. Maybe it's time you ask yourself why." But it wasn't the first time Chance had wondered if there was some truth to that accusation. It had been easier for him once he knew he wouldn't have Lochlan Montgomery to contend with. "The sooner you come to terms with the truth, the better."

"Blackwells always think they know everything. Always think you know what's right." Lochlan shoved himself back in his chair so hard Chance stepped away to avoid being kicked. "Just take what you want, don't matter what anyone else thinks or wants. You keep your Rosie, just like you kept my Maura. Don't want nothing to do with a brat that's half Blackwell."

Chance rose to his full height as the animosity drained out of him. How lost did a man have to be to even think of saying such a thing? Rosie was his granddaughter. His blood. And he was going to throw her away just as he had Maura? "Anytime you want to divest yourself of the Blackwells you're welcome to. Given your daughter's been pulling all your weight for the past few years, we don't need you. And if this is all you have to offer Katie, she doesn't need you, either."

"You kicking me off your land, boy?" Lochlan picked up an empty bottle and tipped it into his mouth even as hope died in his eyes. "Your grandfather wouldn't have any of that. No-good grandsons of his who don't know how sweet they have it."

"Keep talking, Lochlan." As if Chance cared one iota what his grandfather thought or believed. "The deeper you dig, the harder it'll be to climb out."

"You boys leaving broke the old man's heart," Lochlan spat. "All of you, hacking away because he wouldn't bow to your will. Jon with his cattle, Ethan with his schooling. Ben and Ty thinking they were too good for this place and ideas above their station. And you. You took my girl. What have you done with your life other than ruin mine and Maura's? Pathetic, all of you."

"Careful with those stones in that glass house of yours."

Chance waited until Lochlan's gaze flickered to his before he continued. At this point he couldn't be certain if it was the alcohol talking, or if the old man had poisoned himself so long with hate and self-pity he wasn't capable of thinking anything else. "You did the same thing to Maura when she chose to live her own life. You want pathetic, you look in the mirror."

Chance stalked down the hall, poking his head into the rooms until he found Katie's. Aside from the cluttered desk in the corner and a bright purple-and-blue bedspread on the bed, it hadn't changed much since the last time he'd been in this house. A tall, wide, brown paper-wrapped box had been set in the corner, a package Katie hadn't bothered to open. Curious, Chance looked at the return address, a postal annex in Los Angeles. That seemed...odd. As far as he knew Katie didn't know anyone other than him and Maura in LA.

A crash followed by a string of expletives shot through the house, a reminder that Chance wasn't here to snoop, but get Katie enough to get her by for a few days.

Several minutes later, he'd filled a bag with clothes, grabbed a few other items out of the bathroom and from beside her bed, and headed for the door. He could feel Lochlan's eyes on him, lasers burning through his back. Chance was only too happy to take the last word. "If and when you decide to put down those bottles and make something of the years you've got left, you know where to find me. And your daughter. Until then, enjoy your solitude."

CHAPTER SIX

KATIE PETTED HIP on the head as she and the dog stood out of sight, watching Ethan escort an enthralled Rosie around the petting zoo. Hip had been unnaturally attentive today, surpassing even her normal canine-shadow tendencies. Katie didn't think she'd ever been more grateful for anything in her life as she was for her dog.

Hip was, when all was said and done, the only constant she had. The only one who wouldn't judge her. Not for what she'd done. Not for what she'd no doubt be asked to do. It had been almost two weeks since she'd heard from Big E. Two of the best weeks she'd had in a long time. When she'd agreed to be his eyes and ears on the ranch, it had felt as if the old rancher had tied her to him with every dirty trick she was directed to pull on his grandsons. But she also knew better than to expect Big E to have disappeared for good.

He'd be plotting his final hurrah now that the last Blackwell brother had come home.

With Chance's return to the ranch, it was only a matter of time before the last cowboy boot dropped. Probably on Katie's head.

Chance.

Katie took a trembling breath. He was different than she remembered. He'd always had a level countenance and patience about him, even with his head in the clouds when it came to his music and dreams. Of all the Blackwell boys, all of whom had hit the genetic jackpot when it came to being the epitome of rugged, handsome cowboys, Chance had always stood out thanks to his darker hair and eyes, the added spark and attitude in his step. Until she'd seen him again, she hadn't realized she'd still thought of him as a young man, barely out of his teens, with imaginings of stardom and the excitement of true love pushing him onward.

The man who arrived on the ranch yesterday was all man. All tall, dark and determined man, who carried the pain of loss in his wise brown eyes and a smile of fatherly pride on his full, dimple-touched lips.

As unsettling as Katie's interaction with Chance had been, watching her niece slip into the daily routine of ranch life as easily as Katie slid on her boots lifted her dipping spirits. Between the rabbits and llamas, the pigs and the sheep, it seemed the donkeys had captured Rosie's fascination. The donkeys and Billy the goat.

Hip let out a low whine. Katie grinned. "Don't worry, Hip. I think Billy has enough love for both you and Rosie." Hip made a noise that sounded oddly like she was agreeing. Billy the goat had developed what Katie could only describe as a crush on her dog, and while Hip appeared irritated at first, they'd both gotten used to the little guy following them around. "Why don't you go join them?" She patted Hip on the rump and cocked her chin toward the zoo. "Go on. Ethan won't mind."

Hip stared at her, those dark knowing eyes seeing far more than Katie was comfortable with. Forget Jiminy Cricket. Hip could well have a second career as a canine conscience. "I'll be fine. Go play with your new friend."

Hip trotted off and nosed Rosie from behind, which earned her a drop-down neck-squeezing hug.

"Hard to say who's having more fun."

Katie glanced over her shoulder and found Hadley heading her way, wavy blond hair tied back in a flouncy ponytail, her round face sun-kissed pink. Those laser-beam blue eyes of hers never missed a trick. And Katie should know, given how many secrets she'd been hiding.

"I'll put my money on Rosie." Saying her niece's name gave Katie's heart a jolt. How had the little girl settled in so completely that for the first time in years, she felt whole? "I can't stop watching her."

"Kids are miracle workers." Hadley came up beside her and touched her arm, leaned forward to examine her face. "Oh, ouch. I'd hate to see the other guy."

"I've had worse." Katie shrugged. "Out for a morning walk?"

"I can't get enough of this place." Hadley sighed the contented sigh of a woman in love—both with Tyler Blackwell and Montana. Katie had found Tyler's fiancée to be a breath of fresh air when she'd arrived from Portland with Chance's twin last month. Katie had had the distinct impression there was more to the relationship than either had let on, but who was Katie to judge? "I've never seen you stay this still for so long. I didn't know you could."

Katie smiled. Hadley was solid and determined, and made anyone and everyone laugh. Over the past few weeks, the two of them had developed a friendship that reminded Katie of the one she'd shared with Maura. Before...

Katie cleared her throat. "How are things up at the guesthouse?"

"Slow. Our last guests headed out this morning. Nothing on the books for several days at least. But that's expected with school starting up soon." Hadley didn't seem in any rush to head back there. "We're noodling with the idea of approaching schools about field trips and overnight stays. I'll talk to Ty about it when he gets back. What do you think?"

"I think I'm not sure why you're checking with me when it's up to the brothers at this point." Especially since it didn't seem as if Big E was going to grace them with his presence anytime soon. The whole guest-ranch idea had been Zoe's plan. Not surprising, given Big E's aversion to change, at least, where ranching practices were concerned.

"Because I know what everyone else does." Hadley bumped her shoulder against Katie's. "Ty told me this place would have fallen apart without you. Even before Big E took off."

"Ty exaggerates." Still, the sentiment was nice to hear. Being appreciated wasn't something Katie was particularly used to. It wasn't as if Big E heaped praise on anyone, especially a woman looking to make a name for herself outside her sphere. Or so she'd overheard Big E tell her father one day. Not that Katie had let that hold her back. Big E could think whatever he liked about her. Katie loved this land. His land. She'd work it to her dying day if she had her way. He'd come to understand that.

Just in time for him to use it as a weapon against her.

"Ty doesn't exaggerate about important things," Hadley said.

Katie turned and leaned back against the barn wall. "Why do I get the feeling this is leading somewhere?"

"Nowhere weird," Hadley laughed. "But the other night I was talking with Rachel, Grace and Lydia. About the main house. And how much the brothers—"

"Hate it now?" Katie flinched. "Yeah, they aren't the only ones." She might have had to admit Zoe's idea about the petting zoo had been spot-on. And sure, in hindsight opening the ranch to guests for the real "cowboy" experience—if that was what a guest wanted—seemed to be paying off. In pennies, perhaps, but pennies added up. But what Zoe had done to the boys' childhood home should be considered a crime. It was as if she'd ripped the best part of their childhood away from them.

"Well, depending on what happens—"

"You mean if the brothers decide to sell?" Katie's heart seized at the notion. There was a twist she'd bet Big E hadn't seen coming. If the brothers did decide to sell, there went any hope of her ever earning a foreman position. She'd have to start all over again, which on its face wasn't so horrific. But any other ranch wouldn't do. The Blackwell Ranch was her home. She'd do anything to stay. She already had. "Any idea where things stand on that these days?"

"No change, last I heard." Hadley shook her head. "They're tied. Ben wants to sell so he and Rachel can improve the Double T. Ty wants to keep it, obviously, since he's running full steam ahead and hired himself as manager for the guest ranch. Ethan's with him, which makes sense given the large-animal clinic he wants to open on the property."

"Which would bring in more business to the guest portion of the ranch," Katie said. "What about Jon?" The oldest Blackwell brother had his own successful organic cattle ranch nearby. She already suspected which side of selling the brothers each landed on, but it wouldn't do any harm to confirm.

"Jon's for selling. Of course. Big E wouldn't do things his way, so he made it happen himself. Why would he give up what's he's built for this place?"

Katie nodded and agreed with Hadley's somber tone. Why indeed. Big E's ego and bullying had driven his grandsons off this land in the first place. Little did they know it was Big E's selfish agenda that had brought them all back.

With her help. Guilt lodged like a stone in her chest. How she hated the lies.

"Either way, that decor in that house has to go," Hadley said. "The brothers won't want to step foot in it if they keep it, and if we sell, it'll affect the selling price. So we were thinking, as wedding presents for Jon, Ben, Ethan and Ty we'd do a remodel."

"Okay." Katie still didn't understand what this had to do with her. "I'm not an interior designer."

"No, of course not. None of us are. But you know the history of this place. We want to turn it back into something their mother would have liked. Maybe bring back some of the better memories. We were thinking you could help us track down some photographs and stuff? So we know what it looked like before twinkle-toes Zoe got her hands on it?"

"Oh. Yeah, sure." Katie had to admit the idea appealed. It would be nice not to feel nauseated whenever she walked into the main house. "You do like to keep busy, don't you? Isn't there a wedding coming up?"

Jon and Lydia's nuptials this fall were fast becoming the talk of the town. Not just because Falcon Creek loved a reason to celebrate, but it would be the first formal event to be held at the Blackwell Ranch. The first of three weddings, since Ben and Rachel had been their usual practical selves and settled for a quick city-hall ceremony.

"I can take a look around my place," Katie offered. "And Zoe loaded the attic with a ton of boxes of stuff. If you're lucky, there might be some of their parents' stuff there, too."

"Oh, excellent idea. And one thing. This is a secret. We don't want any of the brothers knowing until we get everything locked down and presentable." Hadley turned hopeful eyes to Katie. "You can keep a secret, right?"

Could she keep a secret? Katie turned her attention back to Rosie before the guilt and regret showed on her face. "Better than anyone else you know."

CHANCE PARKED ETHAN'S truck where he'd found it. Blood pounding in his ears, he gripped the steering wheel so tight his fingers went numb. Part of him ached in sympathy for his father-in-law. Chance couldn't imagine how he would go on if something happened to Rosie. But he also knew he'd never turn his back on his daughter, no matter how much he might disagree with her choices.

Which circled Chance back to the question that had been echoing in his mind from the moment he'd stepped foot in the ranch foreman's house.

How did a man get to be where Lochlan Montgomery sat now, saturated with drink and mired in hostility, stuck in a regretful past of his own making? It wasn't as if Maura had planned to sever all ties with Falcon Creek when she left. She'd loved this land almost as much as Katie did, and certainly more than Chance—he couldn't wait to break free of Big E's dream-killing expectations. As much as he was happy to leave, he would have been happy to make visits home with her if only to put a smile on her face.

Instead, Chance watched a piece of her die the day she realized she'd never be able to walk through the front door of the house she'd grown up in without triggering a fight. Or worse, be welcomed by angry silence.

Chance let out a long breath and forced himself to relax. His hands dropped into his lap as he stared across the ranch to where Ethan and Rosie were making the feeding rounds in the petting zoo. All those animals, all the things to do, he'd be lucky if he wasn't forced to take a crowbar to pry his daughter free of this place when it was time to leave.

He jumped at the knock on his window and found Katie standing beside the truck, hands on her hips, her eyes blazing and her jaw locked so tight she reminded him of Lochlan. "Well?"

Her muffled voice echoed through the cab before Chance shoved open the door and climbed out. "Well what?"

"Well what happened?" She took a step back as Chance hauled her bag out of the back of the truck. "What's that?"

"Your clothes. And some other stuff you'll probably need. Anything I missed you can get from Hadley at the guesthouse." He walked right past her into the house. He left her bag at the bottom of the steps and headed into the kitchen for more coffee. A tankard should do. Or maybe he'd just set up an IV line.

The front door slammed shut. "What do you mean stuff I'll probably need?"

"You're not going back there." Chance began putting the dishes she'd left to dry away. "Not for a while at least."

"I'm not?" Katie stood at the end of the counter, arms folded across her chest, looking oddly like the petulant teenager he remembered from his youth. Except she wasn't a teenager any longer. She was a full-grown woman with more spunk and fire than any woman had a right to. "And who are you to tell me where I can and cannot go?"

"The man who just listened to your father call Rosie a Blackwell brat."

Katie's mouth dropped open. "He did not! That doesn't even make any sense."

"Of course it does. She's half-Blackwell. Apparently that's qualification enough to negate the Montgomery side." He slammed a coffee mug onto the shelf. He didn't like thinking that he was the reason Lochlan had turned his feelings of betrayal into hatred for the entire Blackwell family. Chance was the one who had taken Maura away. But now it seemed as if his brothers had been tainted by association. "No way am I letting her anywhere near that man while he's drinking. He's dangerous. I can see it all over your face."

"I've been handling my father on my own for more than a decade, Chance Blackwell. I don't need you riding back into town on your white horse playing hero."

"I'm not playing at anything." Especially hero. He was a man struggling to keep things together. "He's unpredictable, Katie. The only thing keeping him upright at this point is the alcohol coursing through his system. It's not safe for you."

"Again, not your decision. That's my home, Chance."

"It's a house, not a home. And it's not like you're there a lot anyway, right? The only reason you're still there is to take care of him. And he doesn't want that, does he? So you'll stay here. With me and Rosie. She'll love it. She'll think it's a long-term slumber party."

"That's low, even for you, Chance Blackwell." Katie's eyes narrowed. "Using that little girl against me. You can't stop me from going back."

"You're right." Chance planted his hands on the counter and ducked his chin. "I can't. But what I can tell you is that you're only enabling Lochlan. He's got no reason to change or even want to. You make excuses for him. You cover for him. You coddle him and prove there aren't any consequences to his actions. You lied to my brothers about him being gone while he was here soaking up alcohol like a sponge, yet you turn a blind eye to the fact that he doesn't care about anything or anyone."

"I do—"

"Did Big E give you a raise when you took over for Lochlan?" Chance asked. "Did he shift Lochlan's salary over to you and demote him? Or are you doing all the work your father did and more to prevent Lochlan from feeling less than?"

"You'd do the same for your father," Katie growled back.

"No, I wouldn't." Chance cringed, recalling the ghostly images of the father who had died when he was ten. He barely remembered his dad. "I might not have known him, but I know he never would have turned his back on one of his kids because they chose to live their own life. And I know he wouldn't have dived into the bottom of a bottle because dealing with life was just too hard. And if he did, I'd have done anything I could to pull him free of it. Even if it meant cutting off all ties. He certainly wouldn't have—" Chance cut himself off. He'd taken enough swings at Lochlan already; no need to tell Katie about him hanging up on Maura the day of her diagnosis. She had enough to contend with already.

Katie looked at him for a long time. Then, when he thought she might storm out, her arms dropped to her sides and she sagged against the counter. "He's the only family I've got left, Chance. I can't abandon him."

"You mean like Maura did." Chance flinched at the implied accusation. "You think I made her choose between me and your father."

"No." Katie shook her head as she rubbed a finger hard against her temple. "No, I spoke with Maura enough over the years to know Dad was the reason she never came back."

"But you think she should have tried."

Katie looked as if she was debating whether to answer. "It couldn't have hurt. It might have worked. I can't leave him alone, Chance. I'm afraid of what he might do." Tears exploded in her eyes before she looked up at the ceiling and blinked. "I don't want to be alone."

Because a horrible excuse for a father was better than no father at all? Chance wasn't certain he agreed. He knew what it was like to lose a parent—both parents. And he knew, after dealing with Maura and her father, that he'd been dealt the better hand.

"You're not alone, Katie." Chance set down the flatware and walked over to her. He placed his hands on her shoulders and pulled her into a hug. "Do you remember what I told you the day Maura and I left?"

She stood there, stone-stiff in his arms, and nodded.

"I told you that you were my family now. You and Maura were a package deal as far as I was concerned. I promised to be there whenever you needed me. That's what I'm doing now, Katie. You need someone to tell you what you're doing with your father isn't doing anyone any good, especially him. He has to learn on his own there's something to live for. At least give him the chance to try."

"You really think I should stay here?" Katie stepped back, but continued to look at him. "In this palace of pinkness?"

The tip of her hat barely reached his chin. Her eyes were red, her cheeks pink under the bruised skin of her cheek. But those eyes of hers… The sparkling determined eyes lightened his heart and made him forget this was the little girl who used to follow him around and listen to him play the guitar. Or the teenager who had tagged along with him and Maura when they went to the river and eaten so many peanut-butter sandwiches she'd made herself sick. The Katie who, at the age of fourteen, had stared down a runaway stallion and coaxed him back into his stall. She'd never been afraid of anything in her life. She was a woman who did whatever it took to get what she wanted. She was, in a lot of ways, stronger than Maura had ever been. She'd had to be. Because she'd stayed.

Maura...

Chance managed a weak smile even as he felt his heart tip. This was Katie, he reminded himself. Maura's sister. The last thing he should be thinking about was the type of woman she'd become.

"This place isn't so bad." He tried to joke as he resumed cleaning up the kitchen. "Once you get use to the glitter and..." He glanced at the feathered chandelier hanging over the dining table. "Feathers." He shuddered.

"I don't like being told what to do."

"Family trait," Chance told her. "One I'm quite used to, thank you very much."

"I don't need looking after, Chance. I'm a grown woman. I've been taking care of myself for years."

Longer than she should have been, Chance wanted to say, but he refrained from digging the knife in deeper. "Understood."

"Is it? Chance." She touched his arm, startling him speechless as a shock of electric attraction shot straight through him. "I'm not a kid anymore. I don't need you looking after me because of some obligation you feel to Maura."

"That's not what this is." Chance couldn't stop staring at her hand and wished he could ignore the warmth seeping through him. "Believe me, it's not."

"Fine. I'll stay. For a couple of days." She removed her hand and poked a finger into his bicep. "If for no other reason than so I can spend more time with Rosie. If you don't mind?"

He shook his head. "I don't mind. She needs a woman in her life. Someone she can look up to. And admire." And there wasn't anyone more suited to that job than Katie Montgomery.

"Just so we understand each other. Now if you'll excuse me, I need to head out to the stables and check on the foals. I'll choose a room later."

"Sounds like a plan." Chance watched her leave. When he heard the door close with a decisive snap, he gave in to his wobbling knees and sank back against the counter. "What the heck was that?" He brushed his hand over his arm where she'd touched him. Held on to him. She was Maura's sister. He couldn't be attracted to her. Have feelings for her. Could he? "No. Absolutely not." Katie was a friend. She was Rosie's aunt. She was...like a sister to him. A little sister. To all the Blackwell brothers. "Ridiculous."

But as he headed back outside to take Rosie into town for her hat, he swore he heard the familiar, ghostly sound of Maura's gentle laughter on the wind.

CHAPTER SEVEN

"Do you think they'll have a hat to match my boots, Daddy?" Rosie held Chance's hand as she skipped beside him across the street to Brewster Ranch Supply.

"I wouldn't be surprised." Chance bit the inside of his cheek to stop from laughing. Given his brothers' and Katie's reaction to the pink bubble that was the main house, he could only imagine what they'd think of Rosie turning up as a pink cowgirl.

"I love Montana, Daddy." Rosie's matter-of-fact statement set off warning bells in his head. Her own head had been turning back and forth like it was on a swivel as she tried to look everywhere at once. "Don't you?"

"It's all right." He didn't lie to his daughter. Ever. But telling her the truth—that Falcon Creek had always felt more like a prison than a home—seemed a bit harsh to lay on a little girl. "Tell me about the animals you met with Uncle Ethan."

"Ooh, Daddy." Rosie sighed and dragged him onto the sidewalk. "I petted llamas, donkeys and rabbits and there's Billy the goat. Aunt Katie says it's Hippo's boyfriend…"

Rosie's excited chatter was the perfect excuse to distract him from the memories swirling around him. In most ways, time had stood still in Falcon Creek. It was still a town with one traffic light and had the obligatory diner, the Clearwater Café, and a dive bar called the Watering Hole. He spotted the beauty parlor behind them, and a few gift shops and new additions that piqued his curiosity. Familiar faces passed by; some he knew by name while others only niggled at his memory. His face, however, was clearly one people recognized as he caught more than one surprised and wide-eyed expression aimed in his direction.

"And there's a horse named Butterscotch. She just had a baby, Daddy. Her name is BB. A baby horse is called a foal. Did you know that, Daddy?"

"I think I did." He loved that his daughter was a sponge for information and words. One of the things Maura had been able to do, even when she was at her sickest, was to tuck herself into bed, Rosie under one arm, and read to their daughter. He lost track of the hours he'd spent listening to the sound of his wife's voice reciting fairy tales, as magical stories echoed through the bedroom cluttered with medical supplies and prescription bottles. "What else did Uncle Ethan show you?"

"Cows! Oh, Daddy! You should see all the cows on the ranch! There are bazillions of them and their babies are called calafs."

"Calves," Chance corrected.

"Yeah, that. And they're so cute! I wanted to hug one but Uncle Ethan told me that wasn't a good idea."

Uncle Ethan was right. He didn't think the cows would be as amenable to hugs as Hip had been.

"Well, now, who's this?" An old man sitting on the porch of Brewster's leaned forward in his chair and narrowed his eyes at Chance. "Well, I'll be. The last one's come back. Chance Blackwell."

"Hi, Pops." A rush of warmth and affection had him smiling. Talk about a Falcon Creek fixture. Pop Gardner was part mentor, part lie detector, part town conscience with an added chess lesson thrown in for good measure. Chance had found refuge in those games after long hours

spent working the ranch, learning more about life and strat-
egy under Pop's tutelage than he ever had in school. "It's
good to see you."

"It's good to be seen. Hello, little lady." Pop turned his
knowing eyes on Rosie, who, Chance could tell, was about
five seconds away from board destruction. "Do you play?"

"Play what?" Rosie asked as Pops caught her hand before she moved a pawn.

"Chance, don't tell me you haven't started this youngun
playing yet? If she's yours then she's got the aptitude for
it. Your daddy's whip-smart. You know that?"

"Uh-huh." Rosie nodded. "Daddy, are you going to
play?"

"We have time for a few moves. I think." Chance sat in
the same weathered wooden chair he'd last sat in ten years
ago and pulled Rosie between his legs to hold her still.
"Rosie, this is Pop. He kind of runs this place."

"Hi." Rosie leaned forward and examined the pieces.

"It's nice to meet another Blackwell girl," Pop said.
"Funny how Mother Nature is evening things out. You
here for a good while then, Chance?"

"No distracting me while I make my move," Chance
murmured as he pulled Rosie's hand away from the queen.

"Look, Daddy. There's a girl!"

"Of course there is," Pop said. "Most powerful piece
on the board, too. The object of the game is to protect the
king, but I always keep an eye out for this lady."

"Is this like checkers? Do you get to jump pieces?"

"Not quite, Bug." Chance spotted a sleek gray cat slipping around the side of the building. "Looks like you're
about to make another friend." Chance pointed to the animal and, as predicted, Rosie abandoned him and the chess
game to sit on the step and hold out her hand.

"Pretty as a picture."

Chance didn't miss the wistfulness in Pop's voice, nor did Pop cover the misty expression in his eyes.

"Looks like her mama, she does. Sounds like her, too." Pop gave Chance an encouraging smile. "You did real good, boy."

"I'm trying to." Chance shifted his rook across the board and earned a discouraged frown from Pop. "Your move."

"Daddy, look! Kitty likes me!"

Chance glanced over and found Rosie's arms filled with feline affection.

"Name's Whiskers," Pop said, seemingly unconcerned with Rosie's interaction with the animal. "Not always the friendliest of tykes, but she knows who she likes."

"Rosie's a regular Dr. Dolittle," Chance chuckled and swore he saw "help me" on the cat's face as Rosie shifted her over her shoulder.

"Course she is. She's a Blackwell."

Chance cringed. Yeah. That's what he was afraid of.

"You best get to your shopping, boy. This one's going to take some thinking on."

"Yes, sir." Chance got to his feet. "I'll stop back on our way out. Rosie, come on. Leave the cat alone and let's get you your hat."

"And *you* need boots," Pop ordered. "Those things on your feet aren't as citified as those slicksters your brother Ben's been known to wear, but around here, you need boots."

If only to trample through the piles of horse—

"Daddy, Aunt Katie said there are lots of cats and kittens on the ranch."

"Uh-huh." Chance pulled open the door and held it for Rosie to scamper inside. He'd been wondering how long it would take to reignite the "I want a cat" conversation. He supposed he should count himself lucky she didn't want a cow. "Aunt Katie would know."

"I'd be a good kitty mommy, Daddy. I know I would be."

"I know you would be, too. We'll talk about it another time." He bopped her on the behind and steered her down the aisle.

"Chance!" Alice Gardner, store proprietor and mother of his sister-in-law to be Grace welcomed him with a giant smile. "We were wondering when you might turn up. And this must be Rosie."

"Hi. We're here to find a hat. I want a pink one, please."

Chance had never been able to describe the feeling of pride he felt whenever Rosie met new people. She was such a kind soul, so much like her mother in that she had a smile for everyone. Rosie's heart, however, was about ten times the one Maura possessed, which at times left Chance worrying how easily it could be broken.

"It just so happens we have lots to choose from." Alice came around the counter and held out her hand. "Chance, would you like to join us or—" she glanced down at his sneaker-clad feet "—was there something you needed?"

"Boy needs boots!" Pop called in from outside.

Chance felt his cheeks warm.

"Leave him be, Pop." Frank, Alice's husband, appeared from the back office followed by a petite blonde, who had to be Grace.

He'd had a bit of trouble putting a face to the name as he'd done his best to forget everything he could about Falcon Creek. But now that he saw her... Chance grinned. Yeah, he could totally see how she and Ethan ended up together.

"Chance." Her smile made him think of warm sunsets and cool breezes wafting across open fields of wildflowers. Chance's hands clenched as he struggled to keep hold of the thought as he dug for his notebook. "Everyone's so excited all the Blackwell brothers are finally home."

"Everyone?" Chance couldn't imagine it was that big a deal they'd all hit town, even if it was because Big E had pulled a disappearing act a few months back.

"Well, sure." Grace rocked back on her heels. "Although people are starting to lay odds on how long it takes for you all to start stirring up trouble. The town could use a little excitement if you ask me."

"Trouble comes in many forms." Frank grinned and patted a welcoming hand on Chance's shoulder. "Not all of it bad. Can I show you some boots, Chance?"

"Can't hurt to look," Chance lied. He knew looking could hurt. A lot. The last thing he'd wanted to do was step foot onto Blackwell land, let alone slide his feet into boots that felt like anchors to the past.

A few minutes later, after having postponed a decision as long as he dared, he found a pair of black ones that reminded him of the pair his father had worn. He stroked his fingers against the soft leather, felt the dips and dots of the precision stitching, equally delicate and strong. Tradition and history, hard work and reliability. All that went into making a rancher into a legend. And a Blackwell into a man.

"Daddy, look!" Rosie's excited squeal split the air and severed the melancholy hovering around his heart. He peered down as Rosie struck a pose worthy of a runway model. "I love it!"

"It's not pink," he said and refrained from adding "thank goodness."

"But it has pink flowers—look!" Rosie pointed her finger at the narrow band of embossed pink roses. "Misses

Alice says that way I can change it whenever I want, but still keep the hat."

He glanced up to find Alice and Grace covering their mouths to stop from laughing.

"Can I get it, Daddy? Please?"

"It's why we came, isn't it?" Before he changed his mind and let the past continue to define him, he snatched up the boots and followed his daughter to the register. While Rosie wandered the store—with her hands either clapping or in her pockets—he pulled out his wallet. "How much?" The total Frank gave him nearly stopped his heart. Quality gear cost. He knew this. But he'd neglected to consider inflation. Until he had money coming in or until they sold the ranch, he had to consider every penny spent. And Rosie always had to come first. "You know what?" Chance cleared his throat. "I think I've got a pair back at the ranch I can still fit into. Let's just make it the hat."

"You sure?" Frank didn't seem convinced, not that Chance looked him in the eye for long.

"Yeah, just the hat." He could only hope the credit card would go through.

"Chance—" Grace stepped forward, touched a hand to his arm and the instant he looked into her kind, concerned face, he knew she knew.

"My problem," he told her under her breath as humiliation swept over him. "Please, keep this between us."

"Sure." Her hesitation no doubt had to do with keeping secrets from his brother, but it wasn't as if his money issues were a relationship breaker.

"We're going to Jon's place tonight for dinner." Chance was grateful for a reason to change the subject. "Any suggestions on a gift?"

"Lydia's crazy about the Maple Bear Bakery's maple muffins. And they do up a nice little gift box."

"Perfect. Where is it?" He accepted his credit card back with a silent sigh of relief and plastered on a smile.

"Two blocks south," Frank told him. "Right next to the library. Speaking of which." Frank headed over to the town bulletin board and tapped a finger against the flyer. "We're holding a fund-raiser in a couple of weeks at the Silver Stake. Building needs a new roof and there's no money in the town budget. Having a headliner in could bring a lot of attention and donations."

"It sounds great." Chance swallowed hard twice. "I'm, um, not sure how long Rosie and I are staying, though." What a horrible excuse, but it sounded less pathetic than "I'm not in the right mind space to perform in front of anyone now."

"Well, when you are, you let us know. Me and Alice are doing the organizing. We've had trouble finding sponsors in Bozeman and Billings, but if we could attach Chance Blackwell's name—"

"I'll keep it in mind." And pray they found another way to make money. "Thank you both for the help." Chance took an extra moment to look at Grace. "Girl or boy?"

"Not sure." She rubbed her hand around her stomach. "But given the Blackwell boys' track record—" she gestured toward Rosie "—I'm laying odds on a girl."

"We all are," Frank said as Alice joined him behind the counter.

"Thank you for taking care of Rosie," Chance told Alice as he backed away. "I'm sure we'll be back soon."

"I'm sure you will, too," Alice said. "And, Chance?"

"Ma'am?"

"Welcome home."

KATIE SAT ON Starlight and stared out over the hill to where her house sat, silent and accusing. Guilt and regret had accompanied her the rest of the day, a day that was coming to an early close as it was off season both for cattle and guests.

Frustration tightened her stomach into knots as she turned Starlight back to the ranch. On one hand, she knew Chance was right. She had been enabling her father, making excuses for him. Covering for him.

But he was her father. He'd done his best even if his best had brought her more pain than she would have liked. How could she just turn her back on him?

She could imagine Chance's reaction should she go back home. It wasn't anger she was worried about, but disappointment. She couldn't bear the idea of letting any of the Blackwell brothers down, but especially Chance. He was, always had been…different. Special.

Her chest fluttered as she imagined his smile, heard his laughter on the breeze, recalled the pride and love shining in his eyes as he looked at his daughter. It was as if she finally had proof of what she'd always known: Chance Blackwell was a good man.

But that didn't mean he could tell her what to do.

"I can hear you thinking from here."

Katie rolled her eyes as she brought Starlight to a stop by the barn. Chance, arms folded and leaning against the wall like an out-of-time cowboy looking for purpose. He wore simple jeans and a dark T-shirt, and the sneakers on his feet were all kinds of ridiculous for ranching. He was, in essence, a simple man with complexities she couldn't begin to fathom.

Complications she didn't want or need in her life. Complications that would be yet another betrayal.

"You do realize we're putting you to work before dawn." And he'd be flat on his back by noon. "Gotta bring the herd across first thing. Last run for a while."

"I'll do whatever you need me to do," Chance said. "Anything that doesn't include climbing on the back of one of those things."

"You going to let a four-year-old get one over on you?" Katie challenged.

He grinned. "She's almost five. And darn right I am. My ego's just fine on that front, thank you very much. I put Rosie down for a nap. We're going to Jon's for dinner in a few hours."

"Rosie's going to meet her cousins then." Katie's confidence that Rosie would continue to fall in love with the Blackwell Ranch grew. The more attached she became, the harder it would be for Chance to take her away again. Katie bit her lip. Or for Chance to leave.

"Seems that way. You looking for a way to make a break for it?" He jerked his chin toward her house. "Or to go back and check on him without me finding out."

"I wouldn't sneak around like that," Katie lied. "At least not without a plan." Now that Chance would understand. "Want to help me lock things up?"

"Sure. Will you show me Butterscotch and her foal?"

"BB?" Katie froze halfway off Starlight. "Of course." Butterscotch had been his mother's horse and held a special place in all the Blackwell boys' hearts, but especially Chance's. He'd never held an affinity for any animal on the ranch, except Butterscotch. This past year, thanks to Zoe's selfish ignorance, the mare had endured a risky pregnancy that had resulted in a beautiful foal, one that apparently Rosie had taken quite a shine to during her tour of the ranch with her Uncle Ethan, especially once she heard the name. "She's become quite the grand dame around here." She led her horse around and into the stables, stopping in front of Butterscotch's stall to wipe him down. "Here she is. Hey, girl. You've got a special visitor."

Katie was well aware Chance was right behind her as she slid open the bolt and opened the door.

When he didn't respond, she turned to face him. His face had lost all its color. He'd shoved his hands into his pockets and she could hear him breathing. "Chance?"

"She's just as I remember her. She's beautiful. Just like Mom."

His whisper broke her heart. The twenty years since Brenda Blackwell's death disappeared. For an instant, she saw the boy Chance had been, hurting and angry as he'd raced on foot to the river, where he'd screamed himself hoarse. She'd only been eight at the time, but she'd followed him, and stayed hidden as he'd thrown rock after rock into the swollen river that had taken away his parents.

"It's like your mom's still here," Katie told him. "At least that's how I see her. She's a part of this place."

"Yeah." Chance remained frozen as Butterscotch took a slow step forward. Then another. And another. Until she stood before him. And nuzzled his cheek. "Hi, girl." He raised a hand and held her to him, pressing his lips against the side of the horse's face. He closed his eyes. "It's good to see you. What's your little one's name?"

"BB."

"BB. That's an odd name even for a horse." Chance's lips quirked.

"We also call her Blue." Katie waited for the word to sink in. "Butterfly Blue. BB for short."

When Chance opened his eyes, she swore she saw his heart shining in the brown depths. "Really?"

Katie shrugged, as if naming one of their horses after his song was an everyday occurrence. "Seemed right. Maybe you weren't as forgotten as you thought." For a variety of reasons. Katie cleared her throat, blinking back tears as she walked away. "I need to get cleaned up. Just lock the door when you're done, okay?"

"Yes. Thank you, Katie."

"You could have come in here on your own. It's your ranch," Katie told him.

"That's not what I meant." He opened his eyes and for a moment, Katie longed to step into his arms. "Thank you for taking care of her. For taking care of the ranch. For Blue. Just...thank you."

Katie smiled, because she couldn't find the words, not when she wasn't sure they wouldn't erupt without a string of confessions that would destroy all the trust and affection she had, not just for Chance, but for all the Blackwell brothers.

CHAPTER EIGHT

IT HAD TAKEN ten minutes to explain to Rosie why they couldn't ride horses to Jon's house for dinner. He imagined he'd looked quite a sight, standing in the middle of the pink-and-red-striped living room, trying to have a rational conversation with a child, who had clearly had her heart set on arriving at her cousins' house in equine style. At least he told himself that was the reason for Katie's barely suppressed laughter as she'd stood at the foot of the stairs watching them.

She'd only disappeared upstairs when Chance had invited her into the conversation. Smart woman, he'd thought as she'd all but bolted like the Flash. She wasn't about to take sides on this one, especially given how determined she seemed to be to get him on a horse.

"Why don't you like horsies, Daddy?" Rosie asked as he lifted her out of the minivan and placed the pink bakery box in her arms to present to her new aunt Lydia.

"I like horsies—horses—just fine." As long as he wasn't on the back of one. He'd been antsy for the last few hours, with nerves buzzing in his belly like a swarm of angry hornets. He didn't know what he was so worried about. He and Jon got along just fine. And it wasn't as if he was going to be ambushed by all his brothers being in attendance. He scrubbed his palms hard down his jeans. At least he hoped he wasn't. Then again, he supposed it would be the smart move. He'd find it hard to get in a knock-down-drag-out argument with any of his siblings if his daughter was in the vicinity.

Then again, who knew what to expect once all five Blackwell brothers found themselves in the same room after more than a decade. He'd almost come back for Ben's wedding a little more than five years ago, but hadn't wanted the celebration to be marred by the still open wounds inflicted both on Big E's and Chance's part. Given how that day had turned out, clearly he'd made the right decision to stay far away. Chance shuddered.

He still couldn't wrap his brain around Big E wooing Zoe from Ben. Not that he'd have put anything past those large dollar signs in Zoe's eyes. He'd never understood why Ben hadn't seen how superficial she could be.

"This is a pretty house." Rosie peered around the minivan as Chance closed it up. "I like our house better, though, Daddy."

"So do I, Bug."

"I love having all those animals right outside. Billy is so funny, Daddy! And I think I would like a rabbit now, and a cat. But a kitten, so I can help her grow. Llamas would be fun, too."

Chance's stomach dropped to his toes. Rosie was already calling the ranch "our house." Not their home in Los Angeles, but here. Regret and resentment tangled around each other as he began to wish he'd never come back.

Before he could remind Rosie that they lived in California, the front door slammed open and two little girls came barreling outside, followed closely by his brother and a woman Chance assumed was Lydia. The two of them, framed by the front porch and door, arms linked around each others' waists, reminded him of a tourist brochure for the adventurous West.

"We were beginning to wonder if you'd changed your mind," Jon called.

"We had a disagreement on how to get here." He stooped down beside Rosie, a reassuring hand on the small of her back as she shuffled her feet and ducked her head. "Hello, girls. You must be Gen and Abby." Chance held out his hand to each in kind. "I'm your uncle Chance."

"We know." The darker-haired girl had long braids and wore worn cowboy boots, a navy T-shirt and blue jeans. "I'm Abby. I'm your cousin," she told Rosie, gray-blue eyes that matched her sister's sparkling.

"We're your cousins." Gen, a little bit taller with lighter-colored hair, nudged her sister and almost knocked her over. "Do you want to come see our rabbits?"

Rosie looked at Chance, who gave an encouraging nod as he took the bakery box. "Go on. We'll call you when dinner's ready."

"Come on!" Abby grabbed Rosie's hand and dragged her with them as they headed for the nearby barn. Chance rose to his feet, caught in the past as he remembered running around the ranch with his brothers, trying to keep up. Trying to fit in.

"She'll be fine." Lydia walked down the steps and put a gentle hand on his arm, much like the way Grace had at Brewster's, Chance noticed. "We're glad you could come. I'm Lydia."

"Nanny Fantastic." Chance grinned as Lydia's cheeks went bright pink. Where the girls looked like ranch hands, his soon-to-be sister-in-law had a bit more chic to her, with her snug jeans and button-down sleeveless shirt in a hue of blue that accentuated her eyes.

"He can't still be calling me that." She laughed and tugged Chance down the cobblestone path toward the picturesque house.

"Only sometimes in private." Jon winked at her as they stepped inside. "And only since she was promoted to Mom."

"Best promotion of my life. Can I take that for you?" Lydia's eyes went wide and for a moment, she reminded Chance of the twins, all but bouncing on her toes at the prospect of a treat.

"The Gardners suggested you might like these."

"Anything from Maple Bear is welcome." She popped open the lid and took a deep breath. "But muffins are my favorite. Thank you. Breakfast is taken care of. Come on in. Dinner's almost ready. Jon, get your brother a beer."

"Sounds great," Chance told his brother before Jon asked for confirmation. As uneasy as Chance was with the main house on the Blackwell property, he felt instantly at ease here. Now this house was a home. The warm colors were welcoming and soothing, the furniture both practical and attractive. Photographs on the walls, boots lined up on the floor under jackets and coats hanging from hand-turned wooden knobs. In the living room he went to the window to check if he could see the girls.

"Make yourself at home." Jon returned and handed Chance his bottle. "And stop worrying about Rosie. We talked to the girls about the fact that Rosie's never spent time on a ranch or around animals very much. She couldn't have better tour guides."

Chance took a long drink to avoid having to admit that them being perfect tour guides was exactly what he was worried about. He didn't need Rosie getting even more attached than she was already.

"Nice home." And about twice the size of his little bungalow in LA. Lots of space for fun and play. He could imagine the four of them on cold winter nights, huddled around the fireplace and coffee table, playing board games or watching a movie. "It's a good place for you. Your own spread." He took a seat on the sofa, then ran his hand on the crocheted blanket he remembered from their childhood. Grandma Dorothy had given the blue-and-white creation to their mother one Christmas. Out of the corner of his eye he spotted Jon's old fiddle, waiting in the corner as if for a request. "Was it hard leaving the ranch?"

Jon rested an ankle on his knee and shrugged. "Big E didn't give me much of a choice. Change wasn't an option and I still believe the best method to grow the business is to move with the times. Organic is the way to go. As this place proves." He raised his bottle to the window, where the sun was setting over the splay of the Rockies, casting the fields around them in wondrous, sun-kissed hues.

"Guess you showed him."

"We both did. We all did." Jon turned his attention on Chance. "How goes the music?"

One of the many questions he'd been dreading. "It went about the same time Maura died." Chance sat back and scraped his thumb against the bottle. "Trying to get back into it. I have to, or so my agent keeps telling me. I need to if I'm going to keep a roof over Rosie's head."

"Got plenty of roofs around here." Jon didn't miss a beat. Nor did he add in the expected tone of superiority. "Any one of them would be cheaper than Los Angeles."

"That didn't take long." Of all the brothers, Jon was the one who had come the closest to understanding Chance's desire for escape. Not that Jon hadn't tried to talk him out of leaving, but he certainly hadn't held it against him when Chance made up his mind. "But that's not an option for me. This place isn't for me, Jon. It never has been."

"Didn't stop you from coming back, though. Not when you were needed."

"You all need my vote, not me." Not that Chance resented the distinction. "But I get it. You all have a lot riding on what happens with the Blackwell property. It's not quite what I remember, though."

"Zoe's personal touches giving you nightmares?" Lydia joined them, perched herself on the arm of Jon's chair and snagged his beer.

Chance managed a smile while avoiding his brother's concerned gaze. "Something like that. Rosie thinks she's living in Candy Land."

"Place could give anyone cavities," Jon agreed. "I don't even want to think what our mother would say about the place."

Chance only had vague, ghostly memories of their mother—mostly an image of a lovely, happy, salt-of-the-earth ranch wife who'd embraced every moment of the day. It was an image that had brought him an uncertain peace over the years. And inspired more than a few lyrics.

"Zoe's gone for good?" Not that Chance cared one way or the other, but he imagined seeing the fiancée who dumped him at the altar for his grandfather didn't make for the easiest of encounters for their brother Ben.

"One can only hope." Jon took back his beer and toasted the idea. "Chance was just telling me about getting back to his songwriting. You've got a fan, by the way." Jon slipped his arm around Lydia's waist and squeezed. "When she realized my brother was *the* Chance Blackwell, I think she almost fainted."

"There was giddy excitement, maybe." Lydia agreed. "'Butterfly Blue' is one of my favorite songs ever. We're going to use it as our first dance. I don't suppose you'd be willing to sing it live?"

"Because that wouldn't be strange at all," Jon muttered and earned a smack on the arm from his fiancée.

Before his inner voice could scream no, Chance asked, "When's the wedding?"

Lydia let out an excited squeal. "October sixth. But no pressure or anything."

"I'll see if I can work it out," he lied. Guilt swept over Chance like a hot desert wind. How could he not sing at their wedding given that expression on Lydia's pretty face.

"That would be nice." Jon inclined his head. "But you have a bit more to deal with coming home than the rest of them. Can't be easy, seeing Maura everywhere you look. Ghosts can be powerful."

"Actually, it's helped." One of the reasons he'd dreaded coming home was the threat of falling into memories he felt certain would be painful. "All my memories of her here are happy ones. Even with the way we left things."

"The bad always fades," Lydia agreed. "How's Rosie about her mom?"

"She doesn't remember her. Not really. She has…impressions. Like when she smells oranges and vanilla, the perfume Maura wore. I'll hear her whisper 'Mama.' I don't know that she even realizes she does it." But every time she did, his heart broke a little more. "She talks to her when she plays, like an invisible friend."

"Well, I'm sure Katie or Lochlan will help fill in a lot of the blanks."

Chance winced and looked away.

"Yeah. Maybe not Lochlan," Jon said. "Things going okay with Katie?"

Were they? Chance longed for another beer, but knew alcohol wasn't going to solve the questions and uncertainties he had where Maura's sister was concerned. All afternoon he'd found himself thinking about Katie, smiling as he recalled the petulant expression on her face when he'd ordered her to stay at the main house and away from

Lochlan. The way those green eyes of hers sparked like sea glass glinting in the sun. His lips twitched. Boy, she had spirit to spare. "Katie's been great. She's staying at the house for a few days. To be close to Rosie." He didn't think Katie would want it spread around both ranches what had happened with her father.

"That'll be nice." Chance didn't miss Lydia nudging Jon, as if the two of them were sharing a private joke.

"You seen Lochlan yet?" Jon asked.

"Yes." Before he had to elaborate, he pushed to his feet. "Katie showed me Butterscotch this afternoon. Can't believe Mom's mare is still holding court."

"That was the only horse you ever wanted to ride, if memory serves," Jon teased. "Chance here isn't exactly comfortable on a horse," he told Lydia.

"Not everyone is," Lydia said.

"It's heresy for a Blackwell," Jon proclaimed.

"But marrying your grandson's fiancée isn't?" Lydia snatched back Jon's beer and stood. "I think you Blackwells need to get your priorities straight. I'll take a man who knows his limitations over one who doesn't think twice about taking a hatchet to his family any day. Chance, why don't you head outside and get the girls for dinner? They're probably in the barn with Topaz and Garnet. And you." She knocked the bottle against Jon's chest. "Just for that, you're on dish duty."

WITH WORK DONE for the day and the ranch locked down tight, Katie had no reason to feel guilty for ignoring Chance and staying away from her house. It was *her* house. The only one she'd ever lived in. And she sure as shootin' didn't take orders from a wayward son like Chance Blackwell. "Three minutes back in Falcon Creek and he thinks he knows what's best? It's my life. *My* father." And it was her mistake to make if she ended up with things worse than they were now.

Which was why she'd spent the last ten minutes pacing along the side of her house, trying to decide whether to listen to the bad angel or good angel of her nature. She just wanted to make sure he was okay. A quick look in. Chance would never know. Because the last thing she wanted to deal with was arguing with Chance. Again. Truth be told, she was beginning to think it might be best if she kept her distance from him completely. She didn't like thinking—and feeling—all those weird thoughts and emotions that tumbled through her whenever he turned that dimpled smile in her direction.

"Darn it!" For the first time in as long as Katie could remember, she stomped her foot. She stomped it so hard, dust plumed up and coated her jeans. Before she could talk herself out of it—again—she rounded the corner and headed for the porch.

Her hand was on the handle of the screen door when she spun and looked to where her father's ancient pickup normally sat.

It wasn't there.

Dread-tinged fear coated her throat and mouth. Her father hadn't driven in more than six months. He wasn't supposed to, not with his heart condition, and if he'd been drinking...

Katie ripped open the door and plowed inside. "Dad!" Even as she called his name she knew the house was empty. She raced through the kitchen, where she found Snicklefrits lapping at the dripping faucet. The cat let out a muted meow before blinking accusing eyes at her. "Yeah, yeah. I'll feed you in a minute. Dad!" He wasn't in the living room. Or the other bedrooms or bathrooms. The house looked the same as it had when she'd left early this morn-

ing. As messy and unorganized and dirty as it had been
for months. She should have done a better job keeping it
up. Should have spent more than a few hours here each
night catching whatever sleep she could, but that had been
impossible with her ranching duties and being at Big E's
beck and call for the better part of six months.

Katie finally stopped and stood in the doorway of her
father's bedroom. The bed was unmade, sheets and blan-
kets in tangled heaps on the worn mattress. The same Tif-
fany-inspired lamp that had sat on her mother's nightstand
cast a flickering and eerie glow around the grayish room,
which was devoid of personality and memory.

Empty. Her father was gone.

"Oh, no." Katie scrubbed a hand hard against her chest
before she raced into the kitchen and ripped open the pan-
try doors. Three coffee cans sat empty on the shelf. Her
money. All five thousand dollars she'd been saving for the
past ten years was gone.

"Dad, where are you? Where did you go?" Even more
important, what had she done?

"So, ROSIE. WHAT'S your favorite thing about Montana so
far?" Jon asked as they dug into the sloppy-joe dinner
Lydia had made in the slow cooker.

Chance's stomach growled eagerly at the rich aroma of
slow-cooked tomatoes with a kiss of garlic, and the but-
tered Texas toast, which was a nice alternative to the normal hamburger buns he used at home.

"The animals." Rosie's head bobbed excitedly as she
waited for Chance to cut her food. "I love the llamas and
the cats and the goat and the horses. There's Butterscotch
and…" The litany of names and animals turned to white
noise as Chance tried to remember the last time he'd sat
down to a meal with a member of his family who wasn't

under three feet tall. It was odd, seeing the brother he remembered, now married with kids, settled into a life he and his brothers could have only dreamed of growing up. There was a serenity about the evening, despite the inherent chaos of three rambunctious girls spinning about the house like runaway tops.

"Sounds like you've made a lot of new friends." Jon grinned at his wife and then at Chance, who was as proud as a father could be letting Rosie shine. They'd given her a booster seat so she was sitting up at the table. Gen and Abby had apparently outgrown theirs, even though they weren't that much older than Rosie. Then again, Rosie was small for her age. The girls' faces were already smeared with rich sauce as Lydia added salad to each of their plates. Abby immediately picked off her tomatoes and put them on her sister's plate, while Gen gave Abby her cucumbers.

"Uh-huh. I started to name the cows but Uncle Ethan said that wasn't a good idea. Why isn't it a good idea, Daddy?"

Chance's fingers froze around the salad bowl, halting his own salad dispersal. "Um. Because there's so many of them, I suspect."

"But that's why they need names." Rosie rolled her eyes and shook her head. "Splinter's my favorite. He has this mark on his head. Right here." She poked a finger above her nose. "Like a splinter I got at the playground one time. Then there's Norman and Clarence and Jemima and Heather—"

"You can't name the cows, Rosie!" Abby cut her off with a disbelieving laugh. "They won't be here long enough to learn them. Ow! What?" She glared at her sister and leaned down to rub her leg. Lydia reached out and covered Abby's hand with hers. "What?"

"Why?" Rosie frowned and looked around the table. "Where are they going?"

"Um." Chance set down the salad bowl and looked to his brother and soon future sister-in-law for help. "Because they have somewhere else to go."

"Where?" Rosie blinked innocent eyes at him. "Don't the new ranchers want to know their names? I can help. I'm good at naming things. I named Clyde. And Casper and Sangria—"

Jon choked and nearly spit water out his nose. "Sangria?"

"Long story," Chance said before turning his attention back to Rosie. "Bug, I don't think now is the time to talk about the cows."

"Why? You always say we can talk about anything, Daddy. Why can't I name the cows?" Helpless confusion on the face of his little girl did something to a father's insides, twisting them to the point of pain.

"Rosie, honey, the cows are born here and raised for a while before they're taken away," Lydia said. "To another type of ranch."

"Oh. So they'll get their names when they get bigger?"

Abby snorted. This time Lydia shot her a look before pointing to her daughter's plate.

"May I?" Jon asked Chance, who was all too happy to relinquish control of this conversation. Jon had daughters. Ranch daughters. Clearly he'd covered this topic with his girls. Which meant he was two steps ahead of Chance at this point.

"Yes, please." So much for a serene evening.

"Rosie." Jon scooted her chair around so she was facing him. He leaned over so they were eye-to-eye. "We raise cattle, cows, to become food for people. It's where steaks and hamburgers come from, like what we're having for dinner. But the cows are treated well, sweetheart. We make sure of that. And it lets us have lots of land and lots of other animals for you to enjoy."

"You mean people eat cows?" Rosie looked back at Chance with what he could only describe as horror in her eyes. "But cows are nice. They're my friends. Splinter's my friend. He mooed at me and let me pet him." She blinked and giant tears rolled down her cheeks. "I don't want to eat my friend. Daddy, please don't eat Splinter."

Chance looked down at his plate.

"That isn't Splinter." Gen spoke up this time. "Rosie, don't worry. Cows are food. We're learning about it in 4-H."

"Gen, don't." Jon shook his head.

"I don't care!" Rosie cried. "It is a big deal. I don't want to eat Splinter."

"Bug, Splinter is still outside where you saw him earlier," Chance said, trying to appease her.

"Then what's that?" She pointed at her plate. "Is that a cow?"

"Yes." Lydia broke in before the men could. "Rosie, come here." She held out her arms and Rosie slipped down off her chair and walked over to her aunt, who scooped her into her lap. "You know what, you're right. Animals can be our friends." She smoothed back Rosie's hair and rocked her a little. "But some animals serve other purposes and while it might not seem fair to you and you might not like it, it's the way it is."

"Does that mean I have to eat the cows?"

"Absolutely not," Chance said and felt a rush of relief as Lydia nodded.

"How about you and I go into the kitchen and find something else for you to eat." She made a quick motion with her hand to Jon, who picked up Rosie's plate and dumped her food onto his. "And then you and your dad can talk about your food choices later. Will that be okay?" Rosie agreed as Lydia gave her a big squeeze.

"Okay." Rosie sniffled, her lower lip still wobbling. "But what's going to happen to Splinter?" She scrubbed her hands down her cheeks.

"That we'll figure out another time, Bug. But he'll be fine tonight. I promise." First thing when he got back to the ranch, however, he and Katie needed to have a conversation about Splinter the calf.

"How about broccoli, Rosie?" Lydia set Rosie on her feet, took her hand and led her into the kitchen. "Do you like broccoli?"

"Yes. But broccoli is *not* my friend," Chance's daughter announced.

"Thank goodness," Chance muttered. "I'm going to have my hands full with her, aren't I?"

Jon chuckled. "Maybe. Depends."

"On what?"

"On these two." He pointed his fork at his daughters, who looked both shocked and amused at the way the conversation had gone. "Neither of you say one word about the chickens."

"What about them?" Gen went wide-eyed.

Before Chance or Jon could decide whether she was joking, a car door slammed outside.

"Wonder who that is." Jon reached into his pocket for his cell phone. "No one's called. Must not be an emergency." He got up and walked over to the window. "Hey, Chance, anything going on between you and Katie I should know about?"

"Katie? Not really, no. Why?" The second Chance was out of his chair the doorbell rang. And it rang loud.

"It's open!" Jon called on his way to greet her, but he

stopped short in the door frame of the dining room and backed up. "Hey, Katie. What's going on?"

"Is Chance here?"

Anger vibrated across the room the second she stepped into view. Her face was flushed, making the bruise on her cheek all the more defined. She still wore the clothes she'd worked in—mud-splattered jeans, shirt and boots and a fury blazing in her green eyes that would have put Medusa to shame. For an instant, Chance thought perhaps he had turned to stone, given he couldn't move.

"What's wrong?"

"What exactly did you say to my father, Chance?" Katie demanded.

"Nothing he didn't need to hear." Not nearly as much as he'd wanted to. "Why? He show up at the ranch to complain?" He knew he should have stayed close to…home. His stomach churned.

"No, he didn't come to the ranch. Because he's gone."

"What do you mean *gone*?" Chance asked.

"*Gone* as in the house is empty. His truck isn't parked where it's been for the last six months. Something you said drove him away and I want to know what it was."

"Girls, why don't you bring your plates into the kitchen and eat with me and Rosie?" Lydia called from the kitchen door.

"Aw, Mom! This was just getting good," Gen grumbled as she and Abby did as they were told and vanished into the kitchen.

Lydia pressed a finger against her lips before she closed the door.

Chance looked back at Katie. "I told him he was a waste of a human being and should be ashamed of himself for letting hate take over his life."

"Oh, that's just great." Jon closed his eyes, but only for

a moment before he looked at Chance. Then back at Katie. And did a double take. "What happened to your face?" He reached out to touch her.

"Nothing." Katie jerked her face away. "It's fine."

"That's not fine. Lochlan did this to you?" The disbelief in his brother's voice told Chance just how far Lochlan had descended in recent months. "That's what this is about?"

"I do not need you two Blackwell brothers ganging up on my father," Katie ordered. "I had it handled."

"It'll be five once Ben, Ethan and Ty get a look at you when they get back tonight," Jon said. "This time he's gone too far."

"Thank you," Chance muttered.

"Don't thank me," Jon snapped. "It's not like you're the prince of diplomacy where Lochlan Montgomery is concerned. What else did you say to him?"

"Thank you," Katie said, mimicking Chance.

"I told him if he wanted Katie to ever come home he needed to earn it. And that he wasn't allowed to see Rosie until he was stone-cold sober." Not a hint of regret echoed in Chance's voice.

"Which is when he said what he said about Rosie." Katie sagged a little in her boots.

"What?" Jon demanded. "What did he say?"

"It doesn't matter," Chance said. The old man probably didn't remember, anyway.

"This is all such a mess," Katie whispered. "I don't know where he is. As bad as things have gotten, he's never gone off on his own. It's been my one solace, knowing he'd stay put. But if he's been drinking, and if he's driving—" The helpless expression on her face reminded Chance of the one Rosie had worn moments ago.

"Then we need to find him, don't we?" Jon said matter-of-factly. "Chance, you go with Katie and check the west perimeter of the property and up past the river. I'll call Ethan and we'll take the east. Check in with each other in an hour."

"What about Rosie?" As much as Chance agreed they needed to look for the old man, he'd rarely left Rosie behind.

"She'll be fine here," Lydia said as she joined them, an ice pack in hand that she handed over to Katie with an expression of annoyance. "That needs checking."

"It's fine."

This time the words came out of Katie's mouth like sharp shards of glass. Lydia arched an eyebrow. "Don't cop an attitude with me. Tomorrow morning you go into the clinic and get it checked. Or I'll drive into town and bring Doc Grey to the ranch myself. That won't get the rumor mill running in Falcon Creek at all."

"You wouldn't." But Katie didn't look convinced.

"Try me. You all best get going. I'll keep dinner warm for when you get back. Chance, Rosie can sleep over here with the girls. A slumber party." She rubbed a hand down his arm. "And I'll talk to her some more about what happens to the cows."

"You don't have to do that." But even as he said the words, he felt the gratitude slip through him. That said, if he couldn't talk to Rosie about different food sources, how was he ever going to approach the topic of… He felt his face drain of color. "But thank you. She left Clyde, that's her stuffed monster, back at the house. She doesn't usually sleep well without him."

"The girls can loan her a friend for the night."

"Or we can go grab Splinter," Jon said over his shoulder as he pulled on his jacket.

"What's a splinter?" Katie asked as Chance steered her to the door.

"I'll tell you in the car."

CHAPTER NINE

"THANK YOU FOR coming with me." Katie forced the words out beyond the anger and resentment. She pressed her foot on the accelerator as the truck sped into the night. "You didn't have to."

"Yeah, I did." Chance gripped his seat belt and glared at her. "You still drive like a maniac. Am I supposed to be able to see anything other than a gray blur?"

"Boy, that adventurous Blackwell gene just passed you by completely, didn't it?" To annoy him, she added another five miles an hour, but only for a few seconds. Her mind hadn't stopped spinning since she'd arrived at her house. Where would her father have gone? Why now, after all this time, would he have allowed Chance to goad him and needle him into potentially even more reckless behavior than excessive drinking? There weren't good answers to any of her questions.

What if they didn't find him? Guilt mingled into the toxic cocktail she'd been trying not to swallow for years. He knew this land better than anyone. Even better than Big E, who had nearly fifteen years on Lochlan Montgomery. If her father wanted to disappear, he could. But not finding him wasn't the question pushing her over the speed limit.

It was what happened when she did...

"This isn't your fault." Chance's gentle admonition pressed against her nerves like a thistle on a blanket.

"I know it's not. It's yours." Katie flinched. She couldn't

have sounded more bitter if she'd been made of lemons. "Sorry. Out of line. This has been coming on for a while. I'm just worried." *And scared.* She wasn't ready for this— to be on her own. To be alone. She gripped the steering wheel and eased off the gas. "Him taking off like this is the last thing I needed." Not when everything she'd done had been in part to ensure he had a home to die in.

"Lochlan's always excelled at creating problems," Chance said. "You sure he didn't just run out of beer?"

Katie smirked. "Funny. I called the Watering Hole, the Silver Stake and the grocery store. No one's seen him." As far as she knew her father hadn't been into town for so long, people wouldn't even recognize him if he did.

"Then maybe he doesn't want to be found."

Katie pressed her lips together so hard they went numb. The idea of her father, all alone in the elements he'd once embraced fully. Elements he hadn't interacted with in over a year. Elements that could turn on a dime given a nudge.

"I don't want to think of him dying out here." She sagged a little in her seat and sighed. "I love this land. I don't want to look out the window and see his graveyard."

"Yeah. I get that," Chance murmured and covered her hand with his. The squeeze of comfort eased the tension wrapping around her chest. Not completely, but enough that she could breathe without wanting to scream. "Whatever happens, you aren't alone, Katie. I know you think you are, but you're not."

"You don't owe me anything because of Maura, Chance."

"What do you mean?" Chance's hand tightened over hers once before he let go.

"I mean I'm not the helpless little kid sister anymore. You need to see me as a grown woman."

"Believe me, I do."

Katie's heart beat double time. She looked at him, wondering when she'd forgotten how to breathe. Wondering how four simple words could throw her world completely off-kilter. And make her wish, make her want…

Chance was looking at her. In a way she'd never seen before. In a way she couldn't quite fathom. In a way she couldn't let herself think about. He was her sister's husband! Seeing him as anything else was just…wrong. Katie bit her lip. Wasn't it?

He cleared his throat, as if getting the silent message. "What about friends from his ranching days? Anyone you can think of?"

"No." And just like that, they were back on track. At least that's what she told herself. "He doesn't have many friends anymore. They're either dead or stopped talking to him years ago. There wasn't any reason for him to go off like this. Unless…" She trailed off because voicing the fear that had clamped around her heart felt like confirmation.

"Unless he's gone off to harm himself." Even in the darkness she could see Chance wince. "Didn't realize he was sober enough to understand a word I said. He didn't remember hitting you."

While Katie couldn't forget. "I want to check the creek. It's where he used to go after my mom died. I remember me and Maura finding him there after the funeral." She'd been eight. Maura had just turned ten. And it had been the first time they'd had to get him into his truck and drive him home.

"The day Maura learned to drive," Chance murmured.

"She told you about that?" Katie didn't now why she was surprised.

"Maura told me everything. And before you ask, it wasn't leaving your dad that broke her heart. It was leaving you. You could have come with us. She wanted you to."

"I know." Katie leaned forward and peered into the darkness. She eased her foot off the gas, mindful of the long eight-foot ditch off the passenger's side door. "And I thought about it. But those were your dreams to chase. Yours and Maura's." Even if it had taken her months to realize that and stop being angry. "I'd already found mine."

"I guess you did. He doesn't deserve you."

Translation, she shouldn't be out here in the pitch-dark looking for a man who probably didn't want to be found.

"It's not about deserve. It's about doing what's right. He's my father, Chance. Good or bad, I don't have a choice." She glanced at him. "And while I might not like him a whole lot, I do love him."

Chance's lips twitched. "That's exactly what Maura used to say."

"It's what we used to say to each other." She slowed and took the narrow road toward the creek—the road was unpaved so they were jostled in the spring-loaded seats. "He wasn't made to be alone. Mom dying that way, watching her waste away as the cancer killed her—it killed him, too. It's just taking longer." She hesitated, knowing a touchy subject when she crept up to one. "It's one reason he couldn't bring himself to visit Maura. He couldn't watch someone else he loved die the same way."

"Selfish son-of-a—"

"Won't argue with that." How could she when she'd called her father that and worse? "But he's not going to change. I stopped asking him to five years ago. If becoming a grandfather for the first time didn't make an impact, nothing will."

"You've become awfully wise in your young age."

Was that admiration she heard in his voice?

"We might get an awful lot of colors in the sky, but otherwise life out here is pretty black-and-white."

"Great. Everyone's better at this than I am these days." He pulled out his phone and typed something on the screen. "Although at this rate I'll have to give all of you writing credit if I ever get this song finished. Gotta be sure not to tell Felix about it."

"Who's Felix?" Katie eased off the gas and took the dip in the road at a cautious speed. The last thing she needed was a truck repair on top of everything else. That said, she didn't see any new tire tracks or indications her father had driven anywhere in the area.

"Felix is my agent-slash-manager. At least I think he's still my agent. He needs new music to present to producers. Before my career goes stone-cold."

"Maura always said your songs came from your heart. Losing her must have disconnected you from that."

Chance nodded. "You might be the first person to understand. It was Maura I always wrote for, sang to. I still expect her to be in the audience whenever I perform. Not that I do much of that these days."

"I thought you and Ty talked at some dive bar in Los Angeles after a show?"

"We did. Funny how as soon as I think I'm ready, I get pulled back here."

"Maybe you should start over here, then. The Brewsters are hosting…"

"A fund-raiser talent show? Yeah, so they told me this afternoon."

Katie bit the inside of her cheek to stop from grinning. "Already hit you up, did they?"

"Oh, yeah."

"No go?" Chance's silence was all the answer she needed. "What's the matter? Scared?"

"Yep. But not for the reason you might think."

"Go ahead, surprise me." Another glance and she

caught his jaw working overtime. At this rate he'd have a migraine by the time they headed home. "It won't go any further, Chance. I'm not a gossip."

"I know you're not. I wouldn't want to disappoint her."

"Maura?" Now that was a surprise. "Not to make light of my sister dying, but she won't know, Chance."

"Not Maura. Rosie." He leaned his elbow on the door and shoved his hand into his hair. "What if I get on that stage and freeze?"

Katie's heart folded in on itself. The way Chance loved his daughter should be the barometer for all fathers. "Not possible. You're her hero. Anything you do is perfect."

"Until it isn't. I've only ever sung to her, since Maura died. Aside from that one-off before I came out here. It's the only time it's felt right."

"Well, you have plenty of people to test that theory out on while you're here. And besides, you wouldn't want the library closing because you were too chicken to strap on that guitar of yours and sing a few bars of 'Butterfly Blue.'" An idea popped into her head, one she wished she'd thought of earlier. One she wasn't sure she could pull off. But if she could… "At least think about it."

"Anyone ever tell you you're irritating when you're lecturing them?"

"I don't get the chance to lecture anyone very often. But you're a captive audience, so…" She shrugged. "Deep down, you Blackwell brothers are all the same. No matter how hard you try to run from this place, it's where the answers are. However else you see your future."

"Said the girl who's spent her entire life within Blackwell property lines."

"Said the girl who knows where she belongs," Katie countered.

"We've all been pretty successful," Chance argued. "Despite Big E's unrealistic and suffocating expectations."

"Didn't say you weren't." Katie shrugged. "But successful and happy are two different things, aren't they? Four down, I suppose. Now, at least." She arched an eyebrow at him. "You want to give Rosie the best life you can? How about showing her how to face your fears and start over? Be the example for her that Maura was for me. Show her taking the risk, no matter the outcome, is what really matters. Life doesn't have to end because you fail at something. It just means you have to get up and try again."

Hip barked twice.

"Quiet, Hip," Chance said. "If I'd known I was going to be out riding around with you—watch out!"

Katie yelped and caught sight of the mule deer dead ahead. She yanked the wheel hard to the right and sent the truck into a spinning skid. She heard a grinding and then a crack as she struggled to keep from skidding into the ditch. A downed tree, its trunk so massive there was no way to avoid it, loomed. Katie pumped the brakes. Nothing happened.

An image of Rosie flashed in her mind.

She swore, glanced at Chance, who had white knuckles grasping the dashboard. No way was she making her niece an orphan.

"Hang on!" She pulled on the steering wheel to turn into the skid, but didn't have enough body mass to fight the damaged truck. "Come on, come on. Turn." Her butt came up off the seat as she pulled with all her strength, her legs going stiff as she pressed the brake pedal all the way to the floor.

"What the hell are you doing?" Chance yelled as he reached for the wheel. But he was too late. Katie looked out the driver's window as the car plowed sideways into the tree.

And knocked her out cold.

CHANCE'S EARS RANG louder than a heavy-metal guitar solo. Blinking into the darkness of the moonless night, he unlocked his left hand from around the steering wheel and pried his other free from around the top of his seat belt. He groaned. His chest ached and his neck burned, but he could move. Near as he could tell, no damage had been done to the passenger side of the truck. The driver's side, however—

Katie had gone out of her way to make sure she'd taken the brunt of the impact.

"Katie." Her name sounded like a prayer on his lips as he unhooked his belt and turned toward her. She was slumped over, the door wedged against her leg, the front left of the truck mangled to the point of trapping her feet under the dashboard. "Katie." He pressed her back against the seat, pressed his fingers against the side of her neck. Blood trickled down her face and coated his fingers. Hip whined and licked at Katie's face, catching Chance's fingers as well.

Katie groaned about the same time he caught her jumpy pulse. Relief swept over him with the force of a tidal wave. He closed his eyes for a moment, took a shallow breath and shook off the shock. "She's alive, Hip." Hip whined again.

Chance shoved open his door. Thankfully the light came on, dim and flickering, but enough that he could get an idea of their situation. "Come on, girl. Out." He snapped his fingers and pointed outside the truck, oddly grateful as the dog did as she was told. She stuck close to his side, however, her paws sinking and squishing in the muddy ground. Chance dropped a hand on the dog's head, unsure whether the gesture was to comfort her or himself. First things first. He pulled his cell out of his pocket, opened his contacts. But as he dialed Jon's number, the phone beeped. No signal.

Biting back a curse, Chance stepped away from the truck and almost slipped down into the steep ditch still filled with runoff water from the storm. His rubber-soled sneakers may as well have been made of plastic given the lack of traction. He could feel the mud and soil seeping in over the tops of his feet. The chill of the night was dropping over the valley. Temperatures rarely dipped below fifty this time of year, even at night. At least something was working to their advantage.

The smell that permeated the air made his stomach roll. Gasoline.

Chance dived back into the truck, caught Katie's chin in his hand and turned her toward him. "Katie, you need to wake up."

She groaned, tried to raise herself up, but barely moved an inch.

He unbuckled her seat belt and shoved it off her before ducking down and prying her foot free from the wreckage. Chance grabbed hold of her and hauled her out of the truck. He scooped her into his arms, his feet slipping and sliding as he took every step with deliberate care. Hip followed as Chance carried Katie across the road a good distance from the truck. He settled her sitting up, braced against a weed-encrusted hill, no doubt along the path that mule deer had traversed. "Stay with her," Chance ordered as he raced back to the truck and grabbed the toolbox and waterproof container she had stored in the truck bed. Just in case the truck decided to blow, he scooped out all the contents of the glove box, checked under the seats and pulled an extra pair of boots, a thermal blanket and a jug of water out of the back seat.

Once he was back at Katie's side, he used the flashlight app on his phone to search the toolbox, where he found an industrial-strength flashlight that doubled as a lantern. Hip had her muddied paws on Katie's thigh, watching every move Chance made, as if waiting for him to make a mistake. "Come on, work with me." He dug through the toolbox, then the container, until he found what he was looking for. "Thank you for not having complete faith in technology." He clutched the satellite phone and dialed Jon's number. "Stop bleeding, Katie. You hear me?" Chance listened to the phone struggle to connect as he retrieved a first-aid kit. "Jon?" Chance yelled into the phone and earned a grown of annoyance from Katie. She moved her head and winced. "Yeah, Jon, can you hear me?"

"People in Billings can hear you." Katie lifted a hand to her face, but encountered Hip instead. "Hey there." In the light of the lantern, Chance saw her smile. "Which one of you got me out of there? Ow. Oh, man. That hurts." She slid a hand under her knee and pulled up to bend it.

"Stop moving," Chance ordered. "Jon?"

"Yeah? I can barely hear you. What phone—"

"Satellite," Chance interrupted. "There's been an accident. Out by the creek. Katie's hurt." Chance watched the blood trickle afresh down her cheek.

"How bad?" Jon demanded. "No, stop. Turn around. Head to the river. Cut across…" Jon's voice faded. "Don't set off any flares. Fire danger."

"No kidding." Chance hadn't forgotten every ranch lesson he'd ever learned. "But if the truck blows, flares are going to be the least of our problems." The odor of gas hadn't gotten any worse, but he could still smell it. "My cell isn't working out here. We need an—" Ambulance. But the phone had gone dead.

"No ambulance," Katie mumbled as her eyelids flickered. "Just need to sleep."

"No!" Head injuries were nothing to play down. "Jon? Jon?" He banged the phone hard before chucking it back into the toolbox. He grabbed the thermal blanket, the crinkling sound grating on his ears like nails on a chalkboard. He found gauze and antiseptic in the first-aid kit and, after moving Hip aside, did what he could to tend to the gash on Katie's forehead. "Well, that's going to scar." The wound was close to her hairline and continued to bleed profusely.

He drew the lantern closer, making note of the color of her skin, and felt for her pulse, which had evened out. As had her breathing.

He pressed a clean piece of gauze against the wound before tucking the blanket around her. Before he gave it much thought, he wedged himself back against the hill and drew her into his arms. "Up, Hip." He patted his lap and the dog settled half over him, half on Katie, an added layer of warmth against possible chill.

"My hero," Katie mumbled as she pet the dog. "She's worried."

"She's not the only one." Chance tightened his arm around her, needing to confirm she was still alive. Needing to confirm she was still with him. "What were you thinking aiming the car into the tree?"

"Needed to. Otherwise you would have been hurt."

"Yeah, well. You got smacked in the head for your trouble." He pressed his hand gently against her cheek to keep her head still against his shoulder. "Wonder what happened to that deer."

"Ran off. They never stick around." She gave a weak laugh. "Typical man."

"Hey." He ducked his chin and looked down at her. "I'm not going anywhere." And if he had planned on going for help, he wasn't now.

"You're not typical."

Was it his imagination or was she slurring her words?

"Might have caused less damage if you'd taken that truck straight in instead of turning."

"Couldn't risk both of us getting hurt. Rosie needs you." Katie sighed. "Let me sleep, Chance."

"Nope." He jostled her a bit and earned a growl of anger from both her and the dog. "Can't do it, Katie. You need to stay awake." He didn't have to worry about her pulse so much as his own. "You can't go anywhere, Sunshine." Chance bent his head to whisper against her hair. "You've too much to do."

"Sunshine." He felt her lips curve against his chest. "I haven't heard that in years."

"Maura's favorite nickname for you." Until this moment, he didn't realize how apropos it was. "You lightened her heart, Katie. You gave her strength even when she thought she didn't have any left." He needed to keep talking, keep her awake.

"I didn't say goodbye." Katie's hand came up and grabbed his shirt, clutching it in her fist. "I should have been there to say goodbye."

"You were there, Katie." He pressed a kiss to her forehead and embraced the wave of protectiveness washing over him. "She knew you were there in spirit. Katie?" He leaned back as her eyes drifted closed. "Stop, Katie. Wake up. You can't sleep. Not yet."

"Yeah, yeah. I'm sleepy."

"I know, but you have to see a doctor first. Talk to me." His mind raced for questions as he wondered how long it was going to take Jon and Ethan to get here. "Tell me what Big E is doing wrong with the ranch?"

Katie laughed. At least he thought it was a laugh. "Big E is never wrong. You know that."

"Humor me. What would you change if you could?"

"Work with Jon. Organic. Get off antibiotics. Improve the product."

"Jon was right, huh?" Like that was a surprise to anyone. "You going to tell him that or am I?"

"You can. He already knows. So does Big E." Katie sighed. "Need more help. More housing for ranch hands. Tiny homes."

"Tiny…homes." Chance frowned. Now there was something he'd never considered. "You watch a lot of do-it-yourself channels, do you?"

"Background noise. Also thought about working with 4-H and bringing in more kids. Work with the animals."

"As long as they don't get too attached and start naming them," Chance joked.

"Wh-what?" Katie dropped her head back and blinked up at him. "Huh?"

"Rosie started naming the cows. Starting with Splinter."

"Splinter's a cow. Oh, no. No, we don't name the cows, Chance." She patted her hand on his chest. "Tell her we can't name the cows."

"So Jon and Lydia tried to explain. She doesn't like that we eat them."

"Great. Big E will love that."

Chance frowned. "Like he'll ever find out. I'll lay odds the old man isn't ever coming back."

"Never bet against Big E," Katie mumbled. "He knows exactly what he's doing. He knows how to get what he wants."

"You think he's coming back?"

"I know he is." Katie sighed.

He tilted her chin up and smiled down into her barely open eyes. "Hey, you still there?"

"Yeah. I'm here." She lifted her hand to his face. "You got handsomer. You know that?"

"You're delirious." He was going to have so much to tease her about when she recovered.

"Already pretty enough to cause a riot at school. That's what Maura used to say. Maura." Tears glistened in her eyes. "Your Maura."

Chance nodded. "She was mine, yes. And I loved her with all my heart." And he always would. How could he not when he had Rosie? She was a living reminder of all he'd shared with Katie's sister.

"She always got the best," Katie whispered. "Everyone loved her. Dad. Mom. Your brothers. You."

"And you."

"And me." Katie sighed. "I miss her so much."

"I know." Chance did, too, but being back here reminded him just how much of a life he still had to live. Maybe this place was doing all right by him. It was, after all, where he'd started the first time. "It's okay that we do. We just can't live in that place. Not anymore."

"No other place for me," Katie said groggily. "Dad can't forgive her for leaving him or forget."

Her father. In all the chaos of the accident, he'd all but forgotten about Lochlan.

"Why aren't I enough?"

Katie's soft question sliced through his already open heart. "What?"

"Why aren't I enough for anyone? Why doesn't anyone love me like they loved Maura?"

"Katie—" Chance brushed his lips across her forehead, wishing he had the words. But even for him, a man who had made a living crafting the perfect thing to sing, the perfect thing to say, he found no response to heal her pain.

At first he thought he was hearing things, but then a flicker of headlights crested over the hump of the road. No, a pair of headlights. Two trucks. Jon had called in reinforcements. "I'll be right back."

"Uh-huh." Katie propped herself up. "The cavalry has arrived."

"Hip, stay!" Chance moved toward the trucks as the dog shifted more solidly over her master. "About time—" His yell broke off as he realized he didn't recognize the enormous black truck that came to a stop inches from his feet.

The doors popped open. Next thing he knew, he was face-to-face with Ty and Ben, both of whom looked as haggard as he felt.

"I swear when you come home, you pull out all the stops." Ben Blackwell stepped forward and locked Chance in a surprisingly fierce hug. Ethan's twin had never been the most demonstrative of brothers, or even the warmest, but Chance welcomed the enthusiasm for as long as it lasted. And it didn't last long as Ben slapped him on the back before heading over to Katie.

"We were just turning onto the ranch road when Jon called," Ty explained as Jon's truck pulled up behind Ben's. "I think we might have broken the land speed record getting here. What happened?"

"Clinic is expecting us," Jon announced as he got out of his truck. "How is she?"

"*She's* fine. I don't need the clinic," Katie called. "It's just a headache and sore ankle."

"Possible break and definite concussion," Ben called. Chance glanced over his shoulder and saw Ben lifting the light to Katie's eyes. His brother gave Hip an encouraging pet. "Pulse seems steady. She should be okay to move."

"Chance, what happened?" Ty repeated.

"Deer came out of nowhere. Hip tried to warn her." Chance was already replaying the accident over and over in his mind. And he would for the foreseeable future. "She aimed the car at the tree to avoid the ditch." Chance was only now seeing a shadow of what she must have—that given the runoff from the storm, history could have repeated itself and killed them as surely as the accident that had killed his parents.

Ty's vacant stare was aimed directly at Katie's totaled truck.

"She saved my life," Chance told them. "Took the hit so I wouldn't be hurt."

"Sounds like a Montgomery woman to me." Jon gestured to Ethan and together they gathered up everything from Katie's truck and stowed it in the back of his. "Chance, you ride back with Ben and Ty."

"Want me to—" Ben moved to pick up Katie.

"No." Chance grabbed his brother's arm and pulled him away, more firmly than he'd meant to. Ben stared at him and arched an eyebrow in surprise. "No, thanks," Chance said. "I've got her. Just drive carefully." He bent down and gathered Katie into his arms and gave silent thanks when instead of fighting him, she curled her arms around his neck. "I've got you, Sunshine."

He ignored the silent looks from his brothers as he passed them and headed to Ben's truck. She was Maura's sister. That was all.

CHAPTER TEN

"I'VE BEEN HERE hours already." Katie pushed herself up on the thin plastic mattress and tried to ease the numbness in her backside. She hated clinics. She hated hospitals. She hated anything that had the potential of messing with her work schedule. She glared down at the thick bandage wrapped round her ankle and the blue ice molded around it. No wishing that away. Or the blurry vision and the pounding in her head. She was, however, counting her blessings she'd only puked once. Stupid concussions. "When can I go home?"

"Just looking at the final scans now," said Dr. Grey, who, after three years of general practice in Falcon Creek, was still considered a newcomer to town. He continued to examine the X-rays of her foot. "Probably would have been better if you'd broken it. Sprains this bad take a long time to heal."

"Great." Just what she needed. "Don't tell them." She pointed a finger at the door beyond which not one, not two, but all five Blackwell brothers were holed up in the waiting area like a military escort. She hadn't been around that much testosterone in a long time and she oversaw a half-dozen ranch hands. "Give me some crutches, some aspirin and I'll be on my way."

"Always in such a rush to be free of my company." Dr. Grey faced her and, before saying anything else, pulled open the door to the small exam room. "The patient will see you now."

Panic of an entirely different sort set her heart to pounding. "I don't want to see—hey, Chance." She clutched the exam robe closed at her throat. Her jeans were toast and sat shredded in the corner. Her shirt was covered in blood, which meant all she had to wear was the awful saggy faded gown that was way too big. "I'm fine," she said when she caught the concerned look in his eye. "Nothing for you to worry about. Any of you to worry about," she added when four other male faces popped into view behind him. Hip nosed her way through and sat in front of them, an imperious expression on her fuzzy face.

Katie had to admit, seeing all the Blackwell brothers together for the first time in a decade made for a pretty impressive sight. Put that picture on a brochure and they'd have to start hosting singles weekends at the ranch. Geez, she was starting to sound like Ty's fiancée, Hadley. "Seriously, Doc, I'm feeling better. Just let me out of here."

"Not until we get some things straight." Dr. Grey sat down on a stool. "This is your second concussion, which means playtime is over."

"Second? What happened with the first?" Chance demanded, as if Katie wasn't in the room.

Katie set her jaw and narrowed her eyes, something she wished she hadn't done with her head throbbing. "Nothing worth talking about."

"She was kicked in the head by one of her problem children," Dr. Grey said. "What was his name? Faustus?"

"It was just a graze," Katie grumbled. "And he didn't mean it. He got spooked and I was standing in the wrong place."

"Did you know about this?" Chance rounded on Jon, who shook his head.

"I did not." Jon leaned over to glare at her. "Would this coincide with that unexpected few days of vacation you took around Christmas a few years back?"

Katie's mouth twisted. "Maybe."

"A few days?" Dr. Grey's amber-flecked eyes narrowed behind his rimmed glasses. "I told you I wanted you off your feet for two weeks at least."

"Time flies when you work on a ranch." And the dizzy spells had passed soon after she'd gotten back to work. The headaches had taken…longer.

"Did Big E know?" Chance demanded.

"Of course he did," Ben muttered.

"Big E knows everything, remember?" Katie told them. "I believe his advice was to walk it off." Her father had been in a particularly bad way that holiday, the first one since Maura had died. There hadn't been any hint of Christmas to be found in the house that year…or since. "Which I did."

"Which explains why your grandfather doesn't have a medical degree," Dr. Grey snapped. Katie balked. Dr. Adam Grey was one of the most easygoing people she'd ever met in her life. In his midthirties, he'd left a thriving surgical practice in Arizona to take over for his late uncle, who had been the doctor in Falcon Creek for more than thirty years. "It also explains why I'm telling you this in front of witnesses. If you want full mobility in that foot of yours again, I want you off of it completely for at least a week. Which should give your head time to begin healing as well. After a week, come back in and we'll see about getting you fitted for a walking boot. But for that concussion—"

"A week?" She would have screeched the words if it wouldn't have blown her head off her shoulders. "But off it means I can ride, right?" She'd spent every day of her life in the saddle. How was she supposed to—

"It most definitely does not." Dr. Grey's jaw tensed. "The last thing you need is to fall off a horse and hit your head. Again."

Katie's spine stiffened. "I've never fallen off a horse in my life."

"And you won't be starting now. You are, for the foreseeable future, grounded and out of the ranching game. No riding. No walking or, in your case, hobbling around the stables. I want you on your butt, on the sofa, in a chair or in bed. And if I hear from any one of these guys you've disobeyed these instructions, I'll admit you to the hospital in Bozeman and put you in traction."

"Ha ha." Katie forced a laugh. The Blackwell brothers might be many things, but none of them were snitches. "Like any of them would report me."

"I would," Ben said with a carefree shrug.

"Me, too." Ty leaned against the door frame as Jon and Ethan nodded in agreement.

"You know darn well I would," Chance said.

"Seriously?" Katie's mouth dropped open. "After all these years of fighting, *this* is what you agree on?"

"Congratulations, Katie." Ty's grin didn't quite reach his eyes. "You are officially the unifying element for the Blackwell brothers."

"Plus I'm betting once they tell their significant others about your situation, we can add four other spies to the team," Chance said. "And then there's Rosie, of course."

"And Rosie would be?" Dr. Grey asked.

"His secret weapon," Katie mumbled.

"My daughter will like nothing more than playing nurse for her aunt. I hope you like playing Go Fish and Pretty Fairy Princess."

Katie dropped her head back against the table and groaned. "This isn't happening. There's too much to get done." Pressure built up in her chest. "Conner can't handle all those horses on his own! And we're repairing the trenches out in the pastures. You're going to give me a heart attack."

"At least you'll be sitting down for it." Dr. Grey pushed to his feet and slapped her file on the exam table. "In the meantime, I'll get you some painkillers and those crutches."

"I thought you said no walking?" Katie reminded him.

"I thought perhaps you might prefer using them to being carried to the bathroom." Dr. Grey arched an eyebrow in challenge. "You want?"

"I want," Katie grumbled and tried to stop her face from turning red. "This is a nightmare." She scrubbed her hands over her cheeks. "The entire night…" She looked up as the five brothers moved more fully into the room. Had she not known all of them all her life, she might have been intimidated. Might have been *more* intimidated. "Has there been any word on my father?"

Jon shook his head. "Afraid not. I called the sheriff while we were waiting. Filled him in on the situation. He can put out a missing-person bulletin if you want him to. Given Lochlan's history the past few years, he could be considered a danger to himself. What they call a senior in jeopardy."

Katie's mind raced. She chewed on her thumbnail, trying comforting herself to do. She must sit beside someone will be looking for him to be on the lookout. I don't see a downside."

"It would be humiliating for him to be brought home

by the police. Like he's some runaway kid." Katie's insides twisted.

"Would you rather spend your downtime worrying about what might have happened to him?" Jon asked.

"No." Katie cringed. Full circle, she supposed. She'd definitely become the parent in their relationship. "Yeah, let's have them do it. I just wish I had some idea where he might have gone." Tears burned the back of her throat, but she swallowed hard, determined to keep them at bay. "He's just so lost."

"Then we do what we can to bring him home. You're family, Katie." Ethan walked over and patted her shoulder. "That means he is, too."

"Don't worry," Ty said. "Rosie and Hadley'll make sure you're well tended to. You can relax."

"And what about the ranch?" The ranch was her responsibility. Her livelihood. Her *life*. If she let a concussion and sprained ankle take her out, how could she prove herself worthy of the foremanship?

"We'll work all that out in the morning," Chance told her. "For now, let's get you home."

FOR ALL THE worrying she'd done about the ranch, she didn't expect to sleep a wink that night. So when she woke up in the first-floor guest room of the family ranch house, sunlight streaming through the pink curtained window, her foot sticking out of the covers and propped up on a chair of pillows, she wondered if she was still dreaming.

Maura, but if he resented having to check on Katie, she didn't see it.

She spotted the bag Chance brought from her house

on the table by the window, sagging as if it had been relieved of its contents. On the nightstand beside her sat her cell phone, the small butterfly jewelry box that contained nothing more than the pearl earrings that had belonged to her mother and a solitary gold band her grandmother had worn, along with a silver-framed photo of her and Maura, taken a few months before Maura had eloped with Chance.

Katie brushed a finger down the side of the frame, smiling at the image of the two of them laughing at something ridiculous Chance had said. Or done.

Chance.

Her insides did an odd dance that had yet to find its rhythm. What was happening with him? Why did it seem as if ever since he'd come back, she saw him with different eyes? Not a sister-in-law's eyes, not even a friend's eyes. But a woman's.

"Stop looking for trouble," she whispered to herself as she heaved her leg off the pillows and over the side of the bed. Her foot immediately began throbbing, but in conjunction with her head. She groaned and bent over. The worst hangover in her life would be preferable to this. Her head spun while her stomach lurched and jumped stronger than a bucking bronc.

Katie frowned and plucked at the yellow tank top she wore, the matching striped pajama shorts. When had she put these on? She had put them on, right? She tried to remember...

The night was almost a blur, but one thing she remembered with absolute clarity was the way the brother so concerned.

Yet she'd done nothing but never had been so concerned for months. Guilt churned in her empty stomach; guilt that couldn't be eased with a healing hand or kind word or a

Blackwell brother smile. Why had she ever agreed to Big E's ridiculous plan? Why hadn't she stood up to him, told him he was wrong to manipulate his grandsons into coming home? If only she'd refused his offer of keeping him up-to-date on what was happening with the brothers, or refused to open that safe and anonymously send the water-rights documents to Rachel, or not spread those rumors about Ethan starting up a local vet practice... If only. But what choice did she have when doing all those things, and more, would ensure her place as foreman of the Blackwell Family Ranch and thus give her father the peace of mind that he could live out the rest of his days in the only home he'd ever known.

She'd done what everyone always did where Big E was concerned. She'd rolled over and let him use her weakness against her, and where had that gotten her? Trapped in silence while she waited for the next cowboy boot to drop.

Because where Big E was concerned, there was always another boot poised to land on someone's head.

She should come clean, tell all of them, tell Chance, what Big E had been up to these past months. That nothing that had happened since any of them had come home had been in their control. He'd manipulated each and every occurrence, most of the time with her help.

But how did she do all that without admitting she'd betrayed the trust all the Blackwell brothers had placed in it? And what if Chance took the admission as a reason to He already had one sneakered foot out the door. And Katie had to be a way, a time, a place, to tell Chance the truth without destroying every part of her life. Wasn't there?

She grabbed the crutches and hobbled into the bathroom, where, after a few learning curves, she took care of business and lamented over not being able to take a shower. She settled for a sink bath and tied up her hair.

She nearly toppled backward into the tub when she opened the door and found Rosie and Hip waiting for her.

"Good morning, you two." Katie hopped a few extra steps to catch her balance. "Are you my wake-up call?"

"Yes. It's one of my new jobs." Rosie clasped her hands behind her back and swayed back and forth. Katie couldn't help but smile at her cute round face, the sparkly T-shirt, jeans and pink boots she wore constantly. "Daddy is fixing breakfast. He said he can bring you a tray if you'd like."

"I'd prefer the kitchen, actually." She hated lounging around uselessly in bed.

"'Kay." Rosie stepped back and patted her leg for Hip to follow, which the dog did. "Daddy said you can show me how to feed her. He didn't find any dog food in your house."

"Hip doesn't eat dog food." Katie nearly shuddered. "But yes, I can give him that information. She likes to drink a lot of water."

"I know! I also went with her when she pooped and peed."

"I'm sure she appreciated the escort." Katie stuck her tongue in her cheek. She clacked down the hall and her stomach rumbled at the aroma of fresh coffee and toasted bread.

I can get a kitchen _ _ _ _ _ _ _ _ _ no then maybe I don't think he knows that."

"He knows that." Chance rounded the counter. "Good morning, Katie." He motioned for her to sit at the table.

He'd arranged a stack of pillows on a second chair so she could prop up her leg.

"Morning. Smells good." She suddenly realized she hadn't eaten since lunch yesterday. No wonder she was nauseated.

"Scrambled eggs, turkey sausage, toast and—" he set a steaming mug in front of her "—tea."

Katie scowled as she lowered herself slowly into the chair and picked up her leg. Her ankle throbbed beneath the bandage. "I don't like tea."

"Coffee's too acidic for your stomach with these painkillers." He handed her a bottle. "Especially on an empty stomach. See how you do with this dose."

"My stomach's made of cast iron. I don't baby it."

"You do this morning." If Chance was irritated with her grumbling, he didn't let on. "Judging from what was not in your fridge at the foreman house, I'm betting you don't fill it, either. Alice is bringing you some food today, by the way. Lunches and dinners so we only have to worry about breakfast."

"Good eggs, Daddy." Rosie gave him a thumbs-up as she stuffed a forkful into her mouth. "Daddy makes good eggs."

"No talking with your mouth full, please."

"Sorry. Oops." Rosie covered her mouth after she ____ed egg on the table. "Daddy calls me 'his little hea-

sipped ____ like weeds and ____ at Chance as she for the sugar bowl. "What's with the cowboy gear?" She'd peppermint. She reached gotten used to the chambray shirts and jeans, not to men-tion the sneakers. But what the man did for a plain navy

T-shirt and worn Wranglers should be illegal. "Someone playing dress-up?"

"Daddy's going to take care of your horses!" Rosie bit into her toast.

"Is he?" Katie's other eyebrow went up. "Does your daddy even know what a horse looks like?"

"Um." Rosie scrunched up her nose. "Daddy?"

"I know what a horse looks like." He set his own filled plate on the table across from Katie and retrieved an over-size mug of head-swooning coffee. "I also know which end to stay away from, so we can call that progress."

"Hmm. Remains to be seen. You know." Katie cleared her throat. "I'm doing okay with the crutches. I could come out to the stables and—"

"You can't!"

Katie jumped when Rosie, not Chance, protested. "I can't?"

"Nuh-uh. Daddy said you have a cone-cushion. You have to stay here with me. I'm your nurse!"

"Concussion," Chance corrected as he began eating. "And that's right. On your butt, as the doctor said. One week at least. No arguments."

"Oh, there will be arguments," Katie grumbled. "What am I supposed to do for seven days? Stare at the ceiling and count sequins on pillows?"

"You're going to spend time with your niece, read books, take naps and trust us to do what needs doing around this place."

"I wouldn't bet on any of that." Right now she was try-ing to figure out how to steal his coffee. Maybe if she asked him for some jam…

Chance twirled the lazy Susan to display strawberry and orange marmalade. She glared at him. He grinned.

"Don't you want to spend time with me?" Rosie stuck

her lower lip out in a pout that reminded Katie so much of Maura, she lost her breath. "Don't you like me?"

"Of course I like you, Rosie. I love you." Katie reached over and tweaked her nose even while she wondered if Chance had put her up to this. "And yes, I want to spend time with you. I'm just used to having to go to work. It's going to take me some time to get used to doing something different."

"I can help with that. I like different. I am different. Different is good."

Chance nodded. "Different is excellent."

"Whose boots are those?" Katie leaned over and looked at Chance's feet. Ooh, bad idea. Her stomach pitched as her head spun. She pulled herself back up and, without looking at Chance, reached for her tea, which did seem to have a calming effect. Darn it.

"They're my boots."

"Yours?" She'd thought they looked familiar. "From ten years ago? Aren't they too small?"

"A bit." She couldn't have missed the cringe if she'd wanted to. "They'll do for a few days at least."

"In a few days you'll need more bandages than this." She pointed at her foot. "Your grandfather stored some of your father's things in the attic."

Chance's hand froze halfway to his mouth. "He did?"

"I seem to remember there being some boots in one of the boxes. Can't hurt to look. Zoe complained about them when she was emptying this place out for the remodel. There might be a bunch of boxes, actually. Rosie and I could go through them if someone brings them down." And then she did something she'd never done before in her entire life.

She batted her lashes at him.

Chance's smile was slow to form, but when it appeared, his entire face lit up. And Katie's heart swelled.

"You see that look, Bug?" Chance pointed his fork at Katie. "Right there on your aunt's face? That's your mother."

"Is it? Really?" Rosie scrambled onto her knees and leaned over the table to peer closer at Katie. "Can I see it again? I want to see Mama."

Katie's smile faltered as her throat tightened. "I don't do her justice," she choked out as she began eating her eggs around a too tight throat. "Is there any chance you can bring those boxes down? Just stack them in the living room?" Maybe she could find some of those pictures of Chance and the boys' parents and what the house looked like before Hurricane Zoe had gotten her hands on it, all for Hadley's wedding-present surprise.

"I'll head up after breakfast. Ben and Ethan are already out with the other ranch hands finishing up installing the new pipe up on the east pasture."

Katie swallowed hard. "They are? But they have their own work—"

"We're taking shifts, splitting up your jobs. Jon and Ty will head out this afternoon to help bring the cattle over to the northern pasture while I tend to the stables."

"Oh."

"Figure we can meet here for lunch. Hadley's going to bring that by. So before I head out, you just need to fill me in on what needs doing."

Everyone was doing so much to help her. She knew she should be grateful but...

"And FYI, we'll have a full house for dinner. Figure we might as well work out a new schedule between the five of us and the ranch hands so you can stop worrying about whether things will get done. They'll get done. You've trained everyone really well."

"Thanks."

"Don't sound so excited. We're only all rearranging our lives because you ran your truck into a tree."

Katie tried to smile. Her truck. She'd almost forgotten about losing her truck.

"Hey, I'm kidding, Sunshine. It'll all be okay, I promise."

Hearing him call her that last night had filled her with such hope, such longing. This morning, however, the name felt like a butter knife in the heart. A brotherly butter knife.

"The irrigation work in the south pasture is nearly done," she told him. Because focusing on work meant pushing aside all these emotions she didn't want. Emotions that had her longing for a family of her own—Maura's family. Her sister's family. What was she thinking, playing house like this? "We still have at least a dozen ditches and pipes that needed filling and replacing. Then there's the fence we can get a jump on before winter and the cattle needs to be moved out of the north pasture and into the one by the river."

"Write it all down. We'll organize tonight." He picked up his plate and Rosie's, since she'd stopped eating and was playing "pile the scrambled eggs" with her fingers, and carried them to the sink. "You finish up while I head to the attic. This might be something of a treasure hunt. Rosie, you want to come?"

"Uh-huh. Unless you want me to stay, Aunt Katie?" Rosie blinked her overwide eyes at Katie.

"I'm good," Katie responded, but as she watched them head off down the hall, she realized she did want Rosie and Chance to stay.

For good.

CHAPTER ELEVEN

MAYBE IT WAS wearing his father's old boots, or maybe it was because he knew he was working in the stables to help Katie. Whatever the reason, Chance found himself enjoying his time with the horses. As long as someone else—in this case Ethan and Conner—turned them out for their exercise runs while Chance mucked out the stalls. And added new hay. And filled buckets of water and food and...

By the fourth day he'd found his rhythm and even spent some quiet time with Butterscotch and Blue, which made him less leery of the other animals. Now when he walked through the doors in the morning, the horses didn't fidget and neigh. They stuck their heads over their stall doors and waited for him to brush a comforting hand down their noses.

"Morning, Blue."

Butterscotch whinnied as Chance stretched his hand into the stall to stroke Blue's head. The foal was growing every day and would soon be ready to leave her mama. But for now, seeing them together first thing in the morning set the right tone for his day.

"So this is why you get done so early in the day." Ethan strode in, the still rising sun behind him. He set his medical bag on the table inside the stable door. "We've got a pool going on where you disappear to after lunch. Want to give me the inside track?"

"Not really." Chance was all too aware his brothers

were laying odds on his activities. Little did they know Katie filled him in at dinner, which proved how utterly and completely bored she was. Yesterday he'd caught her hopping up the stairs trying to get another box out of the attic. Exactly how she planned to achieve that goal had stymied him, but she'd been determined. What she was doing with all those boxes that had been gone through and put away somewhere else was anyone's guess. About that she'd been increasingly tight-lipped.

But he'd delivered another five boxes to the living room a while later, after tossing her over his shoulder and carrying her back downstairs.

"Come on," Ethan cajoled. "After all I've been doing around here so you don't have to walk these guys—"

"You volunteered," Chance interrupted as he retrieved the manure fork and shovel that had given him calluses and blisters. At his brother's frustrated huff, Chance shook his head. "Let's just say I'm being productive for my other life." Productive was an understatement. He had two new songs already, with a third nearly complete. And all it had taken to get things going was sitting beside that river near where he'd proposed to Maura. In those few hours, the words had flowed as easily as the water. Words he'd never use, but they were words that needed to be purged to allow for the new ideas. New thoughts. New songs.

New feelings.

"Other life, huh?" Ethan opened Dewey's stall and led him out onto the concrete aisle to bridle him for Conner. "Does that mean you're leaning toward selling?"

"No."

"*No* as in leave me alone, or *no* as in you're thinking of voting against the sale?"

"*No* as in I still haven't decided." Chance understood both sides, more than he wanted to. Ben and Jon made good arguments. They could all do with the money the sale would bring. But with Hadley and Ty's marketing plan for the winter that included, thanks to Hadley's actor brother, renting the guest ranch out to a Hollywood film studio for location shooting, and making the Blackwell Family Ranch a premiere go-to destination wedding location, Chance could see this place turning into something really special, not to mention lucrative. Add in the plans for a spa down at the empty barns...and selling it almost felt like giving up. But it would also set him and Rosie up for a good long time in Los Angeles. "I haven't made my mind up yet, Ethan."

"Okay." But the smile on his brother's face was one of hope, and that only increased the burden on Chance's shoulders. Whichever way he voted, he'd be letting down two of his brothers. Given they were all actually getting along for the time being—for Katie's sake, at least—he wasn't in any rush to blow that up.

Katie. His chest tightened. What would happen to Katie if he voted to sell? He had no doubt she could find work on another ranch. References from the Blackwells could set her up anywhere she chose but...

Katie was the first person he saw in the morning and the last one he saw before he went to bed. They'd found an unexpected rapport that left him anxious to seek her out when the workday was done, but she lightened his load enough with Rosie that he could concentrate on his music without having to worry he was ignoring his daughter.

Dinnertime had become his favorite part of the day and made it worthwhile to get up before the sun.

"Rumor has it you're thinking of performing at the library fund-raiser next week." Ethan cinched the bridle and smoothed out the leads.

"That's why they call them rumors." Chance headed

into the now-empty stall. "And while they asked me, I said I'd think about it."

"Running out of time to say yes."

"Hmm. That would be too bad." Nothing clogged up the creative pores more than the stress of having to perform. New songs were one thing. The idea of performing them?

"They're still having trouble finding sponsors. Especially after Saddles and Stirrups from out in Bozeman backed out. That's half the roof fund gone."

"Backed out? When did this happen?" Thoughts of mucking hay evaporated as he faced his brother.

"Two days ago. They've been trying to keep it quiet in case it scares everyone else away. I'd hate to see that library have to close. Remember when Mom used to take us there?"

Did he remember? The library had been his refuge from the ranch. That's where he found his first book on how to write music. And biographies on musicians and composers. When he needed to learn to read music, Mrs. Atherton, the librarian when he was a kid, had special-ordered an entire series of books just for him. And after his parents were killed, he'd hoof it from the ranch after he'd done his chores and hole up at a small table in the back, devouring anything that would take him away from Montana. "I wouldn't be where I am now without that library."

"Shame it's in danger then." Ethan rounded the horse and kept his back to him. "If only there was someone who could step up and help."

"You do know subtlety was never your strong suit, right?"

"I have been told that." Ethan didn't have to be facing Chance for Chance to know he was grinning like a loon. "So, you going to do something?"

Chance stabbed the pitchfork into the manure-laden hay

and tossed it into the nearby wheelbarrow. "Don't suppose an autographed picture or CD would do it?"

"You know Falcon Creek, Montana, Chance. It's all in or all out. And right now, I'd say you're their only hope."

"Awesome." Butterflies the size of canaries swarmed in his stomach. "Even if I did it, chances are it wouldn't be a huge draw. I mean, not a lot of people would come just to hear me."

"A Blackwell brother without an ego. And the one who struck out for fortune and fame no less. Huh."

"Not funny." If there was one thing Maura had excelled at, it was keeping Chance's ego in check.

"Never known you to turn your back on people who need you." Ethan pointed to the pitchfork. "A couple of days ago I would have bet half my income you'd head back to LA before picking up one of those. Now look at you. All to help Katie."

"I'm helping Katie because if we didn't, she'd defy doctor's orders and come out here to do it herself."

"Yeah, but still, you're helping Katie." Ethan had an odd spark in his eye, one that Chance wasn't overly anxious to identify. "She's one of the best people I know, Chance. There's no one who's been more loyal and devoted to our family and this ranch."

"You make her sound like a sheepdog." Chance stabbed the pitchfork harder this time. But he got Ethan's point. "I'm not doing this out of gratitude."

"Didn't say you were. Didn't even think you were. You two look good together, though. Just saying," Ethan added when Chance rounded on him.

"It's not like that."

"Yeah, that sounded convincing. It's okay if you like her, you know. It's okay if you want to be happy again."

Was it okay? Chance gripped the handle so hard he almost gave a blister to his blisters. "She's Maura's sister. Her little sister."

"Katie hasn't been anyone's little anything in a long time. I'm just saying don't turn your back on something you both might need. And it's not like Rosie would mind. She's nuts about her aunt."

"Rosie's nuts about potato bugs," Chance countered. "But point taken. Now butt out."

"Okay. Just one more thing. Chance?" Ethan waited until Chance looked at him. "Maura wouldn't mind."

Chance's heart clenched. "I know. That's what makes it so hard."

If Katie had to play one more round of Pretty Fairy Princess she was going to strangle someone with a string of plastic pink beads.

"You know." Hadley looked up from where she sat on the floor sorting through dozens of old Blackwell family photographs. "It does take a particular level of skill to consistently lose to a four-year-old."

"Four and three-quarters." Katie smirked. At least now she knew whom to strangle.

"I win again!" Rosie scooped up the last of the plastic jewelry and threw them into the air like confetti. "That's six games in a row! Wait till I tell Daddy!"

"You should maybe share some of these beads with him," Katie urged. "And that tiara. Chance would look stunning in a tiara."

"Daddy likes the blue one," Rosie said with a slow nod. "But the earrings pinch his ears."

The image of Chance Blackwell wearing plastic princess jewelry was enough to melt Katie's frustrated, confused heart.

"Now that's a special kind of man," Hadley mumbled.

Katie glowered. She'd have had to be oblivious not to have picked up on Hadley, Grace, Rachel and Lydia's matchmaking tendencies when it came to her and Chance. At least Rachel seemed to be on her side, or so Katie had thought until last night, when dinner with Rachel and Ben had been canceled at the last minute and Lydia had shown up with the twins to take Rosie with them for a sleepover. She and Chance had bonded over bad sci-fi movies and whether popcorn required butter. For the record, it did.

"My brain is bored." Katie reminded herself of an exhausted Rosie the way she was whining. "Can't I help more with this project of yours?" They'd had to be careful with what they said around little ears as the owner of those ears had a very big mouth when it came to secrets.

"Actually, yes. Oh, hey, Rosie, I've run out of sticky notes. Can you go find me some more? I think there are some in Big E's office."

"'Kay!" Ever willing to be helpful, Rosie left her game scattered in Katie's nest on the sofa and darted out of the room.

"If you're playing with me I will kill you." Katie hoisted her foot off the coffee table and shifted it over to the sofa. "I can feel brain cells dying as we speak."

"You've got a laptop, right?"

"Back at the house, yeah."

"Great. There's this new program Grace, Rachel and I found. It's an interior-design program where you scan in pictures of the room and it lets you play with overlays and images to see what colors and designs work. Once we get all these photos digitally stored—" she patted the rather tall pile on one side of her "—then we can start getting to work. We want to have phase one complete and ready to present at Lydia and Jon's reception."

"And let them hire the contractors?"

"Nope." Hadley shook her head. "This is our project. Yours included. Especially when it comes to the contractors."

"Sounds expensive."

"I have a plan for that, too." Hadley wagged a finger in the air. "I've been searching for college design students and interns online. You know a lot of them do construction work on the side to get experience. Might be an untapped market for us and a way to build up their résumés."

"Your brain just works on an entirely different plane than the rest of us, doesn't it?"

"So I've been told. You up for scanning?"

"As long as we have a scanner, sure."

"I'll get you hooked up first thing in the morning. Can you get the laptop?"

"Maybe." Katie bit her lip. What she wouldn't give to get out of this house for an hour or so. Thankfully, Hadley had helped solve her shower dilemma on day two by making a plastic covering for Katie's pseudo cast. Katie's relief when she stood under the water probably meant she'd owe Hadley her first born, but man, it had been worth it. She'd only almost fallen twice. "Hey, Rosie."

"Yes?" Rosie handed Hadley a stack of neon-colored sticky notes before she leaped onto the sofa next to Katie and snuggled in.

"Would you like to see your mom's old room at my house?"

"Ooh, that's just wrong," Hadley laughed under her breath.

"Desperate times." Katie grinned. "How about we ask your dad to take us to my house? That way we can check on Snicklefrits, too."

"Snicklefrits has been making out like a bandit on

tuna," Hadley reminded her. "Lydia and the girls have been feeding her twice a day."

There would never be enough words of thanks to express her gratitude to everyone for all they'd been doing for her. The friendships she'd developed with these women were something completely unexpected. She'd always been one of the boys; how could she not be when she lived and worked on a ranch? With Maura leaving when Katie was only seventeen, she hadn't realized how important female companionship was to her psyche.

"Maybe if I take good care of Snicklefrits like I have Hippo, Daddy will have to say yes to a kitten."

"That does seem logical," Katie agreed with a serious nod.

"But you know what?" Rosie turned those big eyes on her.

"What?"

"I was talking with Gen and Abby and we decided what would really be great is a baby brother or sister."

Hadley choked on her coffee. "Sorry." She held up a hand as she wiped her nose and mouth. "Swallowed wrong."

"Do you think if I asked Daddy for a brother or sister he might get me one instead of a kitten?"

"I think maybe a kitten is a good first step, Little Miss." Katie pulled Rosie into her arms and kissed the top of her head. "How about you keep pushing that and see how it goes."

"Okay." Rosie sighed the heavy sigh only a four-year-old could muster. "But I might ask Daddy for a brother or sister later."

"I would like to be around when you do," Hadley told her. "How about we get all these toys cleared up so we can set up some work space for your aunt?"

"Work space?" Rosie pushed back and frowned. "But I'm your nurse. And I'm supposed to play with you."

"We can still play. Just need to add some new games into our schedule. And speaking of schedule." Katie sat up straighter as Chance strode in the front door. "You're early." She looked him over from head to toe, and didn't see anything broken, amiss or particularly muddy. "You giving up as a stable boy?"

"Hardly." Chance grinned and hung his hat on the hook by the door. "Just have to make a phone call. Didn't have the number in my cell. Oo-o-of. Hey, Bug." He scooped Rosie up when she threw herself into his arms. "Have you been keeping your aunt busy?"

"Uh-huh. I beat her six times at Princess." She wiggled a finger against the plastic earrings.

"Six times, huh? I think that might deserve a medal."

"Or a drink," Katie muttered with what she hoped was a good-natured smile. "Whichever is handier. Who are you calling?"

"Alice. Ethan filled me in on what's going on with the fund-raiser."

"You're going to sing?" Katie sat up on the sofa. "You changed your mind?"

"I don't want my issues to be the reason the library has to close. So yes, I changed my mind."

"Daddy's going to sing!" Rosie's arms went up in the air like she was a practiced cheerleader. "I love it when you sing."

"That's really great of you, Chance," Hadley said with a smile. "I think it'll make all the difference."

"Yeah, well, I'm not so sure." He kissed Rosie and set her back down.

"Daddy, did you know Mama has a room at Aunt Katie's place?" She tugged on his sweaty shirt. "Can I go see it?"

"Ah, how about I talk to your aunt about that before we decide."

Katie's spirits dropped. Of course. She should have realized the house wasn't in any condition for a child.

"You know what, on second thought, Rosie?" Katie leaned forward and held out her hand. "Maybe we can save that for a little while later. When I've had the chance to straighten up."

"Oh, it's all done." Hadley pushed up off the floor and began putting stacks of photos back into boxes. "Lydia, Rachel and I kind of took care of that a few days ago. Hope that's okay."

"Oh, no. You all went in there? It was horrid." Embarrassment and more than a little shame swamped her.

"Hey, life happens," Hadley told her with a dismissive wave. "You work sunup to sundown and beyond. We were happy to help family. Which means you might just get your outing today after all."

"Seriously, don't tease me." Katie patted her heart. "I don't think I can take it."

"No teasing," Chance said. "You've been following the doctor's orders, right?" He glanced at Rosie, who nodded enthusiastically. "I don't see why we shouldn't shake things up tonight. I'll finish up with the horses after I make my call, then how about a picnic dinner by the river. After we stop by your place."

"And I have just the dinner back at the guesthouse." Hadley jumped in a little too quickly for Katie's taste. "In fact, Rosie, how about you come with me and help me fix it up."

"You mean like cook?"

"I mean like pack it up in a pretty basket. I need help choosing between brownies and cookies."

"Can't we have both?"

"No," Chance said.

"Of course," Hadley said with a grin at her future brother-in-law. "That's what favorite aunts are for. Treats."

"You're not her favorite aunt," Katie grumbled.

"Sure I am. Rosie?"

"Um, can't I have two favorite aunts?" She looked up at her father, who nodded. "One for horses and one for cookies?"

"I don't see why not."

"Oh, goodie! Thank you, Daddy." She held up her arms for him to pick her up again.

Katie blinked back tears and hid a smile behind her hand as Rosie squeezed her arms around Chance's neck. "I love it here, Daddy. I don't ever ever ever want to leave."

"I know, Bug," Chance whispered and, for the first time in days, refused to meet Katie's gaze. "I know."

CHAPTER TWELVE

"I FEEL LIKE I've been released from prison."

Chance got Katie settled on her crutches before he led the way to the front door of her house. Rosie, carrying an increasingly beleaguered-looking Clyde, clutched the stuffed monster to her chest and followed close behind, trailed by Hip.

"Given the condition of that house, I can understand why." Chance pulled open the screen door. A few seconds later they were standing in the entryway, steps away from what had looked like a bomb site only a few days before. "Well, gotta hand it to Hadley. This place looks amazing."

He leaned over and clicked on a light. The hardwood floors had been cleaned and there wasn't a speck of dust to be found. Hunting and fishing magazines were piled neatly on the table next to a collection of new candles awaiting their first flame. The bookcases on either side of the fireplace had been straightened, while pictures of Katie, Maura and their mother were arranged on the mantel.

The smell of alcohol and defeat had been replaced by fresh peaches and summer flowers, no doubt thanks to the multiple air fresheners he saw scattered about this room and the dining room.

"How am I ever going to repay everyone for what they've done for me?" Katie sank onto the arm of the sofa and looked around her home as if she'd never seen it before. "This place needed a bulldozer."

"It just needed some attention," Chance told her. "Rosie, how about you see if you can hunt up Snicklefrits. That's his name, right?"

"Yeah," Katie whispered. "Where is he, Chance?" She drew her gaze slowly around the room. "Dad's been gone almost a week. Where is he?"

"I don't know. But they're still looking for him. Jon said the sheriff is going to put out another announcement, this time to some of the local TV stations. See if we get any more information."

"I thought by now we'd have found him. Instead, all I can think is that he drove his car off the road somewhere and he's..." Her voice trailed off in that defeated tone he hated to hear. "What if he's dead?"

"Until we know otherwise, he's fine."

"You don't know that."

"No, I don't. But dwelling on the worst case isn't going to help. Besides, this is your night of freedom. No place for sad faces."

Katie laughed and tilted her chin up. The smile on her face almost reached her eyes. Determined eyes. Sharp, discerning eyes. Eyes that at times seemed to see only him. Chance caught her face in his hand, stroked his thumb across her lips. It would be so easy, one kiss, a brush of lips, just to see, just to test...

"Daddy, I found him!" Rosie squealed a second before she walked into the room, her arms filled with an irritated but resigned cat. "Aunt Katie, I think he's hungry. His tummy is making noises."

Katie's hand came up to catch Chance's. She squeezed her fingers around his once, quick and tight, then pulled free of his hold and pushed back up on her crutches. "We'd best get him settled in for a few more days. At least until I come home. Then we'll go see your mom's room, okay?"

"Okay!" Rosie raced away.

As Katie clicked her way to follow, Chance caught her arm. "Katie."

"Not here, Chance. Not now." She shook her head, but when she looked back at him, for a fraction of a second, he saw the promise. Not here. Not now.

But somewhere else.

And soon.

"Is there anything more beautiful than a Montana sunset?" Katie leaned back on her elbows and stared out at the purple-orange sky. The evening had been perfect, from the weather to Hadley's fried chicken and potato salad, to Rosie getting caught sneaking a second brownie for Clyde before she ran off squealing with Chance chasing her. The late-summer air brushed over them, warm and welcoming, as the river rushed beyond them and meandered through Blackwell land as easily as a bee to its hive.

"I can think of a few things." Chance strummed his guitar, the sound lifting the weight around her heart. Rosie was beginning to sag. She'd laid down on the thick flannel blanket, and rested her head on Hip's stomach as she wiggled and waggled Clyde in the air. When she let out a huge yawn, Hip angled a look at Katie that told her all was well in her dog's world.

"Me playing like this always knocks her out." Chance grinned at Katie in the twilight. "Those weeks after Maura died, when I couldn't sleep, I used to sit outside her nursery when she got fussy and play her back to sleep."

"Did you play for Maura, too?" Katie's heart seized as she thought of her sister's final weeks, her final days.

"I did. She said it took the pain away." His fingers didn't miss a note as he continued to play. "It was the only thing

I could really do at the end. The morphine took care of everything else."

"She called me," Katie said. "A few weeks after the diagnosis. When the doctors told her treatment would just buy her time." The conversation had felt so surreal then, so out of the realm of possibility that Maura would die so young. That she'd leave Katie alone with a father incapable of loving anyone. "She begged me to get tested."

"For the cancer gene she and your mother had? Yeah, she told me." He stopped playing and reached out his hand, which he wrapped around her wrist. "She also told me you tested negative."

"I didn't know whether to laugh or cry. Why her?" Katie heard the anger in her voice. "She had so much more to live for, she had you and Rosie and so much life—"

"No one's life is worth more than someone else's, Katie. She was so relieved to hear you would be okay. I'd be lying if I said she didn't get angry about the cancer. But it was more that she wouldn't have time with Rosie, that she wouldn't see her grow up, get married. Have a family of her own. That we wouldn't have more children."

"Maura always wanted a houseful of them."

"That's an understatement." Chance squeezed her arm before he returned to the guitar. The music helped, she realized, to ease the grief and pull the words and feelings free. "If it had been up to her we would have had a basketball team. Or a backup band. She was so good with Rosie. Nothing rattled her."

"She was the perfect package." Perfect mother and wife and woman. Perfect daughter and sister. Katie could never live up to the life Maura had lived. No matter how hard she tried.

"Is that how you see her? As perfect?"

Katie shrugged. "Wasn't she?"

"Perfect for me, yes. But perfect?" Chance shook his head. "No. She was far from perfect, Katie. She had flaws. She was selfish and stubborn and believed if she ignored something she didn't like or want, it would just go away."

"What are you talking about?" Katie had never heard anyone, especially Chance, talk about Maura in this way. "Chance." Now it was her turn to reach out, to lay a hand on his arm and feel the movement of his muscles as his playing softened. "What don't I know?"

It took a few moments of him staring across the river, before he answered. "She ignored the signs after Rosie was born. She ignored them and hid them from me. She didn't want to take the time away from her, away from us, and once I realized something was wrong, she still wouldn't go to the doctor. No matter how hard I pleaded with her."

Fear pounded in her chest. "What do you mean she wouldn't go to the doctor? Our mother died of uterine cancer before she was forty. She should have been doing everything—"

"I know. But this was six months after Rosie was born. After her first post-op checkup, she stopped going and only took Rosie in. But I didn't know she'd been canceling appointments because she lied to me, told me the checkups were fine. The tests were fine. That she was fine. Until she wasn't. By then it was too late."

"Why would she do that? All her life Maura was terrified she'd get sick like Mama. She knew what could happen." The anger swelled. "Are you telling me the cancer could have been treated?"

"At one time, yes. But as you said, she was terrified she'd end up like your mother. Alone and scared. She was afraid if she got sick, I'd stop loving her. As if her being sick made her unworthy. Less than. Damaged." Chance's eyes sparked in the growing darkness. "Sound familiar?"

Katie swallowed hard as memories she'd long set aside surged. "It sounds like something my father would've said before Mama died. When he'd been drinking." But when he'd been sober, her father had been…working. Out of the house. Away from all of them, leaving ten-year-old Maura as their mother's main caretaker. Katie blinked against the setting sun. "I'd forgotten about that."

"Maura didn't forget. She remembered every moment of your mother's illness, Katie. Every moment of her last days, but that wasn't what stuck with her. It was the way your father refused to deal with it that ultimately cost Maura her life. She was more terrified of losing me than what those test results might tell us. That's what haunts me most, Katie. Not that I lost her. People lose loved ones every day—I was fortunate to have time with her at the end. That we could make some memories for me to share with Rosie when she's old enough. But I will never forgive her for not believing I loved her enough to stay. To fight with her. Every second of every minute. So, see? She wasn't perfect. She lied to me, Katie. About my life. My future. Our future. And because she lied, we lost any chance at one. And my daughter lost her mother."

Katie struggled to breathe. This wasn't possible. Her sister couldn't have…but she could. She did. Katie wanted to believe Maura had lied to protect him, but in the end her sister had hurt Chance even more by keeping the secret.

Secrets. Katie rubbed a hand against her chest as the music from the guitar settled around her. Secrets were as toxic as mercury in the river. Eventually they seeped in, poisoned everyone they came in contact with. Unstoppable. Destroyed all in their path. Nothing was ever the same. "Sometimes people lie for what they think is the right reason, Chance. She never told me any of this. I didn't know."

"I know you didn't." His sad smile brushed against her

heart. "If you had, I don't doubt for a second you would have told me. You've always been honest with me, Katie. Even when it wasn't what I wanted to hear. You've never lied to me." He strummed a final chord and turned that hypnotic, loving smile on her. "And that means the world to me."

"Look at you, boot girl."

Katie stepped back to hold the front door of the main house open for Lydia and the twins, followed quickly by Grace, Hadley and Rachel, who was carrying her ten-month-old baby girl, Poppy.

"Bet you're glad to be off that couch, huh?" Lydia ushered the twins into the kitchen, where Rosie was sitting in her time-out chair after a tantrum of ear-splitting proportions. "Uh-oh. I recognize that pout. What's going on, Rosie?"

"Aunt Katie's mean." Rosie had her arms folded over her chest and her brow was furrowed so deep her eyes practically disappeared. Hip let out a heavy sigh from where she sat by the refrigerator, the only witness to the unfortunate last ten minutes. "She won't let me go riding or visit BB in the stable."

"You slouch any lower your spine is going to collapse." Katie was still getting the hang of the walking boot she'd been fitted with yesterday, but compared to the crutches, she was feeling fancy-free. Her expertise as a disciplinarian, on the other hand, might take a little extra time to develop. Her adorable, sweet little niece had gone from heroine-worshipping cherub to screaming banshee in less than ten seconds. "And maybe you can go riding tomorrow, when someone can be around to watch you."

"I don't need watching. I'm a good rider." Rosie slumped

another inch until her chin was all but level with her knees. "You said so."

"Mean Aunt Katie," Grace said as she walked past them and deposited a cake carrier on the kitchen counter.

"Don't get her started again," Katie muttered as she walked around Ethan's very pregnant fiancée to try to get a peek under the lid. "Chocolate?"

"Maybe." Grace slapped her hand away before she shooed away the twins. "Mom sent it over for after dinner. Unless someone isn't allowed cake because she's sulking?"

Rosie shot up in her chair, the frown vanishing. She started to get up, but Katie held up her hand. "Ah! You still have two minutes."

Rosie sighed and slouched back down.

"Two minutes from when?" Lydia asked in a low voice as Gen and Abby sat on the floor in front of Rosie to entertain her.

"Chance says she gets the same time as her age. So four-and-three-quarters minutes." A snail moved at a faster pace at this point.

"All that happened just before we got here?" Rachel happily handed Poppy over to a finger-wiggling Lydia, who jiggled a giggling and drooling Poppy in the air before locking her onto her hip. "And over a horse?"

"Oh, yeah." Only when Katie had her back to Rosie did she smile. "Makes my heart happy to see how much she loves those horses, but man. That is one stubborn little girl."

"It's the Blackwell," Lydia said. "That's what Jon says, anyway."

"I think she got a double dose thanks to my sister," Katie told them. She'd spent a lot of time last night trying to come to terms with some of the choices her sister had made in the last ten years, but she kept circling back to

Chance and what it must have been like for him to realize that, deep down, Maura had been terrified he would turn away from her, as their father had done to their mother. Her family was even more messed up than she'd realized.

"She really going to ride tomorrow?" Hadley opened the fridge and dragged out the nearly empty pitcher of lemonade tea.

"Dr. Grey says I can go to the stables tomorrow and walk around," Katie told them. "I can get her on one for a few minutes."

"You're not allowed to ride." Rachel grabbed a towel out of her diaper bag and wiped her daughter's grin over Lydia's shoulder. "Remember?"

"Yes, Mom." Katie rolled her eyes. "Conner's got a group coming in for a trail ride tomorrow morning. I was thinking maybe Ben or Ty—"

"Ty's working on some big deal with a law firm in Billings for a corporate retreat," Hadley said.

"Ben's free," Rachel said with a shrug. "I'll talk to him tonight. I only have a few appointments in the morning, so he can be out here."

"You sure Ben will be okay with that? Ah, hey!" Katie glanced over at Rosie, who had stretched one tiny foot to the ground. She yanked her foot back under her. "That's another two minutes, Little Miss."

"Awwww." Rosie's arms went back over her chest in a huff.

"You are good." Rachel looked a bit stunned. "Remind me to send Poppy your way when she gets to that age. And Ben will be fine with it. Good education for him when we put this one on a horse." She pointed at Poppy.

"Dadadadadaaa!" Poppy agreed.

"Yeah, she's Daddy's little girl all right." Rachel beamed with loving pride.

Katie agreed. While Ben wasn't Poppy's biological father, he'd slipped into the role with ease and pride. She'd known Ben her entire life, but she'd never seen him turn to mush as he did when it came to that little girl.

"Hadley said you finished scanning in the house photos." Lydia pressed a loud kiss on Poppy's forehead.

"Yeah, I, um, also did something else." Nerves she didn't know she had suddenly surged to life. "Since Hadley had done a good job sorting out all the photos…" She headed into the living room, where Hadley had set her up with a mini office on the sofa. It was chaotic, but organized chaos. And starting tomorrow, she could work in Big E's office at an actual desk.

"Mom, can we go to the petting zoo?" Gen yelled after them.

"When Rosie's out of time-out," Lydia said. "If Rosie wants to go, that is."

"Yes, please," Rosie, suddenly polite, responded.

Lydia arched an eyebrow at Katie, who glanced at her watch. "A minute thirty."

"You are hard-nosed. I'll let you know when," Lydia called to her girls.

"Everything run okay with the interior-design program?" Hadley asked as they stood around the coffee table and laptop.

"Oh, yeah. That part's great. In fact, I even did some playing around, putting in some details that I remember from growing up."

"Told you I got the right person to do this." Hadley nudged Grace's arm. "Would you sit down? You're making me antsy with all that belly rubbing."

"Sorry." Grace cringed. "She's been swimming up a storm. We might need to add a pool to the ranch."

"Already on the list," Hadley said.

"Sit here." Katie patted the sofa next to her. "I did a little digging around online while the scanner was running and found this family-photo collage program. It also repairs and lightens photos, then you can download them into digital frames or into a projection program. I did a few of them with photos of the boys' parents. I thought maybe we could play them at the wedding, then give them the frames as presents." She pressed Enter and let the collage play through, getting a bit misty at the images of Brenda and Mike from their wedding, to each of the boys' births, to just a few weeks before their deaths. When it was done and only silence hung in the air, she bit her lip. "No good?"

"Oh, Katie." Grace sniffled and leaned her head on Katie's shoulder. "It's beautiful. I'd only seen one or two pictures of them before. The brothers will love it."

"Yeah?" Katie looked at the other women.

"The only problem we're going to have is waiting until Jon and Lydia's wedding. It's wonderful, Katie," Hadley said. "And I'm impressed you managed to keep Big E out of them."

"Don't be. I just bypassed those." Katie's pride dipped. "Maybe someday when they can put everything behind them—"

"Fat chance," Rachel said from where she sat on the arm of the sofa. "When I think of what he put Ben through—"

"What he put them all through," Lydia interrupted. "It's a miracle any of our boys turned out as well as they did. Big E's done more than enough damage to this family. Personally, I hope he doesn't come back. Let them get on with their lives."

Katie bit her lip so hard she tasted blood. None of these women knew Big E the way she did. He hadn't put all this effort into bringing the brothers home only to then stay away himself. He'd want to witness the results of his meticulous plan and bask in his success. But she wasn't about to burst any of these women's bubbles. Not yet, anyway.

"Speaking of getting on with our lives." Hadley retrieved the bag she'd left by the front door and pulled out what had jokingly become known as her Bridal Bible. All the women but Katie groaned. Katie grinned. "We need to finalize some details on your wedding, Lydia. Time's officially up. How many attendants are you going to have?"

"Oh." Lydia sat in the chair by Katie and leaned forward to hold Poppy upright as the little girl stood on still wobbling knees. "Well, it'll be four, obviously. Maybe five if I can talk my friend Meredith into flying out for it."

"Names of the definite?" Hadley flipped through pages and tapped open her pen.

"Hadley, Grace, Rachel and Katie."

Katie gasped as the other women went "awwww" before they all started to talk at once.

"Wait, what?" Katie tried to yell over the excited voices, but no one seemed to hear. She stuck two fingers in her mouth and let out her trademark whistle to bring the room to silence. "You want me to be a bridesmaid?" she asked a beaming Lydia.

"Well, yeah. Of course. You're part of the family, aren't you?"

"I, uh." Katie couldn't decide what to think. Her heart swelled. Her throat tightened. Her eyes burned. "I just never thought—"

"What? That you're one of the girls?" Rachel dropped onto the other side of her, wrapped an arm around Katie's shoulders and squeezed her into a hug. "Hate to tell you, kiddo, but yeah, you kinda are. You've been putting up with the brothers for longer than any of us. And you've lived to tell the tale. That earns you bridesmaid rights for all of us at a minimum."

"All of you?" Katie croaked.

"You're their family, Katie. That means you're ours, too," Lydia told her. "Stop looking so shocked. There's nothing to—oh, no! You're not crying are you?"

"No." Katie sniffled and blinked back tears. "Of course not." She'd never been in anyone's wedding before. Maura and Chance had eloped and she'd never really made friends with anyone else not associated with the ranch or the business.

"Awwww, that's so sweet." Grace wrapped her arms around Katie's and squeezed. "You poor thing. You're one of us whether you want to be or not."

"Whatever happens with Chance," Hadley added and was immediately shushed. "What? Like we aren't all thinking it? Have you seen the way he looks at her?"

"What way?" Katie wasn't sure she could stay on this emotional roller coaster. "No, we're just friends. He's just Chance. He was married to my sister, for crying out loud."

"The important word is *was*," Hadley said. "And you wouldn't be protesting so loudly if there wasn't something on your side of things. I can see it. You like him." She circled a finger in the air in front of Katie's face. "A lot."

"Well, you're just wrong." Katie's voice cracked. It was bad enough she was worried about her growing feelings for Chance, but the idea anyone else had picked up on them? Seen them? *Talked* about them?

Hadley and Lydia grinned.

"Oh, no." Katie shook her head. "No, no…"

"Aunt Katie?" Rosie stood in the living-room doorway, one hand gripping the wall, one leg swinging back and forth. She had her head ducked, but her eyes were looking up at Katie. "Can I come out now?"

"Oh, yes, of course." Katie swiped a hand across her damp cheeks as Rosie walked over to her. Before Katie knew what was happening, Rosie had crawled into her lap and linked her arms around Katie's neck.

"I'm sorry I made you mad, Aunt Katie. You aren't mean. Please don't cry."

"It was—" At Lydia's sharp shake of her head, Katie cut herself off. "It's okay, Little Miss." Katie hugged her back. "All's forgiven." She set Rosie back to look into her face. "You want to go to the petting zoo with your cousins?"

"Uh-huh." Rosie nodded.

"Great! Come on, Rosie!" Abby yelled as she and Gen raced through the living room and out the front door.

"Go have some fun. We'll get someone to go riding with you tomorrow." Katie kissed Rosie's forehead and set her back on her feet.

"Okay. Come on, Hippo! Let's go find Splinter!" The dog raced out faster than the twins.

"Oh, geez." Katie sank her head into her hands as Rosie slammed the door behind her and the other women dissolved into laughter. "I'd forgotten about Splinter."

"She's dodging the subject," Rachel joked as she gave Katie a good shake. "Now back to the matter at hand. Lydia, please tell me you aren't going to make us wear some hideous bridesmaid dresses?"

"Well, it's a fall wedding," Lydia said with a wicked grin. "I was thinking pumpkins and gourds and—"

"No orange!" Grace released Katie and pointed both index fingers at her stomach. "I don't want to be mistaken for a pumpkin. It'll be bad enough to waddle down the aisle."

"I was thinking yellows and burgundy," Hadley countered.

"So corn and wine?" Rachel asked. "That could work. What do you think, Katie?"

What did she think? She couldn't think. "I'm fine with anything."

"Great. So she'll be of no help. Moving on." Rachel patted Katie's leg and faced the bride-to-be. "Let's talk cake."

"We need to focus on her dress," Hadley said.

"Where's the ceremony going to be?"

Katie sank back on the sofa, her mind spinning as the topics and discussion flew over and around her head. She never realized how much she'd been missing out on by not having a tribe of women friends, but clearly she was getting a crash course now. To be included in such an important Blackwell family event, not just one wedding, but three? Where she wouldn't just be on the sidelines observing? That was something she'd never thought possible before.

None of what was happening—not Lydia's wedding, not Hadley taking over the promotion and event planning of the ranch, not Rachel's growing law business with Ben and, in a strange way, not even Grace's pregnancy—would have happened if it wasn't for Big E and his machinations. Which meant everything happening around Katie, all the joy and happiness and hope, was all based on deception and lies.

And Katie was the biggest liar of them all.

CHAPTER THIRTEEN

CHANCE WASN'T SURE what surprised him more the next morning as he strode out of the barn to take a break—that he'd actually been looking forward to the stable chores, or that when he emerged he found his daughter on one of the biggest horses he'd ever seen, his brother Ben behind her in the saddle.

His scalp prickled. His unease had little to do with the idea of Rosie riding than the expression of pure joy on her little face. His little girl had never looked so happy. He leaned the broom against the stable wall and walked over to the round yard, remembering a time when he'd been the one in the saddle. Minus the smile and laughter, of course. Prying Rosie away from this place, away from the animals and family she'd latched onto with the ease of a newborn pup nursing for the first time, was going to be torturous. For both of them. Unless…

Unless they stayed?

His boots made little noise as he joined Katie at the fence line. What a picture she made, standing with her arms draped over the fence, curvy figure looking fit and snug back in her jeans and nonwork T-shirt the color of ripe raspberries. She'd left her hair down and hanging loose from the cowboy hat perched on her head. The only element out of place was the giant black walking boot encasing her left foot up past her calf. Personally he'd have preferred the doctor to have kept her off her feet for another few days at least, but that would mean driving an already bored Katie over the edge. That said, had her convalescence been extended, it would have robbed him of a beautiful late-morning vision.

"She's a natural, isn't she?" Chance took his place beside Katie and smiled at the sound of his daughter's tinkling laughter echoing on the breeze.

"Afraid so." The smile on Katie's face when she glanced over didn't seem quite as bright this morning. There were circles under her eyes, a tension in her jaw he hadn't noticed before. "Sorry?"

"Not really, no. She's a Blackwell and a Montgomery. Nowhere else she belongs other than in a saddle." And with that, Chance pulled out his phone and made note of the thought.

"She apologized to me again this morning," Katie told him. "You have a talk with her?"

"About disrespecting her elders—you bet I did." The idea his Rosie had had a full-blown meltdown with Katie wasn't all bad news. It meant she felt safe with her aunt and it had probably been a good thing for Katie to see that his little Rosie wasn't a perfect angel. That said, the last thing he ever wanted people to think when they saw Rosie was that she was a brat. "You handled it well, giving her the time-out. I wouldn't be surprised if she was testing you."

"Kind of felt that way." Katie's smile eased a bit. "I've been known to have a screaming fit or two. No harm done."

"Except to your eardrums, right?" His heart picked up its pace as Ben kicked Starlight into a trot around the pen.

"Right." Katie's eyes went wide. "Who knew something so tiny could scream so loud? I'm surprised she didn't scare the horses all the way out here in the barn."

"They'll get used to it."

Katie pushed up her hat and faced him fully. "Will they?

Why? You thinking of staying?" Was that accusation on her pretty face or hope?

"I'm thinking about a lot of things." Including kissing Katie. He'd been thinking about it for days now, wondering if those sweet lips of hers tasted like sunshine or rainstorms? Darn it! He rolled his eyes and added another note to his phone, then pocketed it and moved a bit closer. "Things back in LA are complicated."

"Things everywhere are complicated. Doesn't mean there isn't a way to work through them." She turned and leaned back against the fence, hands shoved into the front pockets of her jeans. "Vote to keep the ranch, Chance. Let her have this legacy. Let them all have it."

"You've been waiting for the right time to spring that on me, haven't you?" He inched another step and laid his hand on the fence above her shoulder. The sounds of galloping hooves and Rosie's happiness washed over him. "What about you, Katie? Why don't you ask me to vote to keep it for you?"

Had he not been watching her so closely, had he not been falling into the deep green of her eyes, he might have missed the infinitesimal flinch.

"You mean why don't I tell you that if you sell, I'll probably be out of a job and a place to live? That I'll have to start over, figure out what to do with my father if and when he ever comes home? I can't do that, Chance." Her lips quirked and pulled his gaze down to her mouth. "That wouldn't be playing fair, would it? As much as I want you to keep the ranch, you should vote that way because this is where you and Rosie belong. Not out of some obligation you feel to me because of Maura."

"Is that what you really think?" He lowered his voice and a thrill of excitement shot through him as he saw her shiver. He lifted his hand to her face, stroked a finger down the side of her cheek. "That I only care about you because you're Maura's sister?"

Katie closed her eyes. "Anything more than that would be wrong, Chance." Was that a plea or a statement? But she didn't turn away from him. Instead, she leaned into his touch, her lips brushing against his palm.

"Would it be wrong?" He had dozens of questions swirling in his head, but only one realization, which nearly drove him to his knees. He did care about her. More than he knew he should. Maybe more than he wanted to. And none of his feelings had anything to do with her sister. "I thought my life ended when Maura died. And maybe the life I had before did. But that doesn't mean there isn't another life waiting for me and Rosie." One that could include Katie.

Katie shook her head. "This is crazy, Chance." Her whisper barely reached his ears. "We can't—"

Chance dipped his head and kissed her. Softly. Gently. A brushing of lips, a test, a taste, of what could be. A low whimper escaped her mouth as her hand came up and brushed the side of his face. Soft fingers, trembling fingers. His hand released the fence, brushed down her back. He pressed the flat of his palm into the small of her back. She clutched at his shirt, fisted her fingers. He pulled her in. Tilted his head. And dived deeper.

"Daddy, look at me!"

Rosie's squeal broke the spell, but only enough for Chance to raise his head slightly.

"I see you, Bug." But he didn't take his eyes off Katie. How could he when she looked at him as if a switch had been turned on inside her? "I see *you*, Katie," he whispered.

She caught her lower lip between her teeth, a bright

pink popping up on her cheeks as she patted his chest. "Good to know."

"Daddy, look!"

"Never a private moment," Chance mumbled and looked up to find his brother and Rosie looking past them toward the sheriff's car heading down the road to the main house. "Huh. Wonder what that—"

"Dad." Katie pushed against Chance's chest and darted past him as fast as her booted foot would carry her.

"You got this?" Ben asked as he drew Starlight to a halt beside the fence.

"Yeah. You stay with your uncle Ben, okay, Bug?"

"'Kay, Daddy." She tilted her head back and turned that million-watt smile on her uncle. "We're having fun, yeah?"

"More than expected. Let's have some more." Ben made a clicking sound and kicked his legs. When the horse took off, Chance knew Ben was just trying to get a rise out of him, which he nearly did. As many differences as he and Ben had, he had no doubt his daughter was safe in his brother's hands.

"We don't know what this is about, Katie," Chance told her once he caught up to her. She stood at the base of the porch steps, arms crossed tight over her chest as the white marked sedan pulled to a stop at the end of the house. "Don't worry until there's something to worry about."

"I can't remember the last time the sheriff came out personally, Chance." She couldn't have been standing any straighter and stiffer if her spine had been made of rebar.

"Morning, Sheriff." Katie kicked out her foot to keep the weight off it and shoved her hands in the back pockets of her jeans. Nerves, Chance knew. He'd had enough of them to know.

"Katie." Sheriff Brodie McClasky shoved his hat on his head after climbing out from behind the wheel, an unreadable expression on his thirtysomething tanned face. Chance didn't know much about the man other than what Jon had told him—that he was a onetime Seattle detective who'd left the force under somewhat unusual circumstances. "I called the house but kept getting the machine. Thought I'd drive out to talk to you in person."

"Is it about my dad?" Once again, Katie made a question sound like an accusation.

"Yeah. Can we go inside?"

"Sure. Coffee?" Chance grabbed Katie's shoulders and pivoted her before she could argue. She stumbled up the steps and into the house.

"Wouldn't say no, thanks."

"Is he alive?" They were barely in the kitchen when Katie turned toward the sheriff.

Chance moved to the coffee maker, impressed by the sheriff's calm.

"Yes. He's in Bozeman. Someone recognized his photo from the TV spot we ran and called it in. I drove down last night to check it out to be sure. I wanted to get the details myself before I got your hopes up. Thanks." He toasted Chance with the filled mug before he sipped. "Long morning."

"He drove to Bozeman? Alone?" Katie asked. "Why? We don't know anyone there."

Sheriff McClasky took another long drink and it was then Chance realized he was trying to find the right words. Chance moved in behind Katie, placed his hands on her shoulders and squeezed.

"He checked himself into an alcohol-treatment center. Pricy one, too. Paid cash, from what the doctor told me. Thirty-day plan."

"He… What?" Katie stumbled back. "He's in *rehab*?"

Whatever Chance had been expecting to hear, that certainly wasn't it. Why on earth hadn't the man at least left a note so Katie wouldn't worry? "How's he doing?"

"The doctor and nurse I spoke with said he was doing well. Said it was his last chance. He told them he had a lot of mistakes to make up for before he met his maker."

"So you haven't talked to Lochlan yourself?"

"No." Sheriff McClusky winced and set down his mug. "No. Katie, two days into his treatment, he had a massive heart attack. He's at Bozeman Memorial in a medically induced coma. I'm sorry. But they don't think he's going to make it."

"Hey."

Katie turned dazed eyes from the passenger window and looked at Chance. They'd been on the road for more than two hours. With Hadley, Lydia and the girls off doing wedding stuff, Ty had loaned them his truck while Ben promised to take Rosie with him until Lydia was back with the twins. He'd text them if there were any problems. That Ben had given her a big hug before they'd left told her Chance's older brother fully expected bad news to follow.

"Hey, what?" Katie's voice was raw, as if she'd forgotten how to speak.

"Another half hour, we should be there. You doing okay?" He reached over and took her hand. She stared down at it, unable to sort through her feelings. One second he'd been kissing her, and the next, her life had flipped upside down. And not in a good way.

"I have so many questions. Why didn't anyone call me?"

"Sheriff McClasky said your father left his emergency contact information blank except for one name. Mine."

"Yours?" Katie gasped. "But why on earth—"

"A joke maybe?" Chance shrugged. "They thought so. Putting down the name of a semipopular singer must have seemed like one. Especially when he didn't include a phone number."

"Won't they be in for a surprise when you walk in the door." From the absurd to the ridiculous. She shifted in her seat, tried to work out the kink in her sore leg and had to settle for scrubbing her free hand hard against her thigh. She ached. Everywhere.

"Why would he have gone to Bozeman?" Chance asked. "Why wouldn't he have sought treatment through his own physician?"

"Because his doctor never would have approved a program like that." She'd searched online and found the center in question—a center known for quick detox that focused primarily on the psychological effects of alcoholism and drug dependency. A potentially good solution for someone in good health. Which her father was not. "His heart condition should have precluded him from drastic treatment."

"I'm betting your father probably left that off his paperwork as well. He came in without ID. Left his wallet in the car and used a fake name. Chester Birkham."

Katie might have laughed if she wasn't screaming on the inside. "Mama's old boyfriend from high school. Dad stole her away from him. Or so the story goes. Always a romantic, my dad. And he never forgets a darn thing." She dropped her head back against the headrest and wished she could give in to the exhaustion creeping over her. A sleepless night seemed the least of her problems right now. "At least I know where the money went. I guess I should feel relieved he didn't spend it all on one last binge." Not that the five K would have covered it. Which explained why he'd sold his truck.

"Why didn't you tell me about the money?"

"Because the money didn't matter by comparison." So what if it was her "starting over" fund, her safety net in case the worst happened and she found herself out of a job. She'd been stashing cash for going on ten years. And her father had blown it on a treatment plan that might just have gotten him killed. "Why aren't you telling me he's going to be okay?"

Chance squeezed her hand before he released it. "Because I don't know that for sure. I wouldn't lie to you, Katie. Not about something so important."

"Only about unimportant things, right?" She wanted to make light of the situation, but every time she tried, another piece of her heart broke off and disintegrated.

"Not what I meant and you know it." His slight smile told her that he understood.

"You're probably thinking it would be easier on everyone if he didn't recover."

"Not easier on you." Chance frowned. "And no, actually. I wasn't thinking that. If you want to know the truth, I was thinking how angry I would be if he died before I could have an actual conversation with him. He was blind drunk when I saw him at your house. I bet he doesn't even remember—"

"He remembers." Katie took a shuddering breath. "That's why he put your name down as a contact. If he dies, it'll be his last statement. Stubborn and cruel. Even at the end." Tears burned hot and made her jaw hurt. She wasn't ready to be alone. She wasn't ready to lose the last of her family.

"You don't know that this is the end. And you're not alone, Katie."

"Huh?" She rolled her head around, frowned.

"You said you aren't ready to be alone. You aren't."

She stared at him. She'd said that out loud?

"Despite everything, he's still your dad. It's okay to love him. Even if he doesn't deserve it."

Katie almost smiled. "He'd probably love that you said that. But if we get there and he's gone—"

"What have I told you about that tendency of yours to expect the worst?" He took the final highway exchange with a glance in the rearview mirror.

"Because the worst always happens." The dread that had begun to circle inside of her like a tornado months before had picked up speed. She knew what was coming—the inevitable. The truth always had a way of breaking free of the lies that bound it. It was only a matter of time before Big E came home, and when that happened...

"Just because the worst happens doesn't mean you can't survive it. You get through it. I'm proof of that. Whatever comes at you, Katie, I promise, you won't be alone. I'll be right here. Me and Rosie. Not to mention my brothers and their families. We won't let you fall."

Katie nodded when he looked at her for confirmation she'd heard him, that she understood him.

But deep down, she didn't believe him.

CHANCE SET THE wooden box he'd brought from LA on the table beside Lochlan Montgomery's bed in ICU. Apart from comforting words for Katie, there wasn't anything he could do now other than stand back and be there when she needed him. After all, she was the reason he was here. He certainly wasn't here to give comfort and peace of mind to the old man who had broken his older daughter's heart.

The *beep-beep-beep*s of the machines, the hissing of the ventilator. The uneven pulse rate screaming through the monitors. Every sound of his nightmares echoed at him in stereophonic sound, shooting through his mind and sending him back to those final days Maura had spent in the hospital. Before Chance had taken her home to die.

He didn't want that for Katie. He didn't want her to

watch Lochlan fade away, breath by breath, heartbeat by heartbeat. Not after all this man had put those he'd supposedly loved through. But it wasn't Chance's decision.

And so he stood to the side, hands clenched in his pockets, as he listened to the fiftysomething doctor, who looked oddly like the grim reaper minus the scythe, explain the situation.

"I'm afraid we're in wait-and-see mode, Ms. Montgomery."

"I understand." Katie sat tall in the chair, hands clenched between her knees. "How long has he been like this?"

"Over a week. He was brought in through the emergency room after the night nurse at the treatment facility found him unresponsive."

"He didn't tell them about his heart condition, did he?"

"It's not in the information he provided, no. Once we obtained his real name, I was able to get in touch with his regular doctor."

"Who I'm sure was more than helpful." Katie's mouth twisted. "Dad didn't like him and the feeling was mutual. A patient has to be willing to work on staying alive. He wrote my dad off a long time ago."

"I understand he has a long history of alcohol abuse."

"Twenty years at least. It's been worse the last two. Since my sister died." Katie shook her head. "I know that's not an excuse. I'm sorry." She covered her eyes with one hand and let out a sob that sliced through Chance's heart. "I can't seem to figure out how to feel about this. I don't like to think of him being in pain."

"Of course you don't. And he's not. His heart was significantly weakened by the attack, and his body is still undergoing the detoxification from the alcohol, but we have him on substantial painkillers. In all honesty, if he survives the next couple of days, he'll have gone through the worst without even knowing."

Chance let out a sharp breath. Of course Lochlan would have found the easy way around withdrawal.

"Your father has a DNR order in his medical file," the doctor told Katie. "Do you know about that? If this goes on for more than twenty days, we've been instructed to turn off the machines."

"Yeah, I know."

Finally. Chance's chest loosened. A bit of relief. At least that decision had been taken out of Katie's hands.

"On the chance he does come out of this, what's his prognosis?" Katie wiped her face and clutched her hands in her lap again.

"Uncertain. If he stops drinking and follows medical advice, after a few months of rehabilitation therapy, he could live five, maybe ten more years. But that's only if he wants to live."

"He hasn't wanted to live since my mother died. I don't know what to do. Do I stay here with him? Do I go home and wait? Does he even know I'm here?"

How Chance hated the pleading desperation in her voice. But he also heard her unspoken question: Would Lochlan even care? He ducked his chin to his chest, gnashed his teeth so hard his head ached.

"I'm of the belief that yes, coma patients hear everything going on around them," the doctor said. "There's no proof, of course. And in answer to your other question, it's perfectly understandable if you don't want to stay, Ms. Montgomery. No one will blame you if you go home to Falcon Creek and wait for us to call with news. We have your contact information now. There won't be any further miscommunication."

Katie nodded.

"Thank you, Doctor." Chance pushed away from the window ledge and offered his hand. "We'll let you and the nurses know what she decides."

"If you have any other questions, please have them page me. I'll be in the hospital until five."

"We don't have to rush back." Chance bent down next to Katie. "And if you want to stay, I can book us into a motel." The hell with his budget. Some things were more important than money.

Katie blinked and two big tears plopped onto her cheeks. "I've been so angry with him for so long. But how do I abandon him? How do I justify walking away and let whatever is going to happen, happen? What kind of daughter does that make me?"

"You do what you have to do." He stroked a hand down the back of her hair and wished he could take this pain away. "You do what you have to do for you. Even in his alcoholic haze, when I talked to him that day, he was horrified by what he did, Katie. In his own way, whatever way that was, he loves you. Whatever decision you make, he'll understand."

"I need to get some air." She pushed to her feet and when Chance moved to follow, she held out her hand, shook her head. "I appreciate all you're doing, Chance, but I need some time alone. Just a few minutes."

"Sure." He watched her leave, then once she was out of sight, he stood at the foot of Lochlan's bed, hands shoved into his pockets, and stared at the man who had brought so much pain to the women in his life. "Whatever you're going to do, old man, you do it quick. Don't leave her dangling." He looked at the box beside the bed. The box he'd brought with him from LA. The box that had sat on the mantel of his and Rosie's home for the last two years.

The box Maura herself had chosen.

Anger forced him to move and he picked up the box and set it on the bed. With more care than he realized he had in him, Chance picked up Lochlan's IV-strewn hand and placed it on the box.

He found Katie talking to the nurse at the station at the end of the hall.

"I want to go home," she told him. "I'm sorry, making you drive all the way out here for such a short—"

Chance pressed his lips against hers, waited until he felt the tension in her body ebb. Then he pulled her into his arms and held her while sobs wracked her body. "I've left a box with him," he told the nurse, who had tears glistening in her eyes. "Please make sure whatever happens, I get it back. It's his daughter's ashes."

Katie gasped, but Chance tightened his hold.

"Of course, Mr. Blackwell. We have yours and Ms. Montgomery's numbers. If there's any change, we'll let you know."

"Thank you. Come on, Katie." Chance shifted her against his side, kept his arm locked around her shoulders. "Let's go home."

CHAPTER FOURTEEN

THE REST OF the week ticked by, routine keeping most of them busy and distracted. The passing time also brought Chance closer to not just one, but two things he was dreading: casting his deciding vote on whether they should sell the ranch and…performing at the library fund-raiser.

How he wished he could attribute the empty feeling in the pit of his stomach to concern over Katie and how she was dealing—or rather not dealing—with Lochlan's illness. Instead he had to come to terms with the fact that he was more nervous about tonight than he'd been the first time he'd stepped on stage. Nearly a decade ago there had been no expectations. He and Maura knew they'd take whatever came, good or bad. Now? Not only was Rosie singing his praises—literally, as she walked through the house and across the ranch—but word was tickets had also sold out and they were expecting standing-room-only at the Silver Stake. Hopefully no one was going to ask for their money back.

Which was why, while Rosie took a late-afternoon nap and Katie took a supervisory stroll through the stable, barns and tack room, he sat on the front porch, iced tea at his side, head back and eyes closed, and strummed his new song into some semblance of perfection. Three hours to showtime.

"Don't know what you're worried about." Ben's voice

broke through his meditative practice. "Sounds good to me."

Chance drew his head up, surprised to find not only Ben, but Jon and Tyler also standing at the porch railing, watching him. "Well, this isn't creepy at all. You turning into groupies?" He swung his guitar down and reached for his tea, drinking more out of procrastination than anything. "Or is this some kind of intervention." He glanced around. "You lock Ethan in the shed?"

Ty grinned. "Nah. Katie asked him to come out and check on Gypsy. She hasn't been eating."

"I thought Katie attributed that to her not training with her." Chance recalled Katie worrying about the latest addition to the ranch, but maybe he'd missed something.

"That's the theory. Just want to be sure. Skittish horse. Should be making more progress than she is."

"Once Katie's back in the saddle, she should even out."

"Ben just made a joke." Chance braced his foot on the railing and pushed back. "Now I know something's up. Best be quick about it. Rosie'll be up in a few."

"We need to know where you stand on the ranch," Jon told him.

"For the moment, I'm sitting."

"Chance." Ty shook his head. "As much as we all appreciate your humor—"

"Speak for yourself," Ben muttered.

"We can't keep pushing this down the road," Jon said. "We have to make plans either way."

"And it's my decision on what those plans are. Perfect. Not like I have anything else to worry about these days."

"Look, we know—"

"No," Chance cut off Ben. "You don't know. Because you're not sitting where I am. You each have your own agendas, your own reasons for wanting to sell or stay. And honestly? I can see both sides of the argument. I totally get that the money could make a huge difference to both the Double T and JB Bar. You think I don't realize what that money can do for me and Rosie when we go home?" He ignored the not-so-sly glance Ty shot Jon. "But I also see the progress Ty and Hadley have made with this place. In another couple of years we could make double the amount of money a sale would bring and Ethan can open that large-animal clinic he's been chatting on about."

"He could also pay off his student debt and be done with it." Ben's cool tone told Chance what he already knew: Ben wasn't budging.

"Then there are the kids to consider," Chance told them. "Gen and Abby, and Rosie, maybe even Poppy and however many other kids you all have. One day, this could all be theirs. Think of that legacy."

"Or maybe they won't want this place at all," Ben growled back. "You don't. Or at least you didn't."

No, he didn't. Something shifted inside of Chance. Something primal, possessive. But that was before he saw this place through his daughter's eyes. Through Katie's... "I need to discuss it with Katie."

"I knew it." The frustration in Ben's voice had Chance sitting forward in his chair. "I told you!" he said to Jon.

"Care to explain that comment?"

"Easy, Chance," Jon said. "We're here for a calm discussion, not a confrontation. Or, heaven help us, a fight."

"Maybe that's what we need. A knock-down-drag-out to decide this once and for all," Ben spat. "Why would any of us want to keep a hold of a place that's anchoring us to the past? Staying here, keeping it, is exactly what Big E would want."

"And that's what this is really about for you, isn't it?" Chance argued. "Sticking it to Big E. Selling this place out from under him would be the best revenge you could get on him, wouldn't it?"

"Since when do you defend our grandfather?" Ben glared at him.

"This isn't me defending him, but for crying out loud, Ben, if it hadn't been for Big E, you wouldn't be with Rachel right now. You wouldn't have Poppy or the promise of your own ranch and future. Maybe it's time to admit the old man did you a favor."

"Or maybe you're so worried about Katie and her future that you're fine throwing the rest of us under the bus."

"Okay, enough." Jon held up his hands. "Chance, it's obvious you're leaning toward keeping the place, yeah?"

"Yeah." Until this moment, he hadn't been sure. Now he was.

Ben swore.

"You need to cut it out, Ben," Ty snapped. "We agreed that this might happen when we asked Chance to come home and cast the deciding vote."

"That was before I realized he'd be under a certain someone's feminine influence."

"So much for considering Katie part of the family." Chance grabbed his guitar by the neck, set it against the railing and stood. "You can really look her in the eye and tell her all the work she's put into this place doesn't matter? That her dreams don't matter? This place is as much hers as it is ours!"

"Katie Montgomery can get any job she wants in the state. Hell, I'll hire her if it means unloading this place and leaving Big E in the dust." Ben rose to his full height, danger and anger flashing in his eyes. "You need to get your priorities straight, baby brother, and stop letting her lead you around by your—"

"Heart!" Ty yelled but it was too late.

Chance leaped over the railing and knocked Ben off his feet. Once upon a time Chance wouldn't have been much of a match for a brother who had countless inches and pounds on him, but ten years changed a lot. Now, when Ben kicked out and caught Chance in the chest, Chance knocked his brother's foot to the side and followed through with a fist that caught Ben solidly in the mouth.

"Enough!" Jon roared.

"Not even close." Ben spit blood, shoved himself up and tackled Chance around the waist, driving him backward through the porch railing. The crash exploded in his ears. For a stunned moment, Chance could only lie there, sprawled on his back. He barely heard Ty and Jon yelling before he saw Ben's fist coming at his face. He dodged the punch, whipping his head to the side, and Ben's fist plowed into the porch floor. Chance heard Ben's hiss of pain but ignored it, striking out and catching his brother on the chin.

"Oh, for the love of—"

Chance glanced at his twin, which meant he took his eyes off Ben. His head snapped back. His left eye went dark for an instant, but he only saw red when his vision cleared. He drove his knees up and slammed his feet into Ben's chest, sending him flying off the porch and into the dirt.

Ben rolled, jumped to his feet and advanced, Chance meeting him halfway, but Jon moved in and planted both hands against his brother's chest. "I said enough! You!" He kept one hand planted firmly on Chance. "Back off! And you…" Jon pointed a finger at Ben. "Remember who you're talking about. This place wouldn't still be standing if it wasn't for Katie. If it were anyone else spewing those words, you'd knock their block off, so hold yourself to the same standard."

"He started it," Ben muttered and wiped a hand across his mouth.

"And I'll finish it." Chance dived forward but Ty caught him from behind. "You taking his side now?" Chance swung on his twin.

"I'm taking hers!" Ty pointed at Rosie, who had pushed through the screen door, her sleep-filled eyes wide with fear.

"Daddy? Why are you hurting Uncle Ben?"

The anger whooshed out of him. "Rosie."

"You're scaring me, Daddy." Rosie's eyes filled with tears. "I don't like you to be angry with Uncle Ben."

"I know, Bug. I'm sorry." Chance caught his breath, bent over and planted his hands on his knees. His body ached. His face pounded. The porch was a mess. The railing was toast, laying in broken and splintered chunks of wood, along with the chair, the table and… "Oh, no. No, no, no." He stumbled forward and dropped to his knees. The remains of his guitar, his only prized possession, lay scattered in the rubble. His hand shook as he wrapped his hand around the neck. It came away on its own.

Pain screamed through him as he stared at the dangling, warped strings.

"Daddy?" Rosie squatted beside him, wrapped her tiny hand around his as Chance squeezed his eyes shut to stop the tears. "Mama's guitar."

"It's okay." Chance choked, trying to convince himself as much as Rosie. "It's…okay." But as he sifted through the scraps, it wasn't okay. The guitar was destroyed.

He shouldn't have come home. He shouldn't have believed, even for a minute, that he belonged here. His brothers didn't see him as anything more than a vote for their own individual interests. The bonds he'd felt forming among his brothers over the last few weeks snapped, leaving him what he'd been before he'd come back to Falcon Creek.

Alone.

"Chance—"

Chance swung on his brother, wanting to hurt Ben, wanting him to feel a fraction of the pain that coursed through him like a fire. But the grief on his brother's face, on all his brothers' faces as they looked at the remains of the instrument he'd treasured from the moment he received it, had him shaking his head and reaching for his daughter. Holding her, wrapping his arms around her, was the only thing keeping him together. "It's okay, Rosie." He pressed his lips to the side of her head as he struggled to his feet. "It's okay, Bug. I think maybe it's time we went home."

THE ELATION KATIE felt at having had her first full day back with her horses, and on schedule, was tempered only by the knowledge that her father's life was ticking away. The worry over where Lochlan had disappeared to had been replaced by the understanding he probably wasn't going to recover. Odds were she'd be making funeral, rather than transportation, arrangements.

"Gypsy should be fine now that you're back," Ethan told her as they strode to the main house. "You got her to eat those carrots and apples, so she was just being ornery. Get her into the round yard tomorrow and I'll bet she…"

"You'll bet she what?" Katie skidded to a halt beside Ethan. "What on earth happened here?"

Ben, Jon and Tyler were picking up fragments of wood that she assumed at one time had been the porch railing.

"Disagreement," Ben said without meeting her eyes. He had a stack of shiny, polished pieces in his hands and carried them off to the side. "It's done."

"You got that right," Tyler spat at his brother. "You may as well have taken a sledgehammer to his heart."

"Whose heart?" But even as she asked, Katie knew. "Where's Chance?"

"Inside with Rosie. She had a bit of a fright."

Ethan stepped around Katie and approached his twin. "Ben?"

"It was an accident." His voice was barely a whisper. "He was being so stubborn, and I got so angry, I…" He shook his head and offered the pieces to Katie. "I'm so sorry."

Katie blinked, her eyes catching sight of a familiar piece of wood. The rich grain finish, the splash of dark walnut against oak. The tiny holes that had held the strings tight against the body. "Chance's guitar. Oh, no." Emotion caught in her throat as she accepted the offering. "Where's the rest of it?"

"We're sorting through it all now," Jon said. "We'll save every piece we can. Maybe something can be done with it."

"I doubt it," Ethan said. "Man, that has to hurt. Didn't Maura—"

"Their first Christmas together. She worked a second job on the sly to pay for it." Katie may as well be holding her sister's remains.

"Please, drive the knife in deeper," Ben muttered. "I need to get out of here."

"You're hurt." Katie moved to stop him. "Ben, your hand. You may have broken something. Let me—"

"Trust me, Katie. You don't want to be nice to me right now. Just…don't." Ben stalked off, got into his truck and drove away.

"Is someone going to tell me exactly what happened?" Katie demanded. "Ben and Chance never—"

"It happened a few times, back in the day," Ty said.

"Nothing like this, though. Here. Give me that." He retrieved the guitar pieces and set them into a wooden crate. "You're probably the only person Chance would talk to, so go on inside. We'll take care of all this."

That made two Blackwell brothers who wouldn't look at her. Obviously she'd have to get the details from Chance. She headed inside and after a bit of a search, found Chance and Rosie in her room, Chance sitting on Rosie's bed, watching as she gathered up her toys and clothes.

Her heart twisted. She'd never seen him look so…lost. "Chance?"

"Daddy's sad, Aunt Katie." Rosie walked over to her and handed her Clyde. "Mama's guitar got hurt real bad. I think maybe he wants to cry."

"I'm fine," Chance said, but as he lifted his gaze to Katie, she saw he was anything but. "It's just a guitar."

"No, it's not." Katie hugged Clyde to her chest and sat beside him on the bed. "I'm so sorry, Chance. I wish there was something I could do."

"You're here." He took a hold of her hand and squeezed. "That's enough."

"Rosie, are you packing?" Katie's stomach dropped.

"Uh-huh. Daddy said we're going home." Her chin wobbled. "Will I have time to say goodbye to Splinter and the other animals? And Gen and Abby and Aunt Lydia and Aunt Hadley—"

"We'll have time, Bug. I promise."

"You're leaving?" Katie's heart stuttered as she set aside Clyde. "But why? Because you and Ben had a fight? Over what?"

"What else? The ranch. I told him I was going to vote to keep it."

"But you're leaving. That doesn't make sense."

"I told him I was voting to keep it because of you."

"You're not serious?" Everything was falling apart. Chance was ruining his relationship with his brothers over her? What if they didn't sell and the foremanship would be hers anyway once Big E came home? If he came home. Her stomach churned. It was like waiting for an invisible bomb to go off. She knew one was out there, but where and when it would detonate was anyone's guess. And the collateral damage could be devastating. "Chance, we talked about this." She faced him, and clutched his hand tighter. "I can't factor into this. As much as I want to stay, as much as I love this place, you can't let me be the deciding factor." And yet, for him, she had been. And she loved him for it.

She loved him.

Katie swallowed. Hard. She loved him. Her sister's widow. The boy she'd grown up with. The teenager who had broken her family apart. The man, the loving father he'd become. She loved Chance Blackwell.

"Daddy, I have to go get my games." Rosie walked over and placed her little hands on Chance's knees. "Is that okay?"

"Yes." He brushed a finger down her cheek. "Thank you, Rosie."

"Make Daddy not sad, Aunt Katie." Rosie nudged them together. "Fix him."

Katie smiled as Rosie left the room. "Must be nice to think I have that kind of power. Chance." She pulled free of his hand and cupped his face in her palms. "Chance, you can't make this important decision based on what I want or need. This is your home. Yours and your brothers'. I don't matter."

"Yes, you do." The haze of sadness lifted and she found herself staring into the loving brown depths of Chance's gaze. "You matter a lot, Katie. More than I thought possible."

"Chance—" She didn't want him to say it. Didn't want to hear it. Because once she heard those words…

"I love you, Katie Montgomery. I think maybe it's time we both came to grips with that. Unless…"

"Unless?" She managed a weak laugh. "Oh, boy, Chance, for a man who makes his living putting words to music, you seem to be sorely lacking at the moment. There is no *unless*, Chance. I love you, too. But…"

"But nothing." The corner of his lips quirked and displayed that dimple he shared with his daughter. "You do have a way with words, you know that?"

"Yeah, well." She couldn't remember ever feeling so elated, so joyful. So terrified. "What are you going to do about it?"

"This."

He kissed her. Slowly. Deeply. A kiss that dipped down through her heart, touched her soul and lodged into her very being.

"I can think of worse ways to express your frustrations," she said with a sly smile. She brushed her thumb across his mouth, wondering when and how she'd gotten so lucky as to have Chance Blackwell fall in love with her.

Chance Blackwell was in love with her.

The joy and euphoria vanished under a wave of panic. She had to tell him the truth. About everything. Before the quicksand closed over her head and she couldn't crawl free. He needed to know about Big E, about how she'd spied on them, about his grandfather's plot to bring all the brothers home whether they wanted to come or not. How he'd manipulated each and every one of them with her help. All because she'd been desperate to keep her job and her home, which, in retrospect, didn't matter when compared to losing the man she loved.

"Chance, we need to talk about something."

"Right now?" Chance arched an eyebrow. "We really have to work on this timing thing of yours."

"No, don't joke. This is important. Listen to me, it's about Big E." Katie took a deep breath. Confessing was a little like ripping off a bandage. She had to do it all at once to cause the least amount of pain. "It began a few months ago—"

"Daddy! Aunt Katie! Look! Daddy, you're famous again!" Rosie barreled into the room, a tablet PC in her hands that she shoved into Chance's. "Aunt Hadley says you're everywhere!"

"What?"

Katie glanced up as Hadley stood in the doorway. "Hey. Heard about what happened. Everything okay here?" She eyed Katie specifically.

"Everything's fine." Chance was the one who answered. "But what's this about?" He skimmed through the online news feed.

"Word broke big about your big comeback concert," Hadley said. "I, um, might have spilled the beans about the fund-raiser to a journalist friend of mine who works in entertainment. The good news is the Gardners have raised enough money for the roof."

"What's the bad news?" Katie asked.

"There isn't any." Hadley shrugged. "Unless Chance gets cold feet. It all just hinges on his performance to-night."

And there it was. The combination of fear and doubt on Chance's face that broke through her own needs. Her own desires. What she'd done, admitting to it, would have to wait. Chance needed her help.

"You can do this, Chance," she told him.

"Without a guitar? It's my shield. I can't go out there without it."

"It's Montana," Haldey said. "There's a guitar around very corner."

"We're your shield." Katie turned his face to hers. "You won't be out there alone. And I'll find you a guitar. A special one."

"I don't have time to acclimate to a new one."

"I didn't say it would be new." She kissed him quick. For once, Big E might have provided her with an answer rather than a problem. "Hadley, you and Rosie get Chance cleaned up. I'll meet you at the Silver Stake." She headed for the door.

"Take the spare truck from the guesthouse." Hadley held out her keys. "We've got two hours till showtime."

"Understood. Chance?" Katie swung back to look at him and hoped the shell-shocked expression would disappear. "I'll see you on stage."

CHAPTER FIFTEEN

"WHERE IS SHE?" Chance paced the manager's office of the Silver Stake. Between the desk, a chair, a filing cabinet, two of his brothers, Hadley and his daughter, there was barely enough room to turn around.

"She'll be here," Ty told him for the hundredth time. "Dude, either sit or stand, but you're making me dizzy."

"This one won't work, huh?" Jon set aside his own fiddle, the one he'd been asked to play between acts to entertain the crowd. He hefted a sparkling new guitar into his hands and flipped it over. "Looks good to me."

"It doesn't have any soul." Chance couldn't explain it, but the more an instrument was played, the more it connected to its owner. Going out there without the right equipment was a recipe for failure. He had one shot at this comeback, one shot to make a difference for Falcon Creek and the library and, as of now, he felt as if he had both hands tied behind his back. "It doesn't sound right. It's tinny. There's no depth."

"Or maybe you're hearing what you want to hear." Ty earned a glare from Hadley for that comment.

"Aunt Katie said she'd be here, Daddy. She never lies."

"I know, Bug." Right now that fact was the only thing keeping him steady.

A knock sounded on the door. Hadley sat on the arm of the chair beside Ty so Chance could open it. "Felix!"

"There's my favorite client!" Felix squeezed into the office and took up what space was left. "You aren't returning my calls now? You reinventing yourself all on your own?"

Chance didn't have any words. "What on earth are you wearing?" Laughter bubbled in his chest and he had to cover his mouth to stop it from escaping. The black jeans and button-down shirt might have been okay. And the bolo tie. But add in giant horseshoe cuff links, silver studs on his collar and a hat big enough to serve drinks in, and Felix had obviously decided not to blend in.

"What? It's Montana." Felix held out his arms and did an awkward spin. "I'm a cowboy. Picked up most of this at the airport in Bozeman."

"Sucker born every minute. Ow!" Ty shrank away from Hadley after she smacked his arm. "Geez, enough Blackwell brothers have bruises, thank you very much." She stomped on his foot. "You look great," Ty wheezed.

"T minus ten minutes, right?" Felix looked around the room. "What's going on? Why the gloom and doom? You have some new material, right? Tell me I didn't come out here for another rerun, Chance."

"He has new songs," Rosie announced. "Pretty songs. All about—"

Chance scooped Rosie into his arms and playfully covered her mouth. "It's a secret, remember, Bug?"

She nodded.

"I'm just waiting for my…"

The door shoved open behind Felix and sent him toppling forward. But with nowhere to go, he knocked into Chance and Rosie.

"Sorry I'm late." Katie panted as she stuck her head through the opening. "Not room enough for oxygen in here. I had to change clothes and hey, Hadley? You'll need a new spare for the truck. Blew a tire ten miles out of town. Luckily a Good Samaritan was driving past. Thanks, Ben!" She called over her shoulder. "Okay, everyone out! Chance has to get acquainted with his instrument."

"Is that what they're calling it these days?" Ty's grin faded when Hadley rolled her eyes. "What? Come on, that was funny, wasn't it? Wasn't it? Watch it!" He smacked Jon's hands away as their brother shoved him out the door. "Break a leg, bro."

"At this point that might save me," Chance muttered. "Felix?"

"Oh, right. You want me to…" He pointed to Rosie.

"They've set two seats aside up front," Chance told Felix. "I wasn't expecting you."

"I can sit on Aunt Katie's lap," Rosie told them. She'd cowgirled herself up from head to toe and pushed her hat farther down on her head. "Come on, Uncle Felix. I'll show you where." She kicked her way out of Chance's arms and grabbed Felix's hand.

Katie maneuvered her way into the office, knocking the worn guitar case against the wall as she closed the door. "They really need to add a dressing room to this place." She hoisted the case into both hands. "I think this might be what you need for tonight."

Chance barely gave the case a glance as he set it on the desk. "You look beautiful." He inclined his head, a bit confused. "I'm trying to think of the last time I saw you wearing a dress."

"That would be never." The flirty yellow flowered dress flared at her knees as she kicked up her injured foot. The short yellow sweater grazed over her hips and hugged every curve she hid behind her usual ranch shirts. "Goes with the boot, yeah?"

"And the ballet slipper."

"I don't own any heels. Besides, balance. Open it already, would you?" She dived around him and unlatched the case. He caught a whiff of her perfume that smelled like a spring rainstorm. "You need to get reacquainted."

Chance's breath caught as she exposed the guitar inside. The tour stickers, the carvings, the notches he'd made in the neck for every song he'd learned... "This isn't possible." But as he lifted the guitar free, the instant it sat in his hands, he knew. "Big E told me he burned it." The guitar his grandmother Dorothy had bought for him right after his parents died.

The guitar his grandfather had taken away from him when Chance announced his plans to abandon the ranch and try for a music career. As if losing his instrument would stop him from persuing his dreams.

"Big E said a lot of things," Katie told him.

"But how did you get it? Where did you find it?" He stroked his hand over the body, the ridges and markings a map of his past. How was this possible?

"Tune it up." She sat in the chair and watched him. "Let's hear it."

He sat on the edge of the desk, lifted the guitar and played the opening chord to "Butterfly Blue." Strong. Stable. The vibrations moved through the instrument, through his fingers and straight to his soul. A few more chords, a few improvisations. He twisted the machine heads, sang a few notes, syncing himself with the guitar.

"Well?" He looked at Katie, who was beaming from ear to ear.

"Sounds perfect. You ready?" She gestured to the door. Just beyond, the applause and chants and cheers of excitement grew.

"No." The doubt crept back, sneaky and silent. "I don't like doing this without her."

"I know." Katie stood and walked over to him, put her hands over his where he held the guitar. "But she's here.

With both of us." Katie kissed him, none too softly, with more than a bit of demand. "You need someone to sing to, you look at Rosie. Focus on her. You'll do just fine."

"I'll focus on both of you." He grabbed the back of her head and kissed her hard. "And when tonight is over, we're going to have a talk. About us. Okay?"

Katie nodded. She seemed shaky, uncertain. But her smile was all for him. "Okay."

"Then let's get this over with. I've got a life to live."

"HE GOOD TO GO?" Ty leaned forward as Katie sneaked into her seat in the front row, lifting an excited Rosie onto her lap.

"He's good." Katie managed to tamp down the growing unease by focusing on how proud she was of Chance for going through with this. She knew what losing that guitar meant to him, what it had represented. Being able to give him back a bit of that confidence, even if it was thanks to Big E sending it her way—he said she'd know what to do with it—was something she'd never regret.

The smell of beer and stale cigarettes coated the air, but nothing could ease the excitement pulsing through the bar. There was barely enough room to move. Falcon Creek and fans from neighboring counties had packed the place. Dozens more were standing outside, where speakers and a video feed had been set up. All this time Chance believed he'd been forgotten.

If anything, his popularity had only grown.

"Is Daddy scared?" Rosie leaned back into Katie's arms.

"I think he's nervous," Katie whispered. "But I told him to find us in the crowd and he'd be okay."

The lights dimmed. Applause pounded as screams and shouts accompanied the searching spotlight aiming at the makeshift stage. The second that Chance stepped into view, the place erupted. Katie watched as Jon, standing in the corner of the stage, beamed with pride. Chance headed for the stool and microphone, then seemed to change his mind, and walked over to Jon and talked with him briefly. Whatever he said surprised his brother, but Jon gave him a nod and slap on the shoulder.

Katie looked behind her and found Ty and Hadley, Ethan and Grace, Lydia and the girls, and Ben and Rachel lined up like linemen supporting the quarterback.

"This is incredible," Felix said as he pulled out his phone and started recording. "Couldn't ask for a better comeback."

Chance took his place, shielded his eyes against the spotlight as he searched the crowd. Katie felt the instant he found them, knew the smile on his lips was just for them. She squeezed Rosie and kissed her cheek. "Here we go."

Chance leaned in to the mic and said simply, "It's good to be back. Before we get this started, I want to thank each and every one of you who bought tickets tonight. The Falcon Creek Library and I go way back. It's where I learned about music. It's where I learned to play music. Don't ever let anyone tell you libraries aren't important. It's where our dreams wait to be discovered. And because of you, not only will ours be getting a new roof, but enough money's been raised for a complete upgrade. So my daughter, and all of us who reside in Falcon Creek, can enjoy the library and everything it offers for years to come. Thank you, again. And now—" he strummed the same chord he'd played for her in the office "—'Butterfly Blue.'"

THE SECOND HIS fingers struck the first chord of "Blue," Chance's nerves abated. The lights, the sounds, the people—they all faded as he lost himself in the music, in the words. But not, thankfully, in the memories. Thoughts of

Maura lifted him up. Looking at Rosie's awestruck face as he played some of her favorite songs, seeing Katie's encouraging smile as she rocked and clapped with Rosie and the countless others in the audience...

While he normally preferred the solo performance, asking Jon to play backup had been a natural request. Seeing his oldest brother out there on that stage, hearing him play in much the same way Chance did, on their great-grandfather's fiddle, he knew he had the best support system around. And Jon was good. He listened and improvised and fell into the songs as easily as Chance. But now would be the test. Now was what everyone had come to hear. He played the final chord, held the final note, and sat back as the applause washed over him.

He glanced back at Jon, gave him the sign and Jon nodded, stepping into the shadows and leaving Chance alone on stage.

"As you all know, it's been a difficult few years. Rosie and I lost her mom a while ago and, well, I needed to step back and find my voice again. Find my passion. I spent a good part of my life trying to forget this place, trying to pretend Falcon Creek was never my home. That I never belonged here. But I was wrong. And I know that because this is what I've written since I've been back. So to close the show, I call it 'Sounds Like Home.'"

"With a heavy heart he rolls on,
    Tires dragging, the silence hums.
    Faster than a jackrabbit the past comes,
    Roaring back as the old life fades and starts anew.

"In the distance he sees what he never saw,
    Laughter ringing like wind chimes in a summer storm,

Across rocky tipped horizons and cloudless skies.
And just like that he knows...the sounds of home.

"Colors of the sunrise kissed with gold,
    She eases him into another day.
    Bright green eyes and a smile that lights the dark
places of his heart,
    He listens.
    He waits.
    He hopes.
    For sounds like home.

"Stones tripping over a still lake,
    Ripples echo against his soul.
    The pain fades as a heart awakens
    Like sunshine after a rainstorm.
    The darkness fades and beneath
    It sounds like home.

"Raindrops on the roof.
    Horses on the trail.
    Laughter in the home.
    All the sounds that meld,
    Along a hot desert wind,
    To remind him of Sunshine, saddles and smiles.
    And that he's finally home."

When Chance stopped playing, stopped singing, when
he just stopped, the silence was deafening. No one moved.
He couldn't even hear anyone breathe. For a moment, he
wondered if he'd dreamed he'd played. Maybe he'd just
frozen on stage, forgotten to sing, but then the clapping
started. And increased. And washed through the crowd
like a tidal wave of love and approval. The yells and shouts

and cries were nothing compared to seeing the entire audience rise to their feet.

His body went warm from head to toe as he found his girls—Rosie jumping up and down like a maniac and Katie with tears streaming down her face as she smiled with pride. She touched her hand to her heart, nodded and mouthed "I love you."

He felt a hand on his shoulder and turned to find Jon with tears in his eyes. His brother pulled him off his stool and into a hug. "You did good, baby brother." Jon pushed him back, caught Chance's head in his hand and gave him a good shake. "Shiner and all, you did real good."

Chance breathed easy for the first time in months. Whatever happened now, he'd given it his all. That was what mattered.

The euphoria lasted well into the night, after the last beers had been served, the final CD had been sold and Chance had signed his last autograph. His family had taken up the back corner of the bar, with Gen and Abby lying sprawled and sound asleep under Lydia's protective arms. Rosie had conked out— not in Katie's embrace, but in Ben's. His brother looked over Chance's daughter's head with a nod of approval. And just like that, all was forgiven.

"Chance, man, this could not have gone better. You were a star up there!" Felix flipped off his hat and probably would have tossed it into the air if people weren't still filing out the front door. "That video of you is already going viral. I've had three calls from record companies already and it's only been three hours since I posted it."

"Great." Chance patted Felix on the shoulder. "We have a few things to discuss before you return any of those calls. You hear me, Felix?" Chance had to yell the last question to make sure Felix heard him.

Felix blinked. "Okay. Something wrong?"

"Not from my perspective. You have a place to stay?"

"Hadn't gotten that far."

"You'll stay at the guest ranch. Hadley?" Chance waved her over as she dropped off empty glasses at the bar. "Hadley, can we get Felix set up with a guest cabin?"

"Absolutely. Hi, Felix. Nice to meet you officially. You have a car?"

Chance left them to work out details while he headed to the table for Katie. "Only one thing left I want to do tonight." He held out his hand. "Dance?"

"Oh, Chance, no. I don't know how…and this thing." She kicked out her booted foot, then laughed when he tugged her onto her feet.

"I asked for this one special." He made his way to the stage, helped her up the step and took her in his arms as his favorite cover song filtered through the speakers. "Just one dance, Katie. Before we have to get back to reality."

She melted into him, wrapping her arms around him, and rested her head on his shoulder. "You were wonderful, Chance. That new song, it's perfect. I guess now we all know why you've been disappearing after your chores."

"Not having to worry about Rosie helped take the pressure off. Besides—" he pressed his lips to her forehead "—I had the best inspiration around."

"Montana skies are that," Katie agreed.

"So are you."

She lifted her head and linked her arms behind his neck as they swayed to the music. "You are a romantic, aren't you, Chance Blackwell?"

"Afraid so. That good enough for a cowgirl like you?"

"I think I can work with it. Now shut up and dance."

CHAPTER SIXTEEN

"Nothing like a good kind of tired." Katie rolled her head against the back of the seat and looked behind her to where Rosie slept. After a perfect evening and a quick tire change, Chance drove them home in Hadley's spare truck, following his brothers back to the ranch, where they would continue to celebrate Chance's success. "She was so proud of you, Chance."

"The feeling's mutual." He took her hand and brought it to his lips. "You ready to talk about what comes next?"

"Not really, no." Katie hated the disappointment that flashed across his face and hastened to explain. "We have to talk about something else first, Chance."

"Okay. Talk."

"Not tonight. Tomorrow." She didn't want to ruin this evening, erase all the good that had come of Chance's performing again, by admitting to her role in Big E's scheme. She wanted one more night of perfection. "After that, if you still want to talk about the future, we will."

"That sounds positively dire." He turned onto the main ranch road, the trail of cars slowing as they reached the family house.

And the thirty-foot motor home parked in front.

Katie's body went cold. She tugged her hand free and clutched it to her chest, trying not to shake as she watched the front door of the motor home pop open and the hulking figure of a man drop down to the ground.

Big E.

"What in the world?" Chance leaned forward in his seat and peered over the steering wheel. "Are you freaking kidding me? He chooses tonight of all nights to come back?"

"Looks like." Katie didn't recognize her own voice. She sat frozen in her seat. She couldn't move. Didn't want to move. She just wanted to stay right here, in this moment, in this truck, where she and Chance and Rosie could keep the rest of the world outside. With the truth.

Car doors slammed, voices shot across the night sky. Katie flinched at the anger, the irritation, the frustration. The accusations. The swearing and threats as Ty, Jon, Ben and Ethan circled their grandfather beneath the dim glow of the front porch light.

"Chance, this isn't good for the kids." Katie glanced back as Rosie mumbled in her sleep.

"I know. Can you get her into the house? My brothers and I need to present a united front."

"Yeah. Wait, Chance." She grabbed his arm before he could get out of the car. "I do love you. Whatever happens, try to remember that?"

"Don't think I can forget it." He grinned at her and joined his brothers.

Katie pulled a mumbling Rosie out of the car, carrying her back and around the trucks, taking the long way to the front porch, hoping, praying, to get into the house before Big E saw her. Hip headed her way the second she popped into sight. Maybe she was overreacting. Maybe he had plans she didn't know about as far as what he was going to do now that he was home.

Except she knew what he was going to do. Whether he intended to or not.

"Whew!" Lydia closed the door behind Katie and the

dog and leaned against it. "It got chilly out there all of a sudden. Chance send you in with her like Jon did?"

Katie nodded and held Rosie tight, afraid to let her go. "Girls okay?"

"Out like sacks of potatoes." Hadley bent backward to ease her spine. "Sorry, Lyd, but they're getting too heavy to carry."

"Tell me about it. You want help with Rosie?" Lydia offered.

"No, thanks," Katie said. "I've got her. I'll just be a few minutes."

"Hey." Lydia touched her arm as she headed for the stairs. "You okay? You look pale."

"Long night. Going to be longer, no doubt. Big E has that effect." She gave her a tremulous smile. "I'll be back."

Katie took her time getting Rosie into her pajamas and tucked into bed. She found Clyde and pushed her into Rosie's arms, then stroked her hair before giving her a kiss. "I love you, Little Miss."

"Love you, Aunt Katie."

Rosie's mumblings struck Katie dead center in her heart. She stood in the doorway, gripping the frame so hard her fingers went numb. She could stay in the house with Lydia, Hadley, Grace and Rachel, safe and sound for who knows how much longer. She could keep up the facade, continue the lies, for a few more hours.

Or she could face the fire now.

Before she fell even deeper in love with Chance and his daughter.

"I expected you to be in your pajamas," Lydia laughed, but as she watched Katie descend the stairs, her smile faded. "Katie? What's going on?"

"I'm about to find out." Tears and fear had no place on

the ranch tonight. She knew this day would come and she could only hope she was wrong about Big E.

She stood at the front door, her foot throbbing, but she embraced it. Welcomed it. The pain gave her something to focus on as she pulled open the door and stepped onto the railing-free porch. "Come on, Hip."

"And there she is now, my secret weapon!" Big E's booming voice had Katie cringing as her stomach dropped to her toes. Even faster than she'd anticipated. "You did good, Katie."

In that moment, as much as she wanted to, Katie realized she didn't hate Big E. She wasn't even angry with him. She felt sorry for him. After nearly eighty years, and the only way he could get his family to come home was to plan an elaborate, manipulative hoax. What a pathetic commentary on a life.

The five months away hadn't changed him. Not one iota. He was still the same barreling, booming, balding, commanding presence of a man decked out in a studded cowboy hat, tailor-made jeans and shirt, and a bolo tie whose emblem cost more than her totaled truck. But it was his eyes—piercing blue that didn't miss a trick—that told the story.

Big E was the kind of man who, once he set his mind to something, got it done. No matter who got run over. Collateral damage didn't matter.

"Come on, Katie-girl," Big E ordered with a wave of his hand as if calling her forward to collect a trophy. "Don't be shy. Not after all you did for these boys."

The Blackwell brothers turned as one, to face her, all five pinning their shocked, uncertain gazes on her.

"Katie?" Chance's single-word question pierced her heart.

"I'm fine here, Big E. Thanks." She looked over their

heads, unable to lock eyes with any of them. Unable to shake off the fear and regret that had plagued her these last few months. "Welcome home."

"Welcome home? Are you kidding me?" Ben boomed into the night. "Someone better tell me what's going on around here and fast. Or how about you hop back in that monstrosity of a motor home and get lost again, old man."

Katie tensed and hugged her arms around her torso. She couldn't blame Ben. She couldn't blame any of the brothers for their animosity toward their grandfather. No matter how much time had passed, there was no forgetting Big E had stole Ben's fiancée, refused to listen to Jon's plans for improving the ranch; the difficulties he'd caused Ethan, the obstacles he'd thrown in Ty's way. Or how he'd dismissed Chance's passion for music. He'd driven each and every one of them off this land with his controlling, demanding ways.

And now they were about to learn they'd been brought back by exactly the same means.

"Ben, stop," Jon warned. "The kids are asleep inside."

"Yeah, Ben, stop," Big E commanded. "Wouldn't want to make the same mistake twice in one day. Nice shiner, kid."

Katie's fear abated, and was replaced with anger. "That's enough, Big E. You got what you wanted. They're all home. Don't gloat."

"If anyone should be gloating, should be you, Katie-girl. None of this would have happened without you."

"None of what would have happened?" Chance's voice was so soft Katie wondered if she'd imagined him speaking. She wanted to tell him, tell all of them, that it wasn't what it sounded like. That she hadn't been Big E's partner in crime. That she hadn't spent the last five months lying to each and every one of them and reporting back on the results of Big E's machinations.

But she couldn't. Because that would be a lie.

"Katie?" Chance's voice hardened. "None of what would have happened?"

"All of you coming home, of course," Big E answered before she could draw breath. "I knew if I disappeared that Blackwell obligation would kick in on each of you. Jon couldn't stay away, not when Katie needed help paying the bills and I got rid of all the workers. Sucked you right back here, just like I always said I would."

"Yeah," Jon said without breaking his look at Katie. "Yeah, Katie needed help."

She winced.

"Then there's the water-rights paperwork," Big E went on, as if he had played nothing more than a practical joke on his grandsons rather than turning their lives upside down. "Who do you think sent that paperwork to Rachel, Ben? Only one other person had the combination to my office safe."

"Only one other person." Ben's eyes darkened.

"Don't suppose you had anything to do with the rumors about me starting up a vet practice, did you, Katie?" Ethan asked. "Seeing as you knew good and well I wouldn't have been able to turn anyone away."

"It crossed my mind." What was the point in making excuses now? Big E was making his final play. Katie should have seen this coming miles off, and yet, she'd clung to the hope that things would work out for the better.

Instead, she could see her world shattering before her eyes.

"Awful lot went wrong with the guest cabins when I first came back," Ty said. "That your doing?"

"Actually, no." The guilt over Ty's look of betrayal

nearly drove Katie to her knees. He'd been her right hand since coming back to the ranch, always helpful and encouraging. She couldn't have kept this place running without him. "That was the age of this place lending a hand. But I might have pushed in a few other areas."

"What about me?" The brothers all looked at Chance as he walked toward her. "What games did you play with me, Katie?"

"No games," she whispered. "By then what needed doing was done. You'd all come home. Just like he wanted."

"That's what this was all about? Bringing us back to this place you never bothered to make a home?" Jon demanded of his grandfather, who continued to look as if he'd triumphed over all of them. "To remind us what a callous, manipulative, coldhearted man you are?"

"Jon." Ethan shook his head as if he'd been defeated. "He's not worth it."

"I'll say my piece," Jon growled back. "You've spent the last twenty years systematically destroying this family, Big E. You've bullied and yelled and manipulated us from the day Mom and Dad died. You drove off the only woman you ever loved and tried to replace her with women unfortunate enough to fall in love with you. Then when we'd all settled in to our own lives, you decided you wanted us all back here. In this...*place*."

"The only place you all ever belonged," Big E countered as if he'd scripted his response. "Don't know what you're complaining about, any of you. You've all found good women because of what I did. Even Ben managed to set his ego aside and come back here."

"You think it was my ego keeping me away?" Ben's voice had gone spine-chillingly calm. "It was my loathing of you, old man. I only came back because my brothers needed me. To keep a hold of this place that's clearly nothing more than a pawn in some sick chess game you decided to play."

"The guitar." Chance drew Katie's attention back to him. "He sent you the guitar, didn't he? That was his weapon of choice. He wielded it again, just as he did when I was seventeen and he told me he burned it."

"He did what?" Ethan blurted.

"When I told him I was planning to leave," Chance said. "That ranching wasn't for me. When I got home from school that day, he told me he burned it. And that now I'd have to stay."

Katie blinked against the pain as she heard the front door creak open behind her. "He told me I'd know when to give it to you. He was right."

"Guess I should be glad it wasn't you who broke my other one then, shouldn't I?"

"Chance, no." Katie stood up straight, devastated he'd think her capable of that. "I never would have done that to you."

"Wouldn't you?" And with those two words, he broke her heart. "Can I believe anything you say?"

"Now hold on, all of you." Big E raised his hands as if calling for silence. "No need blaming all this on Katie."

"Oh, we blame you, Big E," Ty said. "She was just along for the ride, weren't you? What did he promise you, Katie? Come on. At this point you can be honest with us. He must have made you a deal. Offered you something in exchange for lying to all of us."

Chance flinched.

Katie ducked her head. "He promised to promote me to foreman. Officially. With back pay and an increase in salary." Along with a vow to allow her and Lochlan to remain in their home for as long as they wanted.

"You lied to me." Chance sounded bewildered, as if

he couldn't comprehend what was happening. "All this time, you knew why he'd brought them all back, brought me back, how he brought us back, and you didn't say anything."

"I tried to. Earlier today. In Rosie's room, remember? I was going to tell you everything."

He looked at her pleading face for a long moment before he shook his head. "After everything I told you about Maura, you still didn't trust me enough. You didn't trust me enough to tell me the truth, Katie."

How else could he see it when it was the truth? "Chance, please, I never wanted—"

"You never wanted what?" Chance boomed. "For me to fall in love with you? To vote against my brothers when it came to this place? Or you never wanted any of this to come out?"

"What do you mean vote against your brothers?" Big E demanded. "What's going on?"

"You got your wish, Big E," Ethan told him. "Your fellow shareholders in the Blackwell Family Ranch are united. Against you. We called a vote on whether to sell this place or not."

"You can't do that!" Big E advanced on the group of them, but Ben stepped out front and center, ready to take whatever Big E dished out.

"You try us, old man. Together we outnumber you. This ranch is ours now that we're all back. We decide what happens to it."

"What about that promotion of Katie's, Big E?" Jon asked. "After all you made her do, it's the least she deserves. So go on. Tell her the job's hers. I dare you."

Big E glanced at Katie and in that moment she realized her mistake. She never should have believed him. Never should have trusted him. He wasn't going to promote her.

Big E would never allow a woman to run the Blackwell Family Ranch. No matter how much she sacrificed for him, including any hope of a future with Chance and Rosie.

"Don't," Katie said as Big E opened his mouth. He'd done enough damage to his family, to his grandsons' lives. To her own. No need to compound the pain by admitting he was a dishonorable fraud who couldn't keep his word. "Don't bother lying, Big E. I quit." The words caught in her throat. "I never should have agreed to your terms. Not when you've never seen me as anything more than Lochlan's tumbleweed daughter. That is what you used to call me, isn't it? Dusty and flighty and never getting very far. Except I got pretty darned far after all, didn't I? This place would have died without me. You would have run it into the ground with the way you've been anchored to the past. You drove Jon away because he disagreed with you. Decided Ben…what? Wasn't good enough for Zoe, so you married her under his nose while you spit on Ethan's, Ty's and Chance's dreams for success beyond this place. They might have all come back, but they came back for each other, not for you."

"Doesn't matter why they're back," Big E boasted. "It's done."

"Yes, it is. And now, for once, you'll have to clean up your own mess. I'm done doing it for you." She headed down the steps, but stopped when Chance caught her arm.

"Why didn't you trust me? Why didn't you tell me what he was doing to you?"

It wasn't a question. It was an accusation. One she knew exactly how to respond to.

"Because just like my sister, I'm not perfect." She tugged free. "I'm sorry I lied to you, Chance. I'm sorry I lied to all of you." She looked at the brothers and wished she could turn back the clock and throw Big E's offer in his face. "I just wanted—" Her voice hitched and the tears burned. "This is my home."

She forced herself to look each of them in the face, but instead of understanding, instead of compassion or forgiveness, all she saw was the stark shock of betrayal. She dared to glance back at the house, to where Hadley, Grace, Rachel and Lydia stood watching in stunned silence.

"Or at least it was."

With that, she snapped her fingers for Hip to follow and headed into the night, back to her house.

Alone.

CHAPTER SEVENTEEN

"DID YOU EVEN SLEEP?" Ty poured himself a cup of coffee and laser-eyed Chance over the rim of the mug as he drank.

"What do you think?" Chance scrubbed his hands over his tired face and stared down at his own coffee, which had grown cold. Because that's what happened when you stare into something blankly for more than an hour. Lydia had taken pity on him and stopped by this morning to pick up Rosie for the day, leaving Chance alone with the one thing he couldn't escape: his thoughts. "What are we doing? What are any of us doing?"

"You mean in general or what are we doing here, at the ranch, just like Big E wanted?"

"Really not in the mood for your jokes right now, Ty."

"Tough." Ty leaned against the counter and picked at the cinnamon rolls Grace's mother had made. "It's what gets me through. In answer to your question, we're here because when all is said and done, this is our home. Big E or not, it's where we belong."

"Speak for yourself."

"I am. Look, Chance." Ty leaned over and met him eye-to-eye. "I get it. He played us. All of us. Better than you play your guitar. And he used a lot of people to do it, including all those ranch hands who just walked away for a tidy severance package. But he was right about one thing last night."

Chance snorted. "Enlighten me."

"I wouldn't trade Hadley for anything. If I hadn't come home, if I hadn't felt the need to try to get out of it by using a fake fiancée—"

Chance actually grinned. "Yeah, I heard about that. Genius move, bro."

"Actually, yes, it was." Ty straightened up. "That's my point. By that same token, Ben wouldn't have Rachel and Poppy. And Ethan—"

"Ethan would have come back eventually and found out about Grace and the baby."

"Maybe. Maybe not. But—"

"I swear if you're about to say you're grateful to Big E for playing us all like fiddles, I'm going to end up with another black eye. And I'll give you one to match."

"Then I won't say it. But I will say this. We weren't the only ones who got played. Katie did, too. And in a much more heartless way. He exploited her, Chance. He knew she'd do anything to help Lochlan, to stay here on the ranch in the job she deserved. And after giving it a good deal of thought, not to mention ingesting a few beers and being lectured by Hadley—"

"I'll bet." Chance smirked and reached across the counter for the coffee to freshen his cup.

"She was alone, Chance. As much as we all fought over the years, as much distance as there was between us, we at least had each other. Katie hasn't had anyone. Not since Maura left. And I for one can't blame her for doing whatever she thought she had to in order to keep hold of the one thing she could."

"She lied to me, Ty." Worse, she sat beside him on that blanket by the river, listened to him pour his heart out about the problems in his marriage—with her sister, no less—and didn't utter a word about her "situation." Why didn't the women in his life trust him? "How do I trust her after that?"

"Would you have forgiven Maura for lying to you?"

"What?" Chance swallowed wrong. He hadn't uttered a word about Maura's deceptions to anyone but Katie.

"Something you said last night. I get the feeling things between you and Maura weren't as perfect as you've led us all to believe."

"That's different," Chance grumbled. "And it's also none of your business."

"Maybe, and okay, that last part is probably true. And I'm not saying what Katie did wasn't seriously screwed up." He popped the last bit of roll into his mouth and finished his coffee. "But I also know, when the truth came out, she owned up. She didn't try to run away from it or hide or make excuses. Might just be me, but that's a woman worthy of a second chance. Or at the very least, the courtesy of a conversation."

"ABOUT TIME YOU showed up."

Katie yelped and clutched a hand to her chest. Hip backed onto her haunches and growled.

"Hadley!" She ducked inside the room she'd been staying in at the main house and quickly shut the door. Ty's fiancée was sitting with her legs over the arm of the chair by the window, tapping away on her cell phone as if it was a typewriter. "What are you doing here?" Katie had purposely waited until she saw the last car—Chance's minivan—pull away from the house and head into town before sneaking in to retrieve her belongings. "You scared the life out of me."

"Returning the favor then." Hadley swung her legs to the ground and sat there, looking at her as Hip trotted over and demanded a pet. "Never took you for a coward, Katie Montgomery."

"You've been watching too many cowboy movies." Katie grabbed her bag and started shoving in her clothes. "Life's more complicated than a Hollywood script."

"Chance's poetry is rubbing off on you. That's good, Katie. So this is what you're going to do now? Just slink off in defeat. Let what Big E did define the rest of your life."

"Big E doesn't define me or my life," Katie snapped as she pushed the framed picture of herself and Maura face-down into the bag. "Not anymore."

"Could have fooled me. You love Chance. Why aren't you fighting for him?"

Katie closed her eyes. She did love Chance. With all her heart. But no amount of love or affection could repair the damage she'd done. She'd done the unforgivable in his eyes: she'd deceived him. Not only him, but also his entire family.

"The brothers will come around, you know," Hadley said. "I already kicked Ty in the butt, so he'll probably be first. But they'll forgive you. And they'll understand. Eventually."

"I lied to you, too, Hadley."

"Nah. Not really. And even if you did, I'm not about to judge you for doing what you thought you had to in order to keep your family together."

"It's not that simple." Katie sank onto the edge of the mattress. Her biggest mistake hadn't been lying to Chance. It had been believing even for a minute that Big E was going to live up to his end of the bargain. The second she'd agreed to his terms, he'd won. "I wish it was, but it's not."

"Not when you're letting fear get in your way it isn't."

"That isn't what I'm doing."

"Sure it is." Hadley got up and sat next to her, wrapped

a sisterly arm around her shoulders and squeezed. "You think I don't know what it's like to love someone so much it aches when it seems like it's over? It's hard to overcome, to see a way over or around or even through. But just walking away without fighting for him? That's just stupid, Katie. And you are not a stupid woman."

"Your pep-talk skills need work."

"I'm still honing them. What are you going to do, Katie? Mope about this and let life decide what's going to happen?"

"I think that's what Maura might have said if she was here." Katie put her head on Hadley's shoulder as Hip walked over and rested her face on Katie's leg. "Except that would be seriously weird since we're talking about Maura's husband."

"Yeah, well, you need to get over that thought. Maura's gone, honey. Chance knows this. He sang it to hundreds of people last night, yourself included. I think the only person keeping her between you is you. Makes for a very convenient excuse."

"I wasn't aware that you had a psychology degree." Katie sniffed. She'd cried more in the last week than she had in the last couple of years. "I appreciate the advice, Hadley, but even if Chance and I could come to an understanding, my time at the ranch is over. I can't stay here and work for them after what I've done. And I sure as heck won't work for Big E anymore. I'll figure something out. But for now." She shrugged. "For now it's best to just let things lie for a while, you know?"

"I know. But I don't agree. Which means I'm not going to stop bugging you about it."

Katie smiled. Maybe she wasn't as alone as she thought. Her phone buzzed in her back pocket. When she read the caller ID, her heart jumped. "It's the hospital." She shot to her feet and answered. "Hello?"

"Ms. Montgomery? This is Chelsea Vittoria at Bozeman Memorial. I'm calling about your father."

"Yes?" Katie clutched a hand to her throat. "Is he—"

"He's taken a turn, Ms. Montgomery. We think you need to be here."

SINCE WHEN DID mucking out stalls and brushing down horses become his coping mechanism?

Chance led Butterscotch back into her stall before treating her to the apple he'd brought from the house. He'd driven into town that morning and was met with hearty thanks and congratulations for all he'd done for the town and the library, which didn't sit well with him. All he'd done was all he could do: he'd sang. He was just fortunate enough that people actually wanted to listen.

He heard crunching footsteps behind him. Without looking, he said, "If you're here for another heart-to-heart, Ty—"

"I don't do heart-to-hearts." His grandfather's voice boomed through the stables. "Thought you would have realized that by now, boy."

Tired anger seeped through Chance's pores. He'd heard Big E was making the rounds to each of his brothers. Not that any of them were giving him the time of day. "Go back to your motor home, Big E. I've got work to do." He grabbed the pitchfork and shovel and headed toward the next stall.

"All those years I spent hounding you about your chores, and all it took was a bit of heartache to get you to do it."

A bit of heartache? Was the old man serious? Unwilling to be goaded into a fight, Chance shrugged. "Yep. That's all it took."

"When do I get to meet that great-granddaughter of mine? Bet she's the spitting image of her mama."

Chance left his tools against the wall and faced his grandfather. Big, tall, proud, arrogant and mean. How many years had Chance spent afraid of him? Avoiding him? Cowering in front of him? He'd never once stood up to him, just accepted his fate in silence and secretly planned his escape. And then, when the day had come, he'd whisked away Maura in the dead of night. What a coward he'd been, trying to earn the respect and love of a man who didn't deserve it.

"Rosie will be back this evening after dinner. We're leaving in the morning."

"Are you?" Big E leaned against the barn door, hands in the pockets of his leather vest. "After all this, you're just going to slink away again? Back to that little hovel in Los Angeles?"

"That little hovel is my home. It was Maura's home. And why do you do that? Why do you feel the need to insult every little thing you don't like? I'm not you, Big E. None of us are."

"Of this I am well aware."

Did Chance imagine it, or had his grandfather flinched?

"I'm a difficult man, Chance. I make no apologies for it. I don't coddle or soothe or comfort. It's not in my nature."

"You don't say?"

"But what is in my nature is family. Blood. This land. And my legacy. And when a man gets to my age, he starts to wonder if what he's leaving behind is strong enough to stand the test of time. I could have gotten one or two of you to come back, run the place, take over once I'm buried in that plot back there under the oak tree. But how long would that last? But together? The five of you? If there's one thing I learned all those years ago, when we lost your folks, it's that the Blackwell brothers are at their strongest when they're together. Bonded. Hate me all you want for doing what I did, but I'm not about to apologize for it."

"You broke Katie's heart."

"Not alone, I didn't. Her daddy started the process years ago. Maura helped, as did you, taking her sister away. But don't stand there and tell me you don't love that girl. You want to keep blaming me for coming between you, you go right ahead. Nothing about that is going to keep you warm or give your little girl the mama she deserves."

"What gives you the right to stand there and lecture me about love and family? You with your endless wives and plots and plans?"

"Nothing," Big E said. "And everything. My land. My family. My life."

"And what a joyous one it's been. Jon was right last night, wasn't he? You weren't ever going to give Katie that foremanship, were you?"

"Doesn't much matter now, does it?" Big E glanced away. "She up and quit on us before I could."

"Katie loves this ranch more than any of us ever will. And more than you ever have."

"You keep on defending her in her absence, Chance. Won't make much of a difference to me."

"Chance!" Hadley's truck came skidding to a stop outside the stable. She was out like a shot and racing toward him, giving a passing glare to Big E as she passed. "Did you stop answering your phone? I've been calling you."

"I turned it off." In case Katie called him. As if that was going to happen. He saw the light die in her eyes last night. If there was one thing he knew for certain about Katie Montgomery, it was that she knew a lost cause when she saw it. "What's wrong? Is it Rosie?"

"No, you buffoon. It's Katie. The hospital in Bozeman

called. It's her dad. Chance." Hadley grabbed his hand. "I know you're angry, but she's all alone. She wouldn't let me go with her. Lochlan isn't going to make it."

His stomach pitched. "She doesn't have a car."

"I loaned her the guest ranch's truck. Please."

"Let's go." Big E ordered as he walked out of the stable.

"What? No way. I'm not driving all that way with you." He'd rather be tied to a runaway stallion.

"Then drive by yourself. Lochlan's been my friend longer than you've been alive. If he's going out of this world, I'm darned well going to see him off. Keys!" He yelled at Hadley as he reached her truck.

"You're a sorry excuse for a man, Elias Blackwell." Hadley slapped the keys hard into his palm. "You just cause pain wherever you go. You hurt Katie again, you do anything else to hurt my family, and I will run you to ground. You hear me?"

In that moment, Chance completely understood how Ty had fallen head over heels for Hadley.

"Hard not to, ma'am." Big E actually grinned. "See this here?" He pointed at his soon-to-be granddaughter-in-law. "Now that's a Blackwell woman."

"Get him out of here, Chance, before I do something I won't regret." She grabbed Chance's arm and looked him hard in the eyes. "Don't you do something you'll regret, Chance. Not many people get a second chance at love. Throwing it away makes you no better than him."

NEARLY FIVE HOURS after she'd arrived at the hospital, Katie was still waiting for her father to wake up.

The doctors had brought him out of the medically induced coma in the hopes of bringing him around, which they had, for a brief moment or two, and that was when they'd called Katie.

Since then, he'd been drifting in and out of consciousness, Katie by his side. The machines continued to beep, the monitors displaying the dismal readouts of his pulse and heart rate.

"Dad." Katie bit her lip and picked up the hand that rested on the wooden box Chance had left at his bedside. "Dad, I don't know if you can hear me, but I want you to know, it's okay if you go. I'll be all right." Somehow she'd find her footing again. Start over. Somewhere as far from the Blackwell Ranch as she could get. As far away from the Blackwell brothers. "Mama's waiting for you. And Maura. I know I'm not enough for you to stay. And that's okay. I understand, Dad. I forgive you."

She wiped a tear from her cheek as the pressure of responsibility and obligation lifted. "I love you, Dad."

Lochlan's hand squeezed hers.

"Dad?" Katie stood up, squeezed his hand back and leaned over. He was so thin, so pale, but as he blinked his eyes open, she saw a spark of life she hadn't seen in years glowing. "Hey. Hi, Dad."

"Katie." His raspy voice was thick. "You came."

"Of course I did." Maybe she should have come sooner. Maybe she shouldn't have let anger and resentment get in the way. *Maybe, maybe, maybe...*

"Saw your mama. And Maura." He moved his hand against the box, frowned. "What's this?"

"Maura's ashes." Katie was beyond the ability to lie now. No matter what the cause. The truth might hurt, but not as much as lies did. "Chance left them with you."

"Chance." Lochlan's eyes dimmed. "Chance Blackwell."

"Daddy, no, please. Don't be angry with him. Not anymore." She lifted her father's hand and sat beside him on the bed, clutching their clasped hands to her chest. "You've let the hate win for so long. Please let it go. For me. If you don't do anything else—"

Lochlan lifted his other hand and caught the tear as it slipped down her cheek. "Okay. For you."

Katie sobbed. "Daddy." She squeezed her eyes shut. "Thank you. He's a good man, Daddy. I swear to you. He was a good husband to Maura."

"I know." Lochlan stared and she could see the thoughts racing across his face. "Wasn't him, Katie. It would have been anyone who took my girls away. You love him. Don't you?"

"Mmm." She nodded and smiled. "So much it hurts. You should see him with Rosie. They're amazing together. She's gorgeous and funny and ornery. She's going to change the world."

"Rosie." Lochlan's eyes filled. "Would have liked to have seen her. One time."

"I know. Maybe if you hadn't run off like that you would have. Why did you leave?"

"I hurt you. So much. So many years. Couldn't face you after what Chance told me." His head lolled to the side. "The bruise. I did that."

"It healed," Katie whispered. "I'm fine."

"Forgive me."

"Of course. I forgive you, Daddy." She squeezed his hand harder, as if she could keep him there. "Daddy?"

"Katie."

She gasped and spun on the bed and found Chance standing in the doorway, Rosie in his arms and Big E right behind him. "Chance." She blinked the grief free.

Rosie stared at her grandfather, eyes wide. "Is that Grampy?"

"Yeah, baby. Come here. Can I?" she asked Chance, who handed Rosie over without hesitation.

Thank you, Katie mouthed. She settled Rosie on her lap and retook her father's hand. "Dad? Daddy? Someone here wants to see you. She wants to meet her grandpa."

Lochlan wheezed and lifted his head, blinked his eyes open.

The beeping monitors began to slow.

"Maura," he whispered as color flooded back to his face. "Maura's little girl."

"Hi, Grampy." Rosie leaned forward and settled down on his chest, her arms sliding around his neck. "Daddy says you're really sick. I'm sorry. I hope you feel better soon."

"Rosie." Lochlan's body shook as he cried. "Rosie."

Katie sobbed as her father looked over at Chance, who moved closer to the bed. "I'm sorry. For everything." He held out his frail hand.

Katie held her breath, waiting for Chance to turn his back and walk away. Or confront him with all the things he'd wanted to say for more than ten years. But he didn't do either of those things.

Instead, he took Lochlan's hand in his and held on. "Me, too."

Katie's heart nearly exploded with love.

"You'll take care of them? Take care of my girls?" Lochlan asked of him, tightening his grip when Chance pulled away.

"Katie doesn't need anyone to take care of her."

Katie closed her eyes.

"I'll be fine, Dad. You can go knowing I'll be fine."

Lochlan looked between Chance and Katie, then down at Rosie, who hadn't moved but clung to her grandfather as if she'd never let him go.

Then he looked over to Big E, who moved in and rested a hand on his old friend's arm. "Lochlan."

"Elias. You fix this. You hear me?" His grip loosened on Chance's hand. "You owe me. Fix. It."

With that, Lochlan Montgomery closed his eyes. His hand went slack in Chance's.

And then he was gone.

CHAPTER EIGHTEEN

"Thank you for driving." Katie sat in the passenger seat of Hadley's truck and stared blankly out at the house she'd lived in all her life. The house that had rarely, if ever, felt like home.

She supposed she should be grateful she hadn't ended up with Big E, but Chance's grandfather had insisted on staying behind to take care of all the paperwork regarding Lochlan's death. Which meant now she'd have something to thank him for. Perfect.

"Is Grampy really in heaven with Mama?" Rosie poked her head between the seats and looked first at Chance, then Katie.

"I think he is," Katie whispered. She was out of tears at this point. But the image of seeing her father embrace his granddaughter before he died was a gift she'd never be able to thank Chance for. "I hear you're going home, Little Miss. You're going to still call me, right? And send me emails and pictures?"

"Uh-huh." Rosie leaned her face against the side of the seat. "I asked Daddy if we could stay forever, but he said our home is in California. We can visit, though. You'll see us again."

"I'm not sure where I'll be living but maybe one day soon, yes. We'll see each other again."

"Why are you moving? You live here. With Uncle Ty

and Aunt Hadley, and who's going to look after Splinter and Billy?"

"There'll be plenty of people to watch out for your friends." Katie pushed open the door and grabbed the bag with her father's possessions. There wouldn't be a service for Lochlan. He hadn't wanted one. He'd be cremated and one day, Katie might return to scatter his ashes on the land he'd loved.

"Where will you go?" Chance asked.

Katie shook her head. "Not sure yet. I have some contacts to reach out to. See if there are any job openings. Won't take me long to move on. Not like I own this place and there's not much I'd want to take with me." What a sad statement for a twenty-seven-year-old woman who had never left home. "I'll get by. Will you come say goodbye when you leave?" She looked at Rosie, but she was talking to Chance.

He gave a sharp nod. "We will."

"Thank you. And thank you again for driving. Although I'm betting that had more to do with you not wanting to spend any more time with Big E." She meant it as a joke, but his lack of response told her she spoke the truth. "Well, good night."

She glanced up at the night sky before heading to her porch, where she found Hip lying down, waiting. The dog whimpered when she kneeled down to pet her. "He's gone, Hip. Guess it's just us now." She pressed her lips to the top of the dog's head and squeezed her eyes shut.

"Katie." Chance slammed the truck door and headed for her.

She stood, unwilling to give herself even the slightest hope that anything had changed. "Yeah?"

"I don't want to leave angry. And wherever you land, Rosie can come visit you. I promise."

Katie's chin trembled. "I appreciate that. I know I screwed up, Chance. All I want is to go back and tell Big E to shove his deal, but I can't do that. I did what I thought I had to do at the time."

"I don't blame you for that, Katie. I know you were only thinking of your dad and your future. I have no claim to that. But if you'd just told me—if you hadn't lied..."

"I know." She'd always known when he found out it was going to be bad. But reality turned out to be so much more harsh than she'd ever expected. "I was wrong again. We Montgomery women make it awfully difficult, I suppose." She looked over his shoulder to where Rosie sat with her nose pressed against the window glass. "I only hope if Rosie ever decides she can't talk to you, you don't hold it against her." *And stop loving her.* "None of us are perfect, Chance. I know you know that. So maybe you should stop expecting us to be."

She took a step forward and reached up to kiss his cheek.

"Katie."

"I hope 'Sounds Like Home' is a huge success. Just remember where the inspiration came from. Montana's your home, Chance. Whether you want it to be or not."

"I CAN'T BELIEVE you left her alone like that. Her father just died, for crying out loud!"

If Chance didn't know better, he'd think his brothers had forgotten what Katie had done to them. The last thing he expected was to be read the riot act by Jon, who had at some point in the last two days re-elevated Katie to the status of saint.

"She didn't give me much of a choice." Chance started to put his foot up on the coffee table in Jon's living room only to collide gazes with Lydia from the kitchen beyond.

She pointed a finger at his foot and glared. He cleared his throat, sat up straighter and lowered his foot. "She insisted she could handle everything herself."

"Idiot," Lydia muttered from the kitchen. "I'm marrying into a family of them."

Jon glanced over his shoulder. "Been a long couple of days."

"No kidding." Ethan strode in, removed his jacket and hung it and his hat up by the front door as Grace walked past all of them straight into the kitchen. "Anyone else getting the silent treatment?"

"I wish," Jon muttered.

"They've closed ranks." Ben carried in a handful of beers and set them on the table by Jon. "Rachel's even got her mother and grandmother on board. Only Poppy's on my side and that's just because I'm her favorite teething toy. Like we don't have the right to be angry. Katie played us. For months. Thought you were leaving today." He took a seat beside Chance.

"My schedule's fluid." The truth was, after driving back and forth to Bozeman yesterday, watching Lochlan take his last breath, then spending a sleepless night worrying about Katie while telling himself he couldn't trust a liar, the last thing he wanted to contend with today was a cranky Rosie, who was adamant she couldn't leave until she'd said goodbye to everyone.

Everyone now included every animal on the Blackwell Ranch and on Jon's. She may as well be going on a worldwide farewell concert tour. "I met with Felix this morning, set some things in motion. Some changes." He scratched at the label on his beer. "Big changes."

"Are you going to make us pry it out of you, or are you going to put it in a song?" Ben asked.

"Please don't irritate him," Jon said. "I'm fond of my porch."

Ethan snickered and ducked into the kitchen.

"I'm turning down the record deals," Chance said. "All of them."

"I'm sorry, what?" Ben choked on his beer. "I thought they offered you high six figures. Are you insane?"

"Maybe. Felix certainly thinks so, but he's on board." And because his manager had decided to stick with him, that was enough confirmation he was making the right move. "I'm going to do an online wide release. Self-producing. I don't want to work for anyone else, not yet, anyway. Maybe if the album takes off—"

"What's this about an album?" Ty came in, followed closely by Hadley, who disappeared into the kitchen and closed the door behind her with a decided thump. "Don't ask. Which offer are you taking?" He hung up his coat and joined his brothers.

"He's not." Ben toasted the air. "Because Chance Blackwell never does the expected. Thought you needed the money."

"I do. I did." Chance took a long pull as his brother waited. "I want to come home."

"You sure about this?" Jon leaned forward. "That's a big leap for you. A lot of memories to leave behind. And an awful lot of change at once."

"It's what's best for Rosie." And if he was honest, for himself. He'd thought about it all night—thought about a lot of things. And about Katie. He loved her. There was no going back on that. "You've seen Rosie here. She loves it. She fits. She loves all of you. Although some I'm not entirely sure why." He glanced at Ben, who gave him a huge grin. "She'll have her cousins and animals and the sky. Out here, I can give my little girl the sky."

"I sense another song coming on." Ty chuckled and lifted his beer in a toast. "To the last Blackwell brother coming home."

"Wait!" Ben sagged back on the sofa and groaned. "Wait just a minute. Does this mean what I think it means?"

"Afraid so." Chance looked to each of his brothers. "I'm voting to keep the ranch." The second the words were out of his mouth, he knew he'd made the right decision.

"We're also giving Big E exactly what he wants," Ben said. "You think about that?"

"Oddly enough, our grandfather didn't figure into this decision." Because he'd only had to focus on two things to find the right answer. "I'm not going to waste any more time on anger and resentment or holding grudges against old men who don't know any better. We've always known who Big E is. Expecting him to change this late in the game is the definition of *futility*. He played us and won. Lochlan taught me that. If he could let go of the hate at the end, then I can sure as heck do it while I've got a life to live."

"You're talking about Katie," Ty said. "You going to try to work things out?"

"I hope to." Chance winced. "If she'll let me."

The kitchen door slammed open and his future sisters-in-laws stampeded into the room. "You mean it?" Lydia demanded. "You're going after her?"

"Going—what do you mean going? She's still here." Chance slowly rose to his feet, dread swirling inside of him. "Isn't she?"

"What do you think she's been doing all day? She's been packing to leave. She's got a rental and a horse trailer. She dropped Snicklefrits off at the guesthouse. Chance, she's loaded up and ready to go!" Hadley looked mildly panicked.

"Where is she?" Chance set down his bottle and dug for his keys.

"She was taking Gypsy for one last ride out by the river," Lydia told him. "At least that was the plan when I last saw her. It might be too late. She was planning on heading out tonight."

"Great. Okay, yeah. I can get there—"

"No way. That's your second beer." Ben yanked the keys out of his hand. "You aren't driving."

"You volunteering after number three?" Chance challenged.

"None of you are driving." Lydia grabbed his coat and shoved his arms into the sleeves. "Jon's going to loan you a horse and you're going to go get her."

"I am?" Jon blinked in shock but at Lydia's glare he nodded. "Yep, I am. Follow me, stable boy. We'll get you a nice one."

"I don't ride." Chance was pushed along by his brothers. All of his brothers. "Guys, seriously, it's been years—"

"I'll go with you," Ty volunteered. "Just to make sure you don't fall off."

"Daddy! Where are you going?" Rosie came racing down the stairs, Abby and Gen hot on her heels. "Can I come, too?"

"No, Bug. I'm going to go see your aunt Katie." And hope he could convince her to forgive him for being such an… He glanced at Lydia. An idiot.

"To say goodbye?" Rosie asked.

"Hopefully not." He kissed his daughter on the top of her head. "You stay here, okay? I'll be back soon."

Ty grabbed his arm and dragged him out of the house, just as he had most days when they were kids. It wasn't that he didn't like horses. They were great. From the ground. He just didn't like being on top of one.

"Geez, I wish there was another way." He skidded to a halt when he saw Jon leading a horse out of the stable. The stallion was stunning, but, man, was he big.

"You show too much fear, Chance. The animal picks up on it," Jon told him. "You want a smooth ride, you just keep imagining Katie's face when you come riding up."

Sure enough, the unease churning inside him faded.

"And that goofy smile will probably help, too. Got another?" Ty asked.

"Coming up behind." One of Jon's stable hands brought a second mare as Chance grasped the saddle horn and Jon leaned over with his hands clasped. "Just like riding a bike, little brother," Jon told him as Chance placed his knee into his brother's hand. "Easy does it." Jon hefted and Chance settled into the saddle. His feet found the stirrups more easily than he expected; his hands grasped the reins as easily as they held a guitar. "Take the south path up past the ranch. Cut across from there. It'll be quicker. And, Chance?"

"Yeah?" Chance called over his shoulder as the mare settled into a trot.

"You bring our Katie home!"

WOULD THIS BE her last Montana sunset?

Katie rested a hand against Gypsy's neck, giving the mare an encouraging pat. It had been her first ride and she'd done great, but Katie could tell she wasn't going to be a horse who liked standing still.

Hip, thrilled for the chance to run free after being cooped up, had raced alongside them as they crested the hill to the river. Listening to the rush of the water as the sun dipped into its watercolor bed was about as perfect a goodbye as she could wish for.

Twenty-seven years and it had taken her less than a day

to pack. It would have taken her even less time if Lydia, Hadley, Grace and Rachel hadn't stopped by to talk her out of leaving. She loved them for it, but she couldn't stay. Not when everyone knew what she'd done, how she'd let Big E manipulate her into betraying the men she loved like brothers. She didn't want to be a daily reminder of how far their grandfather would go to corral them.

She had to think of this as a new beginning. An adventure. Exploring the unknown. Maybe she'd end up in Wyoming. Maybe Arizona or Texas. Or maybe she'd just keep riding until she forgot how much she loved Chance Blackwell.

"Yeah, like that's going to happen." Katie took a deep breath. "Could really use your help again, Maura," Katie said to the sky. "I know you've got your hands full now with Dad, but just one more favor? Like maybe show me which way to turn once I'm on the road?" She waited. "No? Didn't think so." Katie clicked her back teeth and nudged Gypsy around. "Come on, Hip. Time we hit the road."

A flash of movement in the distance had her pulling back on the reins. Two horses headed right for her. No. Make that two men on horseback. And they were practically flying.

Gypsy backed up, two, three steps. Katie could feel the horse tense under her, knew the uncertainty of what was coming toward them had her spooked. "It's okay, girl." Katie tried to soothe the animal, but Gypsy whipped her head back and forth and ripped the reins out of Katie's hands. "Whoa, come on. Steady! Wait, no—ahhhh!"

Gypsy kicked up and, try as she might, Katie couldn't stay in the saddle. She pitched backward and felt herself falling. She landed hard and flat on her back. Arms and legs splayed, she could only lie there and watch as Gypsy raced away, straight back to the Blackwell Ranch.

"Well, that's just perfect." Katie sighed.

"Katie!"

"Chance?" Katie jerked up, then groaned. "Ow."

"Katie, are you okay?"

She leaned up on her elbows and watched as Chance dropped off a horse and dived toward her. Ty came up behind and caught Chance's horse's reins, a look of concern on his face only partially obscured by the coming night.

"You didn't hit your head again, did you?"

"I'm fine. I think." She looked down at her booted foot. "Probably could have stayed in the saddle if it wasn't for that thing. What? Chance Blackwell, are you laughing at me?"

He was laughing, and the sight was beautiful. "You said you'd never fallen off a horse in your life."

"Well, I hadn't. Until now. What are you…? Wait a minute." She grabbed hold of his jacket as he reached down to haul her up. "Did you come out here on horseback?"

"I did." And didn't he look proud of himself for it. "Wasn't as bad as I remembered. Might be sore tomorrow, but it'll be worth it."

"Oh, you'll be sore." But she wouldn't be here to see it. "You really came after me? Why?"

"Because I'm an idiot."

"Oh." Katie frowned.

"Dude." Ty groaned. "You're supposed to be a writer. Get your words straight. Sorry, Katie. He was so worried you'd be gone before he could profess his undying love, he must have left his brain back at Jon's."

"Don't you have somewhere else to be?" Chance growled over his shoulder.

"Nope. I'm the chaperone." His grin lit up the dusky sky. "Proceed. I'll just be over here. Come on, Hip."

"Chance, what's going on?" Katie asked him. "We said

everything there was to say the other day. I don't want to say goodbye again."

"But I didn't say what I should have." He clutched the lapels of her jacket in his hands and hauled her close. "I love you, Katie Montgomery. I was an idiot for not realizing how much. And I didn't until I realized you wouldn't be here. For me and Rosie. Every day. Please stay."

"Chance." Katie had never heard more perfect words, but they weren't enough. "I don't belong here. Not really. I tried to, but this is your ranch. Yours and the brothers'. And Big E's."

"It's more yours than anyone's. At least that's what I told Big E the other day in the stable. Which is why I'm giving you my shares of the ranch."

"You're—you're what?" Katie gasped.

"Yeah, you're what?" Ty demanded.

"Proxy shares. I'm not a rancher, Katie. I never will be. But this place has Rosie's heart. And you have mine. I'm putting the shares in her name with you as executor. You'll have as equal a say as each of my brothers. Until Rosie wants to claim them for herself."

"You… I…" Katie blinked. "What?"

He clasped her face in his hands and kissed her. "Stay here. With me and Rosie. Marry me. Work the ranch. I bet I can convince the other shareholders to hire you as foreman. With back pay. And a house. Either the one you grew up in or we can build a new one."

"But what about… Chance, I lied to you. To all of you." Wasn't that impossible to overcome?

"What's a big lie among family?" Ty called.

"Really don't need your help, Tyler!" Chance yelled.

"You're really going to stay?" Katie whispered. "You really *want* to stay?"

"I do. Montana's where I'm from. But you, Katie." He stared into her eyes. "You're my home."

She smiled and kissed him.

"Is that a yes? Because I have a beer getting warm back at—"

"Shut up, Ty," Chance and Katie said together.

"What do you say?" Chance wrapped his arm around her shoulders and pulled her in close as they headed back to his horse, Hip trailing along behind. "Shall we go tell Rosie we're staying?"

"Yes." Katie hugged him hard. "We'll tell her we're all staying."

EPILOGUE

A MAN DIDN'T make it to eighty years old without making a few enemies. Of course, not every man was Elias Blackwell and most of his enemies were his blood kin. But you took what life gave you.

Or so Big E thought as he sat back in his chair on the front porch of the Blackwell Ranch house and looked out over the family that had come together to celebrate his birthday with a BBQ bash that set the smoke soaring and the meat to roasting. Not that he deserved it. He knew full well the last thing he should have gotten was a wagon load of forgiveness or at least tolerance. But seeing his grandsons back on the ranch, settled and happy, where they belonged, was more than he could have hoped for.

Jon and Lydia would be married in the fall, giving his great-granddaughters Abby and Gen the perfect family they deserved. There would still be arguments; Big E wasn't as open to change as Jon wanted, but he wasn't a fool, either. He knew which way the wind was blowing in the cattle industry. Time to set aside some of his stubbornness and embrace new possibilities.

Ethan and Grace would soon be three and after the arrival of what was sure to be another great-granddaughter, Big E would happily attend their wedding, which, if the bride's holiday spirit was any indication, would be overflowing with Christmas cheer.

That Ben had found his happily-ever-after with the ever-practical Rachel and her adorable daughter, Poppy—not that he'd ever say that out loud—filled Big E with more pride than it should have. He'd dosed that boy with a good deal of animosity, but here Ben was, a doting father and tolerant grandson. They'd never see eye to eye—how could they when Big E had done the unthinkable all those years ago and betrayed him? But he'd been right. In the long run, at least. Zoe never would have looked at Ben the way Rachel did. The way Poppy did. And Ben never would have smiled so much.

Ty and Hadley. Big E sighed. Man, that woman had the Blackwell men wrapped around every finger on her hand, but especially that grandson of his. He couldn't wait to see what they did with this place now that he was officially outvoted on all the big stuff. He had no doubt they'd let him win small victories, but when it came to the battles? He was laying down his guns and surrendering. Hadley and Ty would do big things for the Blackwell Ranch, and they'd all be better for it.

And then there was Chance and Katie and little, precocious Rosie, who had turned Big E into something of a teddy bear of a doting great-grandfather. She'd even talked him into giving Splinter the cow his own private stall in the stable. But he wasn't just doing it for Rosie or Chance. He owed a debt to Lochlan after all he'd put him through—keeping him from his family when they needed him most. He'd been too late to save his friend, but he'd keep Katie close. He'd had a new will drawn up just last week and, when the time came and the afterlife came calling, Katie would be getting his share of the ranch. His boys had enough. But now, with Katie Montgomery, their family was finally complete.

The squeals and screams of laughter, from fathers and daughters and fiancées, echoed across the Montana sky, so Big E got to his feet and went to join the fray. As he filled his plate with the BBQ offerings, right down to the boys' mama's potato salad, baked beans and homemade biscuits that Hadley had perfected and added to the guest ranch menu, he heard a rumbling of an engine coming down the road.

"Who's that?" Rosie asked her father before she squealed after being turned upside down and slung over Chance's shoulder. "Daddy!"

"That's a surprise for your great-grandpa," Katie told Rosie as she arched an eyebrow at Big E.

"Got all I need already, Katie-girl." But as the truck drew closer, something odd buzzed in his chest. He set down his plate as Chance, Ty, Ben, Jon and Ethan all abandoned their food to greet the newcomer.

He saw the silver hair first, but the profile had him blinking in surprise. Dorothy. Last time he'd seen her, he hadn't let himself reminisce or dwell or notice that she hadn't lost a bit of her beauty to the years that had passed. Tall and curvaceous, she wore jeans and a flowered blouse the color of summer lemons and a smile that could light the midnight sky.

"Quid pro quo, Big E." Katie knocked a shoulder against his arm and grinned as the boys escorted their grandmother over to him. "You played matchmaker long enough. Now it's our turn."

"I…uh." Big E blinked, wondering if he was hallucinating. She was back on the ranch. His ranch. Their ranch. "Hello, Dorothy."

"Elias." Her voice still sent chills of excitement and promise down his spine. "Heard you've been messing with my boys. You and me, we've got some catching up to do. Let's say you fix me a plate and we get to chatting."

His grandsons stepped back, all five of them lined up behind the only woman Elias had ever truly loved.

His grandsons.

Back home.

Right where they belonged.

* * * * *

COMING SOON!

We really hope you enjoyed reading this book. If you're looking for more romance, be sure to head to the shops when new books are available on

Thursday 21st February

To see which titles are coming soon, please visit

millsandboon.co.uk/nextmonth

MILLS & BOON

MILLS & BOON

Coming next month

CARRYING THE GREEK TYCOON'S BABY
Jennifer Faye

"I'm pregnant."

Xander stumbled back as though Lea's words had physically slugged him in the chest. The back of his knees hit the edge of the bed. He slumped down onto the mattress. Maybe he'd heard her incorrectly.

"Could you say that again?"

"Xander, I'm pregnant. And you're the father."

That's what he thought she'd said.

But this can't be true. Could it?

Xander knew all too well that it was quite possible. They'd spent that not-so-long-ago weekend in bed…and there was the time on the floor…in the living room—

He halted his rambling memories. He didn't normally let loose like that. In fact, he'd never had a weekend like that one. It was unforgettable. And apparently in more than one way.

The silence dragged on. He should say something. Anything. But what? He'd never been in this position before.

He needed time to think because right now all that was going around in his mind was that he was going to be a father. He wondered if this was what shock felt like.

"I…I need a little time to absorb this," he said. "We'll talk soon."

He wasn't even sure if he said goodbye before disconnecting the call. He had no idea how long he laid there staring into space before an incoming text jarred him back to reality.

I'm going to be a father.

The profound words echoed in his mind.

How could this be? Well, of course he knew how it happened. It was a weekend that he would never forget, much as he had tried. Lea's stunning image was imprinted upon his mind.

Still, he never thought he'd hear that he was going to be a father. A father. His heart was racing and his palms were damp.

His mind slipped back to the time he'd spent on Infinity Island. He never thought that it would change his life. But it had. And now he had to figure out a plan. He was known for thinking on his toes, but this was different. This was a baby. His baby.

And he had to do whatever was best for the child.

But what was that?

Continue reading
CARRYING THE GREEK TYCOON'S BABY
Jennifer Faye

Available next month
www.millsandboon.co.uk